MW01045457

Smudge's Mark

FOR THE ONE WHO ASKED WHAT WAS IN MY HAND.

First published in 2009 by **Be read**
an imprint of Simply Read Books
www.simplyreadbooks.com

Text © 2009 Claudia Osmond
All rights reserved. No part of this publication may be reproduced, stored in a retrieval system, or transmitted, in any form or by any means, electronic, mechanical, photocopying, recording or otherwise, without the written permission of the publisher. The publisher does not have any control over and does not assume any responsibility for author or third-party websites or their content.

LIBRARY AND ARCHIVES CANADA CATALOGUING IN PUBLICATION

Osmond, Claudia, 1968-

Smudge's mark / Claudia Osmond.

ISBN 978-1-894965-69-9

I. Title.

PS8629.S542S66 2009 jC813'.6 C2009-901954-X

We gratefully acknowledge for their financial support of our publishing program the Canada Council for the Arts, the BC Arts Council, and the Government of Canada through the Book Publishing Industry Development Program (BPIDP).

Book design by Elisa Gutiérrez 10 9 8 7 6 5 4 3 2 1 Printed in Canada

Claudia Osmond

Smudge's Mark

Be read

CONTENTS

"ALL THAT IS NECESSARY FOR THE TRIUMPH OF EVIL IS FOR GOOD MEN TO DO NOTHING."

– EDMUND BURKE (1729–1797)

1 O.W.N.O.

My grampa was a wicked prankster.

Usually after working the part-time midnight shift at the mushroom farm, he'd make his way home to 49 Stone Elements Drive in the darkness of the early morning. But not before pulling a stunt on someone. And they weren't just Nicky Nicky Nine Doors kinds of stunts either.

Once he covered all the cars in our neighborhood with dirt and wrote, "Wash me" on the windshields. Another time he made designs all over the sidewalks, driveways, and roads with colored chalk, and the time before that he drew flames on all the windows with what looked like red and orange paint. One time, he even smeared a horrible-smelling soft cheese on everyone's doorknobs.

Needless to say, the neighbors were not happy. Actually, it seemed like they were never happy. Not even on a good, prank-less day. Let's just say the average Grimstown personality matched the environment—bleak at best, downright dead at worst. Once a bunch of people stripped a guy down to his boxers on the steps of Town Hall and pelted him with prunes, just for whistling.

I'd hate to think of what they'd pelt Grampa with if he ever got caught.

Not to mention the idea of Grampa in his boxers. Not a good visual.

Anyways, Grampa was always making a mess of things, and because of it Grimstown had endured a few near water shortages from all the hoses being on at once. Luckily no one in Grimstown, as far as I knew, suspected Grampa. He had amazing skills at working on the sly. The rumor floating around was that the town was cursed by invisible, havoc-wreaking gremlins.

When Grampa wasn't at work or busy "wreaking havoc" on the neighborhood, he was usually in the attic, talking to himself in a mirror.

Using different voices.

Mostly he discussed the weather and how the opposing team was still in the lead. Which opposing team, I have no idea. As far as I knew, Grampa never watched sports. But he was pretty ticked off about it all the same.

Sometimes his conversations got really wacky, like the times he argued with himself. In one argument, part of him said he should leave because Grimstown was getting worse due to the disorder and the other part of him said he should stay because Grimstown was getting worse due to the disorder. I'll admit Grimstown was a super-dreary town where everything was dry and brown. And yeah, it seemed to be getting worse. But that was no different than any other place on Earth, or so I've heard Grampa say. And besides, he was the one causing all the "disorder"!

He sure had a mind of another kind.

I guess if you want to get scientific and bring up the topic of heredity, you could say that's the one thing I inherited from Grampa: a messed-up mind. I have practically no memory from the time I was born to about seven months ago: not of who my parents were, what my favorite childhood toy was, or even where I was born. I could have come from Mars for all I knew. Except my skin's not green like they say a Martian's is. Grampa's ears were kind of pointed (and if he was from Mars, that would sure explain a lot), but he wasn't green, either, so I thought maybe I just came from Colorado or something.

Grampa insisted I was in an accident and that's why my memory was gone. But I just figured he was trying to hide the fact I'd inherited one too many threads from his crazy genes. I mean, surely if I were in an accident, I'd remember something about it. People are always saying things like, "The last thing I remember hearing before the horse kicked me in the head was . . . " or "The last thing I remember seeing before I fell off the cliff was . . . " But I don't remember anything, not even the last thing that happened before the accident.

Grampa has told me the accident had something to do with my parents. He's also told me that my dad's dead. But whether or not he died in the accident, I don't know. And I have no idea about what happened to my mom. He's barely ever mentioned her.

Why? I don't know that either. And every time I've tried asking him questions about my mom or my dad or anything about my past, Grampa would just give me a stinky boiled root to chew on and tell me to go draw. He's never told me anything I wanted to know.

And I sure couldn't count on Griselda for any help in that department. Yeah, her name alone should be a hint. She was the housekeeper-slash-nanny from you-know-where. And I'll bet my right eye she was probably the reason Grampa had gone loopy and spent so much time up in the attic, alone.

And that's how I pretty much spent most of my time, too: alone.

Only I didn't make a habit of pulling pranks and talking to myself.

Although, come to think of it, maybe Grampa was on to something. Maybe sneaking around and talking to an imaginary friend could make life a little more bearable. Especially since I was stuck in Grimstown with no chance of escaping. I had no other living relatives. I was an Orphan with No Options: an O.W.N.O.

And "oh no" pretty much summed up my whole life as I knew it.

2 The Twencil

I wasn't sure if I should follow Grampa or not.

It's not like this is anything new, I thought. Heck, sometimes he stays up there for entire days.

But he did tell me to go look for him if he didn't come back in five minutes. And it had already been fifteen.

I slapped my sketchbook shut, grabbed it off the kitchen table, and headed towards the stairs. Since the house was quiet, I figured Griselda must have been asleep already. And when I heard her snores rattling out from underneath her bedroom door, I knew my tiptoeing wasn't necessary.

It would take more than the sound of a few creaky floorboards to shut that machine off, I thought as I relaxed a bit and walked past her door.

At the end of the hallway on the top floor of the house, just past Griselda's bedroom, was the hatch to the attic. The stairs were hidden in the ceiling, and when you unlatched the hook and pulled down on the rope, the stairs creaked open and came down to meet the floor. Luckily Grampa had left the hatch open.

I climbed the creaky, narrow staircase that led to the open attic area. It was what Griselda called "the loft." It was full of boxes, crates, suitcases, mannequins with important body parts missing, and racks and racks full of Griselda's old costumes.

The attic smelled musty, and I could see the dust floating around under the light of the few bare bulbs that hung from the rafters. I decided to stay hidden on the stairs below floor level and spy on Grampa for a while, before I let him know I was there. I'd spied on Grampa lots of times before. That's how I knew he talked to himself. It's amazing what you can find out when people don't know you're watching.

Sure enough, Grampa was sitting on his red leather chair in front of a metal-framed mirror, talking to himself.

"I can't believe it!" I heard Grampa say in one of his other voices as I got comfortable on the step. "Not remembering!"

"I don't underthtand what'th going on!" he interrupted himself with his regular lisp. Grampa's two front teeth were missing, so he spit through the gap whenever he talked. "I ekthplain everything to him every morning during breakfatht, but ath the day goeth on, it theems he forgetths everything. And by the very nektht morning I have to thtart all over again! I bet he doethn't even remember a thing I told him thith morning!"

It was obvious Grampa was talking about me, so I strained my brain trying to remember what we'd talked about over breakfast. Besides his demonstration of how he finds it hard to eat an overripe pear because of the gap in his teeth, I drew a total blank.

"But he hath been drawing a lot, jutht like I told him to. I've theen the picturth mythelf. But I thought the rootth would work better at bringing the memoryth back. I have a thneaking feeling he'th not eating them! He'th got to eat them for them to work!"

Grampa was speaking so forcefully I thought his massive comb-over that hid his bald spot would unravel at any second. Yes, I said unravel. I'd often considered suggesting he shellac it into place. At least it could double as a helmet that way.

"And tonight—"

"Yeth, yeth, I know," he interrupted himself again. "It'th almotht midnight."

"I know! Give him the graphite implement. Don't wait for him to come up here. Go back down and give it to him—now."

"Yeth, yeth! Brilliant idea! Jutht what I was thinking!" he congratulated himself. "He hath to begin to remember—*thomething* becauth time ith running out and he'th definitely—"

"Needed."

My skin prickled and I shivered. I'm needed? I thought. What am I needed for?

As if I had thought those words out loud, Grampa suddenly turned in his chair and looked towards the stairs. I sucked in a sharp breath and impulsively crouched down, ducking out of sight.

If I had thought about it, I would have remembered that Grampa had actually told me to look for him, so it really wouldn't have been a big deal if he saw me there. But I guess I just didn't want him to know I'd caught him in the middle of a conversation with himself.

Especially since he'd been talking about me. What the heck was that all about? And, yeah, I'd been drawing a lot since Grampa had given me the sketchbook a few months ago and told me to draw whatever came into my head. But the roots? I didn't know that eating those horrible-smelling things was supposed to help bring back my memory. Every time Grampa gave me one and told me to chew on it, I'd pretended to do it while secretly dropping it down the heater vent.

And what was it that he'd been telling me every morning that I couldn't remember? Most likely something more important than not being able to take a bite out of a pear. Would the roots have helped me remember that, too?

After a few quiet seconds, I slowly straightened up so I could peek back over the edge of the attic floor. I wanted to hear more.

I just about swallowed my tongue in fright when I saw a magnified eyeball staring back at me from the other side of the railing. Grampa was lying on the floor, commando style, behind one of the posts. Only half of his face was visible.

"What took you tho long?" His huge eyeballs blinked a couple of times behind his pop bottle–thick glasses.

"I . . . uh, I—" I stammered.

"Thtay there!" He slithered away on his belly.

I heard some movement from the other side of the attic and few things fell to the floor. Then I heard Grampa chant his silly rhyme. The one that went like this:

The seventh sun, the seventh sun
Lives so pie in the sky
Unawares he is
Of the job that's his
To do lest we all die.

Grampa always chanted this meaningless rhyme whenever he was busy doing stuff around the house. I think it was kind of like a habit, like whistling is for some people.

I rose up onto my knees to see what he was doing when something long and thin came rolling across the floor and under the railing, right towards me. I crouched again and leaned to the side, letting the thing fall off the edge of the attic floor and onto the stairs. It bounced down a couple of steps.

"I know you're thtill there," I heard Grampa whisper, just above me. "Take it!"

I sat down on the stair and bum-bounced down a couple steps and picked it up. It was a twig with a piece of paper wrapped around it, held on by a rubber band.

I looked up at him, wondering what he wanted me to do with it.

"It'th for your birthday!" Grampa said with his head hanging over the edge of the attic floor.

I wiped the spit from his lisp off my face with my sleeve.

"Uh, thanks, Grampa," I said.

I mean, I was surprised. And confused. On one hand, I couldn't believe he'd remembered my birthday!

But on the other hand, a twig?

"The paper is jutht the wrapping," he said. "Thorry it'th not fanthy. I didn't have time to find a gift bag. When you unwrap it you can jutht throw the paper away."

"Uh, okay," I said. "So what should I do with it? After I . . . uh . . . unwrap it."

"Draw with it!" he said, as if that was the obvious answer.

"With . . . with a twig?" I asked.

"It'th not jutht a twig!" he snorted. "Look clother."

I turned the twig around in my hands.

"Look at it'th tip," Grampa said.

That's when I saw it was a pencil. A twig pencil.

A *twencil*, I said to myself, nodding and smiling.

"You mutht draw thirculth around all your drawingth with it," said Grampa, jabbing a crooked pinky finger at the sketchbook I was still holding.

I slid over on the step and twisted my back so I could look up at him.

"Circles? Why?" I asked. I could barely see Grampa's glass-covered eyes blinking back at me in the dim light.

"Becauth I thaid tho!" he said. "And becauth you haven't been eating thoth rootth, have you?"

"Uh . . . " I wondered what eating stinky roots had to do with drawing circles around my pictures with a twig.

"No, you haven't. And that'th really thlowing thingth down. There'th nothing I can do about the ackthident that wrecked your memory, but I can try to help you remember. You mutht draw thirculth right away," he lisped. "Tonight! Before you go to bed."

"Uh, okay," I said.

Suddenly there was a thud from somewhere down the hallway and then the faint sound of clacking heels.

Grampa gasped and stuck his arm down, touching the top of my head with the tips of his fingers. "You mutht go now! She'th coming! Don't forget to draw the thirculth!"

He disappeared back under the railing. I heard a few more bumps and shuffles from up above, and then Griselda's bedroom door opened. The dim orange light from her room spilled onto the hallway floor. The heavy smell of scented candles filled the air, and the steady rhythm of heels click-clacked towards the attic stairs.

I straightened one leg so I could jam the twencil into my pajama pocket. I think that's when she saw me.

Enter Griselda.

There she was, staring up at me from the bottom of the stairs with her jaw hanging open. She was fully dressed, complete with a feathered scarf wrapped around her neck.

The funny thing about Griselda—if "funny" is the word—was that her warty face, bald head, big behind, and long, hooked nose didn't stop her from constantly walking around like she was some kind of beauty queen. She always wore a bleach-blonde wig, pearls, high—high!—heels, bright-red lipstick, an evening gown, and long white gloves.

And she was furiously taking off those gloves, a finger at a time.

Does she really wear all that to bed? I thought.

I guess you've got to give her credit for at least trying to cover up her hideousness.

She motioned with a flick of her gloves and a jerk of her arm for me to come down.

I did.

"What are you doing out of your room, you sneaky little urchin?" she hissed.

I wanted to ask her the same thing. But I would have called her something else.

I tried to slink past her, but she grabbed my arm and dug her long red nails into my flesh. Too bad she'd taken her gloves off.

"Get back downstairs before I make you trim my toenails!"

Ugh! I had to do that once before, and trust me, I couldn't eat for a week.

"Ith that you, Grithelda?" Grampa called from the attic.

Griselda cleared her throat and narrowed her eyes. "Don't you move," she mouthed to me as she gave my arm another squeeze.

"Yes, yes it is, Horace, dear," she said in a drippy sweet voice. She was such a good faker when she had to be. Apparently, she used to star in movies.

Probably *The Bride of Frankenstein*.

Griselda carefully climbed a few steps towards the attic. She threw a quick dart at me with her eyes before she popped her head above the attic floor.

"Are you in the loft, Horace?"

"I'm thorry," Grampa said. "I didn't mean to wake you."

"Don't worry," said Griselda. "I'm sure it wasn't you. Probably just one of the pests in the walls—or on the stairs. We really should call an exterminator," she said through gritted teeth as she shot another quick dart my way.

"Yeth, yeth. Firtht thing in the morning when I get home from work," said Grampa.

"Well, I'll just go down and get a drink and then head back to bed," Griselda said in her sickeningly sweet tone. "And by the way, I don't think the dinner dishes have been done yet, so if you don't mind . . . I've had an excruciatingly long day. And the cats would probably appreciate the leftovers, too."

"Yeth, of courth," Grampa replied.

It was beyond me why he'd hire a housekeeper when he had to do everything himself anyways.

"See you in the morning," Griselda said as she steadied herself on the steps and turned to come back down. Her ankles wobbled as she tried to keep her balance on the crazy stilts she had strapped to the bottoms of her feet.

Her eyes immediately fixed on mine when she safely landed on the hallway floor. She flung her feathered scarf behind her shoulders and grabbed my sketchbook. She held it at arm's length as though it were a dead mouse.

"Trash," she said as she dangled the book in front of me by the back cover. She clamped her hand on my arm again and whispered into my ear with a hot, hateful breath, "How much longer do I have to put up with you and your trash?"

Her spit from the "t" hit me between the eyes, and I wanted to gag.

She tightened her grip on my arm with her claws and dragged me down the hallway, still holding my sketchbook as if she were holding a dead mouse by its tail. She nudged me down both flights of stairs ahead of her, tripping on the hem of her gown the whole way. At the sound of the scuffle, her cats appeared. They ran up and down the stairs beside us, meowing madly, almost as if they couldn't contain their excitement of witnessing my capture.

Either that or my book reminded them of a dead mouse, too.

Griselda twisted her ankle as she missed the final bottom step when one of her cats darted in front of her. She cursed—at me, of course.

She opened my bedroom door and pushed me inside, throwing my sketchbook in after me and slamming the door.

"And stay in there!" she hissed.

Then I heard her "ouch" and "ooch" as she limped all the way back up the basement stairs.

3 Voices

I picked up my sketchbook off the floor, smoothed out the crinkled pages, and laid it on my bed.

Griselda's heavy, lopsided footsteps thudded across the floor above my head. My bedroom was right below the living room. I figured Griselda was about to claim her usual place, on the overstuffed chair. Sure enough, I heard the chair springs creak and the TV turn on: *Gone with the Wind*.

"Rhett . . . Rhett . . . if you go, where shall I go? What shall I do?"

"Frankly my dear, I don't give a damn!"

Griselda's bad-actor voice rose higher than the TV volume as she tried to imitate the characters in the movie.

Maybe having no memory wasn't so bad. Remembering seven months of my life with Griselda was long enough. I think I'd have gone totally nuts by now if I had memories of the past thirteen and a half years.

I took the twencil out of my pocket and sat on my bed. I took the rubber band off and shot it, gun style, at the ceiling towards where I thought Griselda's chair was. It hit its mark, pinged off, and fell to the floor.

Suddenly the TV volume lowered.

No way, I thought. There's no way she heard that!

I quickly crumpled up the piece of wrapping paper and shoved it—along with my sketchbook and twig—

under my mattress, just in case Griselda had suddenly grown bat ears and was on her way back down to see what I was up to.

The chair springs groaned as Griselda must have stood up. But before I even had the chance to lie down and pretend I was asleep, I heard the doorbell and realized she was headed towards the front hallway.

The doorbell rang again.

"If you ring that bell one more time, I'll ram it down your throat," I heard Griselda say as she limped out of the living room.

After a few seconds of silence, muffled voices came through the air vent at the top of the wall. I pushed my dresser under the vent and pulled my chair up to it. Then I climbed up and stood on top of the dresser so I could press my ear against the grate. The voices were still pretty muffled, but at least I could make out what they were saying.

" . . . And so, I do apologize for the hour," I heard a man say. "But I just wanted to introduce myself as the new headmaster at the Grimstown Academy for Orphans in the valley. I had heard that perhaps there might be an orphan boy living in this dwelling."

"Oh . . . well, actually, dear sir, there is," said a woman. Was that Griselda? She sounded so . . . pleasant.

"Perhaps we might discuss the educational opportunities the academy could offer this . . . ahem . . . young lad."

"Oh, yes . . . I'd love to," said Griselda, "but I regret that I can't invite you in at the moment. You see, his grandfather is home and . . . " She lowered her voice so I couldn't hear what she said after that.

"Yes, yes, of course," replied the man. "I had thought that perhaps he may not be in agreement. Living relatives very rarely ever are. And that is precisely why I chose to drop by now. I thought he may have already left for work, so the two of us could discuss the issue without bias. However, I understand the bind this might put you in, so I'll be on my way and then perhaps some other time down the road . . . Oh—I do beg your forgiveness . . . I know this is off topic, but I just can't help but speak what's in my heart. I am completely taken with your beauty, my dear lady. You truly are a goddess."

Gag! Is this guy blind?

Griselda *giggled*. "Oh, why, thank you," she said. "You can call me Griselda."

"Griselda . . . ahhh . . . music to my ears. And you, lovely lady, may call me Edgar."

"Edgaaaaar," repeated Griselda.

"Now, I must be on my way," Edgar said, "but before I go, perhaps I should just make mention that you are welcome to bring the boy around to our esteemed academy at any time, considering the burden he must be on you."

"Oh, trust me!" said Griselda. "If I had it my way, I'd bring him first thing in the morning. If only Horace weren't around."

"Indeed," said Edgar. "I can only begin to imagine how difficult it must be for you to endure what you do. I've heard about this Horace. Pure injustice for a goddess such as yourself to be subject to such slavery, I say. And am I correct in assuming that he also requires you to homeschool the boy?"

If you consider her watching *Gone with the Wind* while I work through textbooks on my own "homeschooling."

"Yes," said Griselda. "And it's absolute torture."

"Indeed," said Edgar. "That is why I'm offering my services. Now, I must be on my way. But please, I beg our acquaintance not stop here. Will you join me for dinner sometime? Perhaps I could offer . . . employment alternatives. I am a shareholder with the theatre, after all."

"Really?" asked Griselda in a giddy voice. "That's right up my alley."

"How coincidental," said Edgar. "Shall we discuss it?"

"Oh, that would be lovely, Edgaaaar," cooed Griselda.

"Dinner?" asked Edgar.

"Oh, yes, yes. That would be . . . divine."

"Well, I really must run. I have one other appointment tonight that I simply must keep. Until then. And remember, dear lady, you may bring the boy around at any time, should opportunity present itself."

"Yes," she replied. "If the temptation to commit a double homicide doesn't overwhelm me before then."

They both laughed, but it didn't sound to me like they were laughing at a joke.

Then I heard the door close.

So she secretly wants to send me off to that academy for orphans, I thought. I wonder what Grampa would say if he knew that?

I could tell Griselda was making her way back into the living room by the sound of her limping footsteps. Just as I heard the chair springs creak again and the volume on the TV go up, a set of lighter footsteps shuffled into the room above my head.

"You are thtill up," I heard Grampa say. "Who were you talking to at thith hour of the night?" His voice came loud and clear through the vent, since he was standing pretty much right above me.

"I was just . . . er . . . just talking on the phone to my mother," said Griselda. The TV volume turned up.

I heard the floorboards creak as someone—probably Grampa—walked to the TV and shut it off.

"I thought your mother wath dead," said Grampa.

"I didn't say 'mother,'" said Griselda. "I said . . . 'brother.' Now, if you'll excuse me, I tripped down the stairs earlier on and twisted my ankle. I must go soak my foot before the swelling reaches my throat and chokes the life right out of me."

"Yeth, of courth," said Grampa.

I heard the chair springs groan as Griselda stood up again. "Oh, and don't forget the dinner dishes," she said before leaving the room. "You need to do those before you head off to work. I hate waking up to a mess in the kitchen."

I heard her "ouch" and "ooch" all the way up to the top floor of the house. That was followed by a huge sigh, an "Oh, woe is me!" and a door slamming shut.

Movie star, no doubt.

I slid off the dresser and onto the chair and then jumped onto my mattress.

She can't send me away without Grampa's permission, can she? I wondered.

I knew what I had to do. First thing in the morning, as soon as Grampa came home from work and when Griselda was sure to be snoring, I was going to tell him about the man who came to the house. And about why he came to the house.

And this time I'd try really hard to remember what Grampa wanted to tell me, too.

I heard Grampa start his seventh sun rhyme as he shuffled his way to the kitchen to do the dishes.

"The theventh thun, the theventh thun
Liveth tho pie in the thky
Unawareth he ith
Of the job that'th hith
To do letht we all die."

As I listened to the slow, steady rhythm of "The Seventh Sun," I suddenly remembered the twencil Grampa had given me and what I was supposed to do with it. I took it and the sketchbook out from under my mattress. I flipped the book open and fanned through the pages. Since Grampa had given me the sketchbook, I'd drawn lots of different pictures. I had no clue where the ideas came from, but I hoped that if I just did what Grampa told me to do, what he had said might happen would happen, that drawing my thoughts might help me start remembering stuff. And I wanted to remember, so I kept drawing whatever popped into my head. I have become a pretty good artist, if I may say so myself, but I can't say it's helped bring back memories.

I tightened my grip on the twencil and drew a circle, just like Grampa had told me to, around the first picture, a waterfall. I sat back to see if anything would happen.

Nothing did.

I drew a circle around the castle with the statues. And then the eagle.

Nothing happened.

By the time I heard Grampa leave for work, I had drawn circles around every single picture I had in my book, including the faces and the old-fashioned key.

Still nothing happened.

Oh well, I thought as I closed my sketchbook and yawned. Whatever. At least he remembered my birthday.

I stuck my book and twencil back under my mattress, switched off the lamp, and curled up under the covers.

Tomorrow is Saturday.

July 7.

My fourteenth birthday.

And Grampa remembered.

I couldn't stop a smile from spreading across my face.

I pulled my thin blanket up around my shoulders and closed my eyes.

"Happy Birthday to me," I said.

4 Frightmare

Sleep wasn't usually something to be taken for granted at Grampa's place, thanks to the way Griselda usually watched *Gone with the Wind* at high volume through all hours of the night. It was a wonder I ever fell asleep at all.

Luckily she was off quietly soaking her foot, so at some point before the clock struck twelve I fell asleep.

But not so luckily, I found myself in a vivid dream.

It started out with a blinding flash of light that felt like it stabbed right through my eyes and got stuck in my brain. I actually thought the pain had woken me up, but when I opened my burning eyes, I was straddling the body of an enormous eagle. From what I could see while sitting on its back, it was mostly black, but it had a thick white band of feathers across each wing and rich brown feathers across the back of each shoulder. For some reason, the eagle looked strangely familiar, but I couldn't think of where I might have seen it before.

Talk about barebacking it! And the strange thing was that I was totally at ease, as if I'd taken eagle-back flying lessons and was an old pro. I guess that's the weird thing about dreams: you magically know how to do things you don't really know how to do.

I squeezed my legs the best I could around the bird's body to keep my balance and tightened my grip on the brown, oily feathers on the back of its neck as it took off.

All of a sudden the eagle turned upwards and flapped its wings like a speed demon. My knuckles turned white from holding on so tight. I could feel the mist of the clouds on my face as we continued climbing up, up, up, and then as we dove straight down.

Luckily a tunnel opened up in the earth below to make way for us or we would have splattered all over the ground. The eagle's huge wings pumped hard as we dove deeper and deeper. I gulped the humid air, trying not to puke. Talk about butterflies in my stomach. I felt like spewing a few thousand of the half-digested little suckers all over myself.

When the tunnel leveled out into an open space, the eagle landed. Strangely it seemed like we were above ground again.

The eagle wanted me to get off its back, so I hopped down. Actually it was a little more complicated than that: the eagle had to lie down and pretty much roll over before I got the hint. After I got off, the bird stood back up and took a couple of long strides as it maneuvered its massive body around to face me. It was only then that I noticed its beak was mostly yellow, but the surface of it turned an intense fire-red close to the eyes.

I heard a rustling sound as the eagle slowly walked circles around me. Its legs were covered in deep-red, armorlike scales, and each talon was about the shape and size of the Grim Reaper's sickle.

The eagle nudged me and squawked. It stopped behind me and pushed me forward with its strong head. I had no idea where the bird wanted me to go, so I waited for each shove before taking another awkward step in the direction its head pushed me.

We walked like that—shove, step, shove, step—for quite a while, along a river and towards an enormous rocky waterfall. I looked up—way up. As soon as my eyes met the top of the waterfall, another blazing flash of white light burned my eyes. I suddenly had the feeling I'd been there before, like I was having déjà vu. Or maybe I'd just had this dream before.

Massive rocks jutted out from both sides of the waterfall, all the way up to the top. And the rocks below shattered the water into a bazillion glistening droplets.

When we reached the base of the waterfall, I stopped walking, but the eagle gave me a final hefty shove into the rocks. I took it as my cue to start climbing. We continued up beside the waterfall, over the rocks and then along a narrow, slick ledge that led behind the sheet of solid water that continued to break itself on the rocks below. The roar was deafening.

Behind the waterfall was the entrance to a cave. The eagle prodded me through the entrance and along a winding tunnel that was lined with flickering torches. We finally ended up in front of a stone archway. It was so dark past it that I couldn't see what was on the other side.

Four statues guarded the archway. They were made of stone, but their hair was real. Well, it wasn't real hair, like you have on top of your head. One had hair made of water, one had hair made of leaves, one had hair made of fire, and the other one had hair made of, well, nothing. It didn't have hair. It had a cyclone-type thing sitting on the top of its head like an upside-down swirling sugar cone.

The statues' eyes were closed and their hands held empty bowls.

Then, with its wings stretched out on either side of its body, the eagle ruffled its feathers as a beautiful angel-like creature appeared under the archway. I had to squint and shield my eyes so I could see because the angel gave off such a bright light. In the near-blinding glow, I could see she was wearing an ivory-colored gown and strands of her long dark-brown hair were gently flying around her perfect face.

Suddenly another bright flash went off in my head. It was whiter and hotter than the others had been. I covered my eyes and screamed.

When the light faded and my eyes refocused on the angel, I saw her in a totally different way, as if my eyeballs had been burnt out of my head and exchanged for another set.

Her laugh . . . her eyes . . . and her smell . . .

Bubble gum!

She smelled like bubble gum! And in that moment, it was like I'd smelled nothing but bubble gum my entire life. It was the most familiar, comforting smell in the whole world.

And from somewhere deep down inside, I knew that was my mom's smell.

"Happy Birthday, darling," she said. And laughed.

And then suddenly, from that same place deep down inside, I knew that was my mom's laugh.

She blew a huge pink bubble as she unhooked something from a long silver chain she was wearing around her neck. She held out her hand like she wanted me to take what she was holding.

It was a key.

When I hesitated, she nodded, smiled, and blew another bubble.

I took the key.

Suddenly the statue with the cyclone hair raised her heavy stone arm and pointed to the key. I took a closer look. It wasn't the flat, cookie-cutter kind you use to start a car. It was solid, heavy, and old-fashioned looking. I think it was made of brass. It had four holes cut into the widest, flattest part at the top. The part you put into a lock was chunky and smooth and kind of shaped like the capital letter *E*. I turned the key around and saw that the backside was totally flat, as if someone had taken a supersharp knife and sliced the key in half from end to end, all the way from the top to the bottom.

"The time has come to fulfill your purpose as prophesied in the ancient foretelling," the angel said.

What? What did she just say? I have a purpose that was prophesied in an ancient foretelling?

I searched her eyes, waiting for her to continue. She smiled and blew another bubble. "You must keep it safe," she said when the bubble popped. She nodded towards the key and pointed to my pocket.

I put the key in my pocket.

Suddenly the eagle let out an ear-piercing squawk. As I turned to look at it, it raised its head high and squawked again, sounding like it was in pain. Then the bird's feathers shimmered and wavered until its whole body became transparent. With one more squawk the eagle evaporated like mist rising into the air.

Through the haze of the mist, I heard a voice, but it was very different from the angel's soothing voice. "Simon," it said, not very loud, but just so I could hear it. "I've been looking for you."

As I turned to see who had spoken, I was surprised that it was the angel. But the moment we made eye contact I knew those weren't her eyes anymore. They had become narrow vertical slits, and one eye blazed with a piercing green light.

Her skin suddenly turned pale, crusty, and oily, and black fangs stuck out through grinning cracked lips. Her gown ripped and frayed and turned black. Her hair frizzled and crackled and burned right off her scalp, leaving horrible red patches and a few stringy strands hanging to her shoulders.

The creature gagged and spit the wad of pink bubble gum onto the ground.

"Welcome to my world," it hissed. Its white, boney fingers reached for my throat.

I turned to run.

The creature laughed. "Yes, run," it said. "Turn away and run."

As I kicked into high gear, there was another shriek of laughter. Everything faded to black, and I ran blindly through the darkness. Even though I couldn't see anything, I ran and ran and ran as far away from that creature as I could, hoping I would somehow run myself right out of the dream.

But then, as if I hadn't been running anywhere at all, I heard the creature's voice very close to my ear. "Cowardly little imp," it whispered.

What felt like a strong jolt of electricity zipped through my body as I gasped and woke up.

"What the heck was that?" I said, swallowing hard to push my heart back down into my chest where it belonged. Drenched in sweat, I desperately fought to catch my breath.

My sketches! I thought as I suddenly remembered where I'd seen the eagle and waterfall before.

With a shaky hand, I reached underneath my mattress and took the sketchbook out. I switched on the lamp and flipped through the pages. Something had changed.

Actually, some pictures had changed.

Some of the pictures I had drawn circles around had grown details—details I'd never included. And even though they were still flat pencil sketches, the transformed pictures took on a freakishly realistic look, as if they could just step right off the page.

The eagle had grown the same intense eyes and oily feathers the bird in my dream had.

The waterfall had grown rocks and a ledge that was visible behind the water.

And one of the faces—a woman's face—had grown a body. And a smile.

"Mom?" I asked. I put my hand on the picture. I could have sworn I heard her laugh again.

The twencil and those flashes must have changed my sketches into memories! I thought. I think I remember those things. My mom. And the eagle— he's . . . he's her guardian! And I know that waterfall, I just don't know from where.

I put the book on my mattress and got up. I needed to pace.

When I stood up, I felt something cold and hard skid down my leg, under my pajama pants. I immediately assumed it was some huge beetle or something that had just found a warm place to sleep for the night.

But when I heard a "clink" on the floor, I knew it was no beetle.

It was a key.

Or at least half of a key.

I picked it up.

It was exactly like the key in my dream.

I jumped back onto my mattress and flipped through the pages of my sketchbook.

The key.

But it hadn't grown any extra details. In fact it had lost some.

It was just a flat outline now.

With a shaky hand, I laid the brass key on the paper, flat side down, and slid it over top of the sketch.

It fit the shape exactly.

Then the line circling the key uncurled and reformed itself into two words:

FIND IT.

5 The Rat

I couldn't get back to sleep.

I stayed up the rest of the night staring at the sketches.

Was this what Grampa had in mind when he gave me the twencil? Did he know this would happen?

Of course he did! I thought.

It took every ounce of self-control I had (which isn't much, I'll let you know!) to keep myself from running to the other side of Grimstown in the dark to the mushroom farm to ask him what the heck was going on. I all but chained myself to the wall like a prisoner, passing the hours by pacing and bouncing my legs as I sat, staring at the sketches.

I spent most of those hours really concentrating on the angel, because I wanted to memorize every detail so I'd never, ever forget her again.

As I flipped through some of the other pictures, the ones that hadn't entered my dream, I noticed a big black patch on the very last page—a big black patch I hadn't put there.

I slapped my sketchbook shut. I couldn't wait any longer. I had to go upstairs and at least sit in the kitchen until Grampa came home. I had no idea what time it was, but I knew he wasn't home yet because I hadn't heard the kitchen door slam shut. I got dressed and grabbed my sketchbook and the twencil, and put the key in my pants pocket.

I swung the kitchen door open. Instead of walking into an empty kitchen like I'd expected, I saw Griselda sitting cross-legged on the counter, a half-eaten onion in one hand and a cigarette in the other.

No wonder she always smelled so bad.

Her gown was slit up the side, and her hairy legs were in plain view. Her crossed leg (which was swollen at the ankle) was bouncing up and down, and one of her high-heeled shoes was dangling off her big toe.

I quickly shoved my book and twencil into my back pocket.

"It's about time you got up!" she snapped, spitting onion all over the floor like bits of apple. "Here, eat this." As she tossed a bowl of cold porridge onto the table, her bouncing leg flew up, sending the shoe that had been hanging on for dear life flying off her toe and across the room. "Get that for me! And be quick about it. We have to go."

"Go?" I asked.

"Yes, go."

"But I want to wait for Grampa," I said as I picked up the shoe and handed it to her. She put it back on her toe and started bouncing her leg again.

"Oh, he's gone." Griselda exhaled a steady stream of smoke through her nostrils.

"Gone?"

Griselda's mouth slowly turned up at the corners. "Oh, yes," she said as she threw her onion in the sink and pulled a knife out of the wooden block.

"When's . . . when's he coming back?" I asked.

"Oh, I don't think he will be," she said calmly, smiling again.

Did she kill him? I thought as I watched her study the blade.

"Where is he?" I asked, trying to steady myself.

Griselda rolled her eyes. "He left."

"He left? Why?"

"To get away from you! Now eat! And be quick about it! We need to leave in five minutes."

"Where are we going?"

Her eyes narrowed. "The Grimstown Academy for Orphans," she said.

"You can't just take me away without Grampa's permission!"

"Without his permission? Oh, I have his permission all right!" She shoved the knife back into the block. "Here. Read this. It's a good thing I found it or else you might never have believed me." She threw a scrap of thick, torn paper at me. It said:

Simon,
Will
you
get
lost.
Grampa

It was written in Grampa's messy handwriting.

"What's this supposed to mean?" I asked.

"What do you think it's supposed to mean? He wants you to get lost! And . . . he told me to take you to the academy. He wants you out or else . . . he won't come back." She smiled again. "You didn't expect he'd want to keep you forever, did you?"

"Where did you find this?" I asked in disbelief, holding up the note.

"Taped onto your bedroom door," she said as she took another puff of her cigarette.

"Right."

"What? Do you think I'm making it up? You can see that he wrote it himself!"

She did have a point there. That was definitely Grampa's writing. But I couldn't believe he'd want me to go to the academy or that he would tell me to get lost. It just didn't make sense.

But then again I could probably count on one hand the number of times that Grampa did something that made sense.

Then I suddenly thought of something else.

"But it's July," I said, sitting at the table. I put the spoon into the porridge. It stood straight up on its own.

"And your point is...?" she said.

"Uh, well, I'm on summer vacation."

Well, I was, in theory, anyways. I don't think many people would call spending all summer at home, sleeping in a basement, a vacation.

"And your point is . . . ?" she said again.

"There aren't any classes in the summer."

Griselda laughed. "Ah, funny boy. The academy has classes all year round. Why, where do you think all the little orphans would go if they had summer vacation?"

"But I thought you told me Grampa doesn't want me at that school," I said. "He thinks they're all incompetent."

"Well, I guess he doesn't think so anymore!" Her eyes narrowed again. "Eat! We have to go." She butted out her cigarette on a dish rag, straightened her shoe, hopped off the counter with a thud, and walked out of the kitchen. "Get your things! I'll be waiting in the car!" she hollered from the hallway. I heard the jingling of keys, and then the front door slammed.

I picked up the bowl of porridge by the upright spoon and threw the whole thing in the garbage. It would have taken me a week to scrape that bowl clean.

I went into the hallway and grabbed a backpack from the closet.

The grandfather clock chimed seven-thirty.

It didn't look like Grampa was coming home.

I read the note again. My heart started aching.

I guess he really does want me gone, I thought. There was no second-guessing what the words meant. I shoved the paper into my pocket.

I went down to my room and put everything I owned (which was pretty much just a couple T-shirts, boxer shorts, a grey zippered hoodie, a couple of pairs of jeans and socks, pajamas, and a toothbrush) into the backpack and zipped it up.

I double-checked to make sure I had the key in my pocket.

I guess I'll never get to tell Grampa about this, I thought. Or show him my sketches. Or tell him about my dream.

And I guess I'll never know what it was he wanted me to know.

I closed my bedroom door and stood there for a few seconds as these thoughts sunk in.

I've often wanted to have a different life—a life away from here. But now that it was actually about to happen, all I really wanted to do was stay. Things had literally changed overnight, in a big way, and I was suddenly desperate to ask Grampa if he knew anything about the "ancient foretelling" and show him my key. I wanted to tell Grampa I was ready to do anything it took to remember, even eat those horrible-smelling roots.

I slowly headed up the stairs and out the front door.

• • •

The ancient stone building of the academy stood in a secluded valley. Before we could make our way up the winding driveway, we had to get through the heavy, black iron gate. The gate had "Grimstown Academy for Orphans" twisted right into the bars, as if the letters had tried to escape and got trapped in the metal.

Griselda stopped the car in front of the gate and laid on the horn.

The gate creaked open, and the gatekeeper waved us through with his one arm and all three of his fingers. The gate clanged shut behind us.

If I'd slept the whole way there and just woke up, I would have thought we had accidentally driven to Alcatraz instead of an academy. The school building was covered with spindly vines that looked more like barbed wire, rocks crumbled from the walls, black crows flew above the flat rooftops, and all the windows were narrow and dark.

The only things missing were bars on the windows and a gallows in the playground.

As we drove up the driveway, I noticed a dark figure of a man slip out through the doorway at the top of the school's massive stone steps. He was tall and thin and dressed entirely in black.

I was suddenly blinded by a flash of white-hot light — the exact same kind of flash I'd had in my dream. This flash was really short, but it was really intense. It felt like knives had been shoved into my eyes and pulled back out.

"What are you groaning for?" Griselda spat.

"Uh, just a . . . headache," I said.

As my eyes refocused on the building, I couldn't figure out why that flash had happened. I couldn't remember drawing anything like the school in my book. The only building I'd drawn was a castle, and this place didn't look anything like it.

I quietly took my sketchbook out of my pocket and flipped through the pages behind Griselda's seat. None of my sketches had changed, but something was happening to the black spot on the last page. A shape was emerging from the middle of it, as if the lead was being lifted off the paper with the edge of an eraser. The shape formed into a three-point star.

"Whoa," I said out loud, without thinking.

"Yeah," snorted Griselda. "Enjoy your new home."

Stunned, I closed my sketchbook and looked back out the window.

Before the car had even stopped, Griselda said, "Get out." She pounded the gear shift into park, turned around, and knelt on her seat. She reached back to where I was sitting, unlocked my door, and pushed it open. "I said, get out." She threw my backpack out onto the unpaved driveway.

I'll miss you, too, I thought as I got out and picked up my pack. I slung it over my shoulder and put my sketchbook back into my pocket.

Griselda was just about to pull the car door shut when something caught her attention. I followed her gaze to see what it was. It was the man at the top of the stairs. He gave a little nod and walked down the stairs towards the car. He held on to the rusted railing as he descended, and seemed to test each step with his toes before putting his full weight on them.

Griselda spun around in her seat and straightened her wig. She quickly lit another cigarette, slid out of the car, and leaned casually on the side of the hood, as if she'd been standing there watching the sunrise.

"Griselda?" the man called as he slowly approached the car. "Is that you? I had a sneaking suspicion I would see you again soon."

It was the man whose voice I'd heard through the vent the night before.

Griselda took a long drag of her cigarette and exhaled slowly. "Why, Mr. Ratsworth," she said.

Ratsworth. Now that's funny, I thought.

Only he didn't look too funny. He had the thinnest face I'd ever seen. It looked like the only thing keeping his bulging eyeballs from popping right out of his tightly pulled eye slits was a combination of his high cheekbones and his thick Neanderthal brow.

That and the darkly tinted eyeglass that was secured over his left eye with what looked like a hinge attached by a massive staple. The hinge and staple were crusted over with dried blood. His other uncovered eye wandered wildly around his eye socket.

I knew there was a reason he thought Griselda was pretty. He can't see straight!

"Oh, please, do call me Edgar," he replied as he held his hand out to her. She put her hand in his and he kissed it.

"Then Edgaaar it is," Griselda said in her syrupy voice.

"Truly enchanted once again," he said, bowing.

Griselda cleared her throat. "Um . . . your . . . eye . . . "

"Ah, yes. Nothing really. Just an unfortunate accident.

Not to worry about." He patted the eyeglass with a long white finger.

I must have let my heebie-jeebies show because the rat-faced man said, "Oh, I suppose this is the boy. Just as rude and obnoxious as his grandfather, I see." He stepped towards me, his one "good" eye trying to focus on my face.

He leaned in and . . . did he just sniff me? He did! Like a dog sniffs another dog. Did I forget my deodorant?

The Rat Man reached out. It seemed like he was about to cuff me up the side of my head, maybe because he thought I stunk. But his hand stopped suddenly just inches from my ear. I felt a kind of a buzz shoot up through my body and out my temple to his hand, kind of like an electrical shock but with the repelling force of two north-poled magnets.

The Rat Man let out an odd grunting sound and flapped his hand in the air, as if he'd gotten a bee sting or a shock or something.

"Yes, just as rude and twice as obnoxious," said Griselda, oblivious to The Rat Man's odd reaction to me.

"Yessss," hissed The Rat Man as he blew, as discreetly as possible, onto the palm of his hand. "And am I to assume, being graced with your exquisite presence, that the obnoxious old man has suddenly been called away on . . . urgent business?"

"I guess," said Griselda. "He just woke me up late last night and told me he had to leave for a few days."

"All the better for us then," said The Rat Man as he took Griselda's hand and kissed it again.

"Oh, yes," she said, fanning herself.

"Well, I suppose I should be getting him inside," said The Rat Man, letting go of Griselda's hand.

"Yes, I suppose," said Griselda with a sigh.

"And please, when you do see the old man again, be sure to let him know that the boy is in very competent hands. I will most certainly take care of him," he said, looking down his nose at me. I swear I saw a trace of a smile quiver from the left corner of his mouth. "One way or another." He spit into his hand and, as he slicked back his black, stringy hair, I noticed a red mark on his palm.

That's really strange, I thought. I wonder how I'd done that.

"And we must meet again," said The Rat Man. "Over dinner. I feel we could make beautiful music together."

Griselda giggled. "Charmed," she said.

"I was hoping so," said The Rat Man, winking at her with his uncovered wandering eye.

He helped Griselda back into her car and closed the door for her. She rolled down the window.

"Until then," he said.

"Yes, until then," she replied.

Griselda put the car in reverse, carefully backed out of the parking space, and slowly drove down the driveway. The three-fingered gatekeeper waved her out and closed the gate behind her.

And then I was alone with The Rat.

6 Blonde-haired, Blue-eyed Praying Mantis

Our shoes crunched across the gravel as The Rat led me towards the enormous set of stone steps that ended at the building's front door. He muttered curses under his breath and shot me harsh sideways glances. He blew and spit into his palm again, and I noticed the red mark had turned into a blister.

If only I knew how I'd done that.

As soon as we stepped onto the top landing, the door swung open on its own with a deep, drawn out creak. I followed The Rat inside and the door closed behind us.

The Rat walked to the table and reached for the candelabrum, and as he held up the flickering candles, he turned and stared at me. His eyeglass glinted in the candlelight. The spot above where it was attached to the browbone looked puffy and bruised. Whatever happened to his eye couldn't have been that long ago. Even Griselda was surprised by it, so it must have happened after he visited her at the house.

His voice echoed loudly in the darkness of the entry hall.

"Tessa!" he shouted.

I heard the echo of someone's heels clacking across the stone tiles behind me. If he hadn't called the name "Tessa," I'd have thought Griselda had returned by the sound of those shoes.

As we stood in an uncomfortable silence, with me looking at the floor, the clacking heels suddenly stepped into the splotch of candlelight. I looked up to see the rest of the body that was attached to them.

Holy crow!

I mean, okay, I'd never really been into girls before. I'd never really had a reason to be. I mean, when your school has a grand student population of one, there aren't too many female options.

"Yes, Mr. Ratsworth?" asked the blonde-haired, blue-eyed angel that stood beside me.

"Ah, Tessa. Would you please direct young *Simon Mugford* here to the boys' dormitory?"

"Yes, sir," she said, and then said to me, "Right this way." She gestured towards the staircase.

But I couldn't walk. My feet wouldn't work. My heart was racing. Aw, geez. What's wrong with me? Get with it, man!

I was drooling, for Pete's sake.

"You! Boy!" barked The Rat.

"Uh, yeah, yeah. Right that way," I said. I shifted my backpack to the other shoulder. Bits of gravel fell and bounced on the stone floor. I concentrated hard to take a step.

"Oh, and Mr. *Mugford*," The Rat continued.

I really wasn't liking the way he said my name: low and gravelly, like it was a bad taste in his mouth.

"Yes?"

"Since it is the summer semester, you are not required to wear uniform; however, there will still be no running, laughing, or singing in the halls; you are to wake up at 6 a.m., turn the lights out at 10 p.m., eat breakfast at 7:30, lunch at 12 noon, and dinner at 5 p.m. sharp."

Oh, and one more thing, Mr. *Mugford*—Happy Birthday, I said to myself on his behalf, since he had obviously forgotten.

"Understood?"

"Yes, sir."

He sniffed again.

He was making me really self-conscious.

The Rat passed Tessa a candle from the candelabrum. Then he carefully walked up the left side of the creaky, winding staircase.

The dark hall was really quiet.

Tessa looked amazing standing there, softly lit by flickering candlelight. Her smooth, glowing skin reminded me of warm peanut butter on toast.

"So . . . so I guess you're going to show me to the boys' dorm now?" I managed to splutter.

Suddenly the soft light was uncomfortably close—and hot—as she shoved the candle towards my face.

"Do I look like your slave?" she asked. "I'll have you know my name is Tessa Olivia Tasselbaum—the Tessa Olivia Tasselbaum of Tasselbaum Estates in the upper-middle section of the northeast corner of

Grimstown. I'm sure you've heard of it! And since I am the *only* student on campus who is *not* an orphan, I will not have you treating me like I'm some sort of slave!"

Who was this demon? It may very well have been the dim lighting playing tricks on my eyes, but I could have sworn she sprouted fangs.

"I'm talking to you! Are you listening to me?"

Was she growling at me? And to think my heart started racing when I first saw her! Now it raced again, but for a whole different reason: my mind flashed to a story I'd heard about the mating habits of the praying mantis.

"Who do you think you are?" she demanded.

Okay, so you play that way, do you?

"I," I said, emphasizing the word so loudly it echoed off the walls, "am none other than Simon Mugford. The Simon Mugford of Mugford Estates in the lower bottom basement of 49 Stone Elements Drive in the southwest corner of Grimstown. I'm sure you've heard of me as well," I added as I offered her a chance to kiss my hand.

"You're a moron," she said as she shoved my hand away. "I can tell I'm going to have to keep a close eye on you. Mugfords are bad news. Mr. Ratsworth told me that, in case you're wondering. He said, 'Tessa, you must keep an extra-close eye on the new boy who's coming. He's bad news, just like his grandfather was back in my day.' And now I can clearly see that his delineation of you is correct."

Delineation?

"So you, young Mugford, can find your room by yourself. And don't be late. Lunch is at 12 noon sharp." She cupped her hand in front of her candle and took off up the stairs.

So there I was, forced to find my own room in the dark.

Which was just as well, because I really didn't want Miss Delineation yapping at me the whole way to the boys' dorm anyways.

7 Spy and Seek

Believe it or not, what ended up being my biggest torture at the academy wasn't Tessa, although we did end up having quite a few more run-ins during my first week there.

And it wasn't the guys who knocked me down in the dark hallway and stepped over me on my first night at the school either.

And, believe it or not, my biggest torture wasn't even the teachers. Well, except for The Rat, that is. And maybe the tattooed cook, who was always wielding a butcher knife, whether he was in the kitchen or not. Sometimes I wondered if he slept with it.

No, my biggest torture—the thing that kept me awake at night—was the key.

What purpose could I possibly have that was prophesied in an ancient foretelling?

And supposing I did find the other half of the key, what was it supposed to unlock? And how could I find out? Since being put in the school, my sketches hadn't done any strange things anymore. I wasn't getting any more flashes or messages or clues or anything. No more dreams either. As far as I was concerned, Griselda had dropped me off at a dead end.

So I spent most of my free time alone in my room, drawing and staring at the drawings that had changed. I wanted—no, needed—more memory flashes.

A few days after being dropped off, as I was staring at the picture of the key, I figured I might as well get off my butt and start trying to solve the mystery behind it—right here, right now. I mean, I knew it would probably be a one in a billion chance that I'd actually find the other half, and probably a one in two billion chance I'd find what it actually unlocked, but there was nothing else to do in my free time.

So I began daily explorations throughout the halls of the school. And it turned out to be the best decision I'd ever made in my fourteen years of life. During my first week alone I discovered passageways and hallways behind rotating bookshelves, fireplaces, and sliding picture frames; underneath loose floorboards; above ceiling fans; and inside wardrobes. Most of the rooms in these secret passageways were locked. You obviously can't unlock doors with half a key. But that didn't stop me from trying. And just because I couldn't get in didn't mean I couldn't find out what kind of room it was that I wasn't getting into; I peeked through the keyholes. But, I'm sorry to say, most of the rooms were either empty or the furniture in them was covered with dusty sheets, which made for a pretty low excitement factor.

A couple of weeks after I said my sweet good-byes to Griselda, I had some time to kill before dinner, so I decided I'd go exploring again. Just as I was passing the mail room, I heard a voice shout out, "Hey! Young Master Mugford! I've got some mail for you today!"

Mail for me? Who'd be sending me mail? I thought. I spun around on my heels and headed into the room.

"Good thing I saw you pass by," said Mr. Greer, the cheerful, round man responsible for the mail. Mr. Greer had a medium-length white beard, a shaved head, and wire-rimmed specs, and wore a red zippered sweater every day. "I think this is finally your lucky day! Ho, ho, ho!"

Well, he didn't really say, "ho, ho, ho." I added that part. I just thought he should say it. He was the jolliest person in the entire school, probably in the entire world.

He totally didn't fit in with the school's other prison staff.

Mr. Greer nodded towards a huge, flat, oval gift-wrapped package leaning up against the wall. Then he went back to rifling envelopes into the mail slots.

"That?" I asked. "No way!"

"Yes way," Mr. Greer chuckled. "It's got your name on it! Take a looky!"

Sure enough, there was a big white sticker in the middle of the wrapping with my name and the school's address typed in heavy black ink. About five different stamps were stuck along the top right edge.

"Came by courier about an hour ago," Mr. Greer said. "By the look of how much they paid for postage, whoever it was that sent it to you must have wanted you to have it in an awful hurry! Need some help taking it to your room?"

"Uh, I think I'll be okay," I said as I lifted the package. "It's not too heavy."

"All-righty then!" Mr. Greer winked at me as he fired a bright orange envelope into a slot. He never missed a shot.

To think! I, Simon, got mail. Big mail.

If the package hadn't been so awkward to carry, I'd have run all the way to my room. But I had to settle for a speed-walk instead.

When I got there, I managed to open my door and drag the present inside. I leaned it against my desk.

"Grampa?" I said as I stood staring at the package. Who else would it be from? Definitely not Griselda.

I took the tag off the gift and sat on my bed. It looked like the tag had been torn. Somehow it seemed familiar.

The words said:

Dear
This
help
not
Too
Love,

And it was written in Grampa's messy handwriting.

Hang on a minute.

I went over to my desk and rifled through the drawers until I found what I was looking for: a torn piece of thick paper with writing on one side—the piece of paper Griselda had thrown at me in the kitchen the day she brought me to the academy.

Come to think of it, I'm not really sure why I kept it. It wasn't like it was cheery or anything. But it did have Grampa's writing on it.

Sure enough, when I held the two pieces of paper together along the torn edges, I saw the full message:

Dear Simon,
This will
help you
not get
too lost.
Love, Grampa

What?!

He didn't want me to get lost after all!

I got up and ran to the window. I looked up and down the driveway, as if I would see Grampa strolling away. Of course I didn't see anyone.

I picked up the package, sat back on my bed, and tore the wrapping off.

It was a mirror. It had a narrow metal frame around it.

It was the same mirror Grampa used to talk to himself in.

"Your mirror?" I said. "Why would you send me your mirror?"

I couldn't figure out why Grampa would just send me a mirror instead of coming to rescue me. He might not have wanted to get rid of me, but it was obvious now that he knew where I'd ended up.

And what the heck did that note mean? Knowing him, probably nothing. It was probably just another goofy rhyme. Except it didn't rhyme.

"Thanks anyways, Grampa," I whispered. I took a lot of comfort from thinking that obviously he didn't really hate me after all.

I put the mirror on my desk and leaned it against the wall. I threw the wrapping paper in the garbage and lay on my bed, staring at the glass. But I didn't stay there for long. Even though I was thankful for the gift, lying there and thinking about Grampa hurt too much.

I left my room and found my way to a hallway I'd accidentally stumbled into a couple of nights before. Just as I was crouching down to peek through a keyhole, a boy passed by me. Actually, he snuck up behind me and . . .

"ACHOOOOO!"

"Holy crow! What the heck are you doing?" I asked as I straightened up and put my hand on my damp skin. "Oh, sick," I said when I realized, too late, that I probably shouldn't have done that.

"I'm s-sorry. I didn't m-mean to s-sneeze on you. I'm al-llergic, you know."

"Yeah, well, next time warn me first so I can get out of the way," I said as I used my sleeve to wipe the wet stuff off my neck.

"I'm Gilbert M-Miller," he said. "I've s-seen you in class."

"I'm Simon. Simon Mugford. I've seen you, too."

"W-what w-were you l-looking at?" asked Gilbert.

"Oh, nothing," I said, suddenly feeling kind of stupid for getting caught.

"Oh, I thought m-maybe you'd found the girls' changing room or s-something."

Hey, I'd never even thought of that.

"No, it's just some dark, empty room," I said.

"S-so why are you p-peeking into a dark, em-mpty room?"

"Long story. Let's just say I'm doing it to pass the time. Why are you wandering down a deserted hallway?"

"I got l-lost l-looking for a sh-short-cut t-to dinner," he said.

"Yeah? Not a hard thing to do in this place," I said. "I've been lost a ton of times."

"You haven't accidentally s-stumbled into the . . . Det-tention Hallway, have you?" he asked with wide eyes.

"The Detention Hallway?"

"You've never h-heard of it?" His mouth hung open in shock.

"Uh, no."

"Creepers! You need to g-get out m-more! The Det-tention Hallway's just the m-most s-scariest p-place in the s-school! The horror st-stories about it are enough t-to m-make your s-skin . . . "

He stopped before he finished his sentence. Right where the floorboards and the baseboards met, a green wormy-type thing suddenly popped out of the crack. It snaked its way up the wall and spread out into branches, unfolding leaves as it climbed.

The vines from outside the building were finding cracks and coming inside!

"Whoa!" I said as I jumped back.

"Yeah. That's just s-started l-lately," Gilbert replied.

Just as soon as the leaves unfolded, they died, turning brown and crisp. Some of them even snapped off the vine with little popping sounds and fell to the floor.

"This s-school has always b-been w-weird, though," said Gilbert. "It used t-to b-be a m-monastery for a s-strange, old religion."

"So that's why there are so many empty rooms and passageways."

"Yeah, b-but even s-so, the s-school w-wasn't always s-so creepy. Just s-since . . . M-Mr. Ratsw-worth arrived." He said The Rat's name in a whisper. Then he leaned in close to me and looked around, as if he thought the vines could hear. "Can't t-talk ab-bout it here," he whispered. I figured "it" meant the Detention Hall. He didn't seem too concerned about the vines. "M-Mr. Ratsw-worth's orders. And it's am-mazing the th-things he finds out ab-bout. I l-liked it a l-lot b-better b-before he came along."

"The Rat's orders, huh? Oh, okay," I said. I made a mental note to remember to find the Detention Hallway on my next outing.

"W-what did you just call him?" Gilbert asked, his mouth hanging open in shock again.

"The Rat."

"Oh. That's w-what I t-thought."

We stood there staring at the dead vines for a while.

Okaaaay . . . somebody has to say something! Say something, say something. . .

"So, you've got a stutter, huh?" I blurted out.

Aw, geez . . . really intelligent!

"Uh, yeah," he said as his face turned red. He started tapping the baseboards with the toe of his shoe.

"I'm sorry. I shouldn't have said anything about it. I'm not making fun of you, honest. I just didn't know what else—"

"God just h-hiccupped w-when he m-made m-me, th-that's all," Gilbert said, cutting me off. "No b-biggie. Don't w-worry ab-bout it. Uh, s-so . . . how old are you?" he asked, changing the subject.

"I just turned fourteen."

"Really? S-so did I. W-when's your b-birthday?"

"July 7."

"M-mine's the twenty-first. Just a f-few days ago. Uh, you got s-something on your f-face," Gilbert said, pointing. "L-looks like s-some dirt or s-something; m-maybe from the keyhole. It's a dark s-smudge, right th-there." He poked my cheek.

Not again.

"Oh, yeah, that," I said as I tried wiping my face clean with my hand. "Pencil smudges."

Gilbert looked at me like I had ten heads. "You rub p-pencils on your f-face?"

"No, of course not. I like to draw—especially in class when things get boring, you know. And I get wicked pencil smudges." I showed him the side of my left hand. It was pretty much black from all the pencil lead smudged on it from that day's sketches.

"C-cool," said Gilbert.

"Yeah," I said.

"W-what do you d-draw?"

My hand instinctively went to my back pocket. But I just hooked my thumb over the edge of it and let my hand hang there.

"Oh, you know. Just . . . stuff," I said. I didn't want to tell him what kind of stuff. That was a bit too private to share with someone I hardly knew.

"Huh," said Gilbert, nodding.

There was another uncomfortable silence.

I cleared my throat and wiped my face harder.

"It's not getting any b-better," said Gilbert. "M-maybe you should t-try the other h-hand."

"Yeah," I said as I switched hands.

More silence.

"S-so you w-wanna go to dinner w-with m-me, S-Smudge?"

Smudge?

"Did you just call me 'Smudge'?" I asked.

"Uh, yeah, cause . . . w-well . . . I figured s-since you called M-Mr. Ratsw-worth . . . " Gilbert's face got redder and redder as he talked. "Uh . . . you know, s-so I figured that I could . . . uh, w-well . . . cause of the . . . s-smudges . . .

and all . . . " He stopped talking and looked down at the floor. I never knew a face could turn that shade of red.

"Oh, really? I never would have figured that one out." I tried to sound overly sarcastic to lighten things up a bit. I actually didn't mind the sound of "Smudge." I kind of liked it.

And it sure beat O.W.N.O.

"S-sorry. I w-won't call you that again," he said, turning even redder, if that was even possible.

Apparently he didn't understand sarcasm.

"No, no," I said. "I like it."

He peeked up at me without lifting his head. "Really?" he asked.

"Yeah, sure. Why not?"

The red from his face drained out of his cheeks as he sighed and wiped his forehead. I hadn't noticed until then, but he was sweating bucketloads. I noticed huge wet spots under his armpits.

"Okay, S-Smudge," he said. Then he laughed.

"So what are we waiting for?" I asked. "I'm starving. Let's go eat . . . *Gil.*"

8 Blind Eyes

Gil and I hung out together every day after that afternoon. As it turned out, neither of us had a roommate, so we decided to bunk together. We didn't ask if we could. We just did. And I don't see why it would have mattered to anyone anyways. There were so many empty rooms in the school just waiting to be filled. Even though each room had two sets of bunk beds in them, every kid at the academy had their own private room. Heck, you could have spread your stuff out into two rooms if you wanted.

We ate every meal together, did our homework together, and even sat beside each other in all our classes. Before I knew it, two more weeks had passed and we were already a week into August.

And sitting in the middle of an excruciating primeval history class.

"Turn in your textbooks to page sixty-six where we will begin today's lesson by discussing the significance of blood in ancient practices of . . . "

The Rat's voice slowly turned into a background hum as I took a little mind trip out the classroom window. Primeval history was the worst class to have right after lunch. All anyone wants to do is nap.

The classroom had floor-to-ceiling windows all along one wall that looked out into the courtyard garden.

My desk just happened to be next to one of them. And considering the snail's pace of the lesson, my brain was on the other side of the glass before The Rat said anything about the significance of blood in the ancient practices of whatever.

The garden wasn't really the kind you'd want to play in. I mean, the only times I'd ever been out there was when I had to be, like when Professor Hester took us out there to play horseshoes during P.E. classes. It was an overgrown garden, tangled with dead vines, rosebushes, and other thorny plants. There was no soft grass to walk or play on, only sharp chips of stone that cut into your knees and the palms of your hands if you tripped and fell.

As my eyes traveled along the pathway, I focused on the massive stone dragon in the center of the garden. On some nights the dragon looked real as its red jeweled eyes flashed, reflecting the outdoor torch lights. It almost looked as if it hadn't eaten in years and was dying for a good meal.

That'd be great to add to my sketches, I thought as I reached for my sketchbook, pulled it out, and flipped it open to a blank page. I started sketching the dragon, beginning with its angry eyes. I wondered if I had a red colored pencil in my pencil case. A bit of color would make the eyes perfect.

Before I had the chance to add the evil glint to the second eye, I was harshly brought back to reality by the sound of fingernails scraping down the blackboard.

Everyone jumped in their seats and groaned, covering their ears. The sound made my skin crawl.

"Have I made myself clear?" asked The Rat.

"Yes, sir," said everyone.

Everyone except me.

"I'm not exactly sure Sludge knows what you just said, Mr. Ratsworth," said Tessa from the desk behind me. By now my new nickname had caught on, but Tessa enjoyed putting her own little twist on it.

I closed my sketchbook and slid it under my notebook just as The Rat started walking down my aisle, pointing a long spindly finger in my direction.

"Is that so?" he said as he stopped beside my desk. He was about to poke his finger onto my forehead when I suddenly felt that same electrical, magnetic, repelling feeling shooting from my head. The Rat growled, flapped his hand in the air a few times, and stuck his finger in his mouth.

"Sir?" I asked.

"Mr. Mugford, would you please repeat what I'd just said?" The Rat said as best he could with the middle finger of his left hand in his mouth while tapping the unclipped fingernails of his right hand on my desk.

I had no idea how I kept zapping him, but I liked it. I had to try really hard not to smile this time.

"I'm waiting . . . "

Aw, geez.

"Uh, you said . . . uh . . . " I stammered. Whatever trace of a smile I had sneaking around inside vanished.

"You! Boy!" he shouted while wagging his red finger at me. "I would have expected you to begin applying yourself here, at this academy, by now. You've certainly got a long way to go before you will ever make a passing grade, so I suggest you begin following along in class! Now, can you even tell me what we were discussing?"

"Uh . . . well . . . uh . . . we were discussing the significance of . . . uh . . . blood in ancient practices of . . . uh—"

"Maybe you should refer to your notes," Tessa butted in. "You were taking notes, weren't you? I'm certain I saw you writing in your book."

I seriously wondered what the chances were of the stone dragon coming to life, crashing into our classroom, and eating Tessa.

"My notes . . . well, uh . . . "

"Yes, you know. Surely you couldn't have forgotten already. You only closed your book a few moments ago," she insisted.

"Well, Mr. *Mugford*? I'm waiting," said The Rat. "And you know how I detest waiting. Will you show me your notes, or shall I find them for you?" He leaned towards me and sniffed near my shoulder a few times.

Geez, I had a shower this morning, I thought.

"Mr. *Mugford*?"

With his face so close to mine, I couldn't help but notice that the spot where his eyeglass was attached had been cleaned and had formed a scab. It still looked horribly painful.

"Oh, th-those notes," Gil piped up in a shaky voice.

The Rat's head snapped around to face Gil.

Gil grabbed a few pieces of paper from his desk and held them up. "Th-they fell on the floor w-while you w-were b-busy looking up th-the reference on the b-board, S-Smudge," he said, careful not to make eye contact with The Rat.

The Rat glared at Gil and snatched the papers from him. He held the notes close to his face and then far away as he tried to focus his wandering eye on them. The Rat's eyesight was really bad, considering one of his eyes was covered over and the other couldn't focus on anything. Everyone knew that he could barely see past the end of his own nose. And everyone also knew that he'd never admit it.

The Rat let out a low growl. "Don't be so careless next time, Mr. *Mugford*," he said, slapping the papers onto my desk.

Tessa's jaw dropped.

"But, Mr. Ratsworth," she protested. "I suggest you take a closer look at—"

"Not now, Tessa," he said as he raised his hand to silence her. "And you," he said, turning to Gil. "Mr. Miller, it's best you just be concerned about yourself in the future."

He raised his eyebrows at Gil and gave him a nod and a twisted little smile. Then he turned sharply and walked back to the front of the classroom.

"Wh-what's that supposed t-to mean?" Gil whispered to me when The Rat was a few desks away.

I shrugged. How should I know?

Tessa's eyes narrowed as she glared at Gil.

Gil's face went red and his forehead immediately got damp as he buried his face in his textbook.

I looked at the papers that lay crumpled on my desk. They were pages from one of Gil's mystery magazines, a set of handwritten clues suggesting the whereabouts of a murder weapon that was stashed somewhere on a dairy farm in the Midwest.

The Rat really was blind!

Good old Gil.

Just then the bell rang.

"Ah, yes, the recess bell," said The Rat. "A shame you won't be able to heed its call. Since Mr. *Mugford* used up much of our valuable class time, you all will now copy the tables on pages sixty-seven and sixty-eight into your notebooks. You can all thank Mr. *Mugford*."

The whole class groaned.

Except for Tessa. She just smiled and said, "Yes, Mr. Ratsworth."

He turned and walked back down the aisle and sat on the corner of his desk. His long yellow fingernails tapped on the desktop as he stared at me.

I decided I'd better get to work this time. I opened my books and started copying the tables: T5—Blood

Rituals of the Ancient World and T6—Tools Used for the Releasing of Blood. Sheesh.

Before I knew it, the bell suddenly rang again, jolting The Rat out of his evil glare and signaling the end of recess and the beginning of a different class.

"Now get out! All of you!" The Rat slammed his fist down on his desk, sending pencils and a stack of paper flying to the floor.

"Mr. Miller, a word," The Rat said with his eyebrows raised at Gil.

Gil looked at me with terror in his eyes.

"Alone," said The Rat, staring at me.

I slowly got out of my seat and walked towards the door. I looked back to see Gil, his face still frozen in fear, watching me leave.

"Alone," The Rat said again.

9 Scared Spitless

"So he just asked you to clean up his papers for him?" I asked, still stunned, as Gil and I started our homework in the dorm room that night. Over dinner, Gil had told me the reason The Rat had kept him in after class. I had thought for sure he was a goner when I left him alone in the classroom. I thought maybe The Rat had clued in to the mystery magazine papers or something. "That's it?"

"Y-yeah. Pretty m-much."

"Pretty much?"

"W-well, he just s-said I should b-be less concerned ab-bout you and s-start thinking ab-bout m-myself m-more," Gil said as he sat on the floor and pulled his pencil case out of his school bag.

"And? What did you say?"

"I just nodded and s-said, 'Ok-kay.'"

"Did he say anything else?" I asked.

"W-well, he did ask m-me one thing," Gil said, sharpening his pencil.

"Well, what was it?"

Gil reached out and tapped my arm. "I w-was right."

"What? What are you doing?"

"He asked m-me w-what happens when I t-touch you. And I t-told him nothing happens. Actually, w-when he asked m-me I didn't really know b-because I didn't remember ever t-touching you, so I just guessed. I guess I g-guessed right."

"What did he say when you told him that?" I asked.

"At first he l-looked like he w-was going to b-blow his t-top. He w-was carrying on s-something ab-bout curses. Or w-was he cursing s-something ab-bout carrying on? W-Whatever he w-was doing, he event-tually just ended up s-smiling and s-saying, 'Good.' Then he t-told m-me to w-worry less ab-bout you and m-more ab-bout m-myself again."

"Did you ask him why?"

"Are you crazy? I just w-wanted to get out of there as fast as I could. I w-wasn't ab-bout to s-start a conversation w-with him." The tip of Gil's pencil broke off halfway through writing a word.

"Geez, Gil! For a guy who loves solving mysteries, you sure aren't too into this one!"

"Oh yeah?" he said, looking up at me. "W-well, all those m-mysteries I read are ab-bout other p-people's m-murders, not m-mine. And I'd rather do everything I can t-to avoid h-having m-my m-murder be the t-top s-story in next m-month's issue of M-Mysteriously M-Mystifying M-Mysteries!"

"Okay, okay," I said as I sat down and emptied my school bag onto my bed. "I get your point."

So The Rat's trying to figure out if I have the same effect on other people or not, I thought.

"Well, I'm just glad you didn't get in trouble 'cause of me. Thanks again for bailing me out, by the way."

"No p-problem," he said, sharpening his pencil again. "Just don't st-tart m-making a real habit out of it."

"Uh, Gil?"

"Yeah?"

"Do I smell?"

"W-what?"

"Do I smell?"

"I don't th-think s-so."

"Come here." I lifted my arm. "Smell."

Gil scrunched up his nose and stuck it in my armpit.

"S-smells fine to m-me," he said as he sat back down on his bed. "W-why?"

"It's just that The Rat always seems to be sniffing me."

"M-maybe you just th-think he is," Gil said. "You know he's kind of s-strange. M-maybe he's just got a nose tw-witch or s-something."

"Yeah, maybe. Oh, here are your mag pages back. You're a genius, you know that? I don't know what I'd do without you."

"P-probably get yourself k-killed." Gil took the papers and slid them back into his magazine. "S-so, w-why do you th-think M-Mr. Rats-sworth hates you s-so m-much?"

"I have no idea. Well, actually, I think it has something to do with my grampa."

"Your grampa?"

"Yeah . . . he seems to think I'm just as—how did he put it? Oh yeah—that I'm just as 'rude and obnoxious' as my grampa."

"Ouch. S-seems they've got s-some kind of history t-together."

"Yeah. I guess. But I don't know what that has to do with me."

"Uh, could b-be 'cause you're his g-grandson?"

Did I just detect a hint of sarcasm?

"Maybe, but there is one thing I do know," I said, changing the subject. I really didn't want to talk about my grampa.

"Yeah? W-what's th-that?"

"Tessa has to pay."

"Uh, w-why does she have t-to p-pay? You hardly got into t-trouble t-today," said Gil.

"Doesn't matter. She can't think she got away with what she did. If we let her get away with this, she'll keep trying until she gets us into real trouble."

"Yeah, I s-see w-where you're h-headed." Gil's eyes got really wide. "One of th-these days she m-might get us s-sent to . . . the Det-tention Hall!" He jumped onto his bed, pulling the covers up over his head.

I still had no idea what it was about that place that had him so terrified.

Gil peeked out from under his blanket.

"Exactly," I said. "So we need to let her know she can't keep messing with us. We need to send her a strong message that says, 'Keep your nose out of our business.'"

Gil blinked a few times. "Yeah." He lowered the blanket a bit. "Yeah, you're right." He slowly lowered the blanket all the way.

"So what's with this Detention Hall anyways?" I asked after a short silence.

Gil grabbed his blanket in his fists and let out a little squeak. "It's just the m-most s-scariest p-place in the w-whole s-school," he whispered.

"Yeah, okay, you've told me that before, but why? Why's it so scary?"

"Creep-pers. Everyone knows!"

"Hey, I just got here a few weeks ago, remember?"

"You r-really don't know? Is . . . is the d-door locked?" Gil whispered, looking at it as if it had just grown ears.

I got up and checked.

"It is now," I said. "Why does the door need to be locked?"

"M-Mr. Ratsw-worth . . . has forbidden anyone to t-talk ab-bout it," he whispered.

"Riiiight," I said, playing along as if I believed we were being watched, too. "Well, the door's locked, and I'm almost positive there's no one in here besides us, so—"

"Ok-kay," he said. "W-well, I guess no one really knows exactly w-what hap-ppened, cause no one w-was actually th-there, b-but just a few w-weeks ago, p-probably just a day or t-two b-before you got here, M-Mr. Rats-sworth locked a guy named M-Maximillian S-Snute in Det-tention Hall. He w-was a few years older than m-me, s-so I don't really know m-much ab-bout him. Actually, n-no one really knows m-much ab-bout him 'cause he w-was a new kid—only got here that day. And no one knows w-what he did to deserve the p-punishment he got, b-but it's b-believed to have b-been the w-worst p-punishment ever in hum-man history."

"So what happened?" I asked.

"Rumor has it that just as M-Mr. Ratsw-worth locked him in, M-Maxim-millian s-started b-beating on the b-bolted door w-when all of a s-sudden the frosted glass w-window sh-shattered and a s-sliver caught M-Mr. Ratsw-worth right in the eye. Ever w-wonder w-why he w-wears that glass p-patch over his l-left eye? Yeah, w-well, that's w-why. And w-when the w-window glass got him in the eye, M-Mr. Ratsw-worth let out a b-blood curdling s-scream that p-pierced the halls of the academy. Th-that p-part's t-true, for sure, 'cause I heard it m-myself!"

Gil reached into his bedside table drawer and took an inhaler out. He shook it and sucked in a long puff.

"I didn't know you had one of those," I said.

He nodded as he held in his breath for a few more seconds. "I haven't needed it m-much lately," he said on a steady exhale. "Usually just w-when I've b-been running. Or really s-stressed."

"Oh."

I wasn't sure if I should push him to go on with the story or not, so I didn't say anything else. But he continued anyways.

"B-but w-what they s-say happened next is t-too horrible for w-words. T-too m-much b-blood and s-stuff. They s-say it's t-taken Mr. Lurch, the custodian, all this t-time just to get all the b-blood s-stains out of the w-walls and drapes."

"Whoa," I said, totally at a loss for words.

"Y-yeah. T-tell m-me ab-bout it. And no one knows w-what happened to M-Maximillian after th-that. No one ever s-saw him again." Gil leaned in closer to me and whispered, "I think M-Mr. Ratsw-worth killed him."

"Are you serious?"

"Yeah. W-why else w-wouldn't M-Mr. Ratsw-worth ever w-want anyone t-talking about M-Maximillian or the Det-tention Hall? And all the rumors ab-bout the b-blood and st-tuff—"

"I don't know," I said.

Gil nodded. "I'm t-telling you, he p-probably killed him and b-buried his b-body under the floorb-boards."

"Gil, maybe you're reading too many of those magazines of yours."

"M-maybe," he said. "B-but you just never know w-with s-someone l-like that. If you ask m-me, I th-think this whole s-school is cursed. B-between M-Mr. Ratsw-worth, M-Maximillian S-Snute, and M-Marion B-Bates, the w-whole s-school's s-scared s-spitless."

"Marion Bates?"

"Y-ea-ah!" he said as if I was supposed to know who Marion Bates was. "Just the b-biggest, m-meanest kid in t-tenth grade! Everyone knows M-Marion!"

"Oh, you mean Mad Dog?" I'd seen the aftershocks of Mad Dog, including the way he'd spray-painted his demon eyes symbol on the bathroom walls and on his victims' locker doors. "You mean to tell me the biggest, meanest kid in school has a girl's name?" I asked, snorting back a laugh.

"Y-you have j-just proven the p-point," Gil said, nodding his head. "W-wouldn't you have anger i-issues if your parents named you M-Marion . . . and you were a b-boy?"

"I guess," I said, laughing. But the look on Gil's face told me Marion's name wasn't a laughing matter, so I stopped.

"You d-don't want to do that around h-him," he said. "In c-case you h-haven't heard, M-Marion's the guy who 'accidentally' mistook P-Professor Hester's leg for a stake while playing Horseshoes."

10 Threats for Breakfast

I decided not to bring up the topic of my revenge on Tessa again that night. Gil was so exhausted from talking about his encounter with The Rat after class, what happened to Maximillian Snute, and why I shouldn't laugh at Marion Bates's name that he fell asleep on his bed while I went to the bathroom. And that was really too bad because I was thinking of going spying. And I was thinking of finally inviting Gil to go with me. But he looked so worn out, lying there sprawled across his bed, that I decided to just let him sleep and ask him some other time.

As I peeked into the first keyhole, I also decided that even if Gil did go spying with me sometime, I'd keep the key a secret from him. I mean, how do you go about explaining that your mother—who showed up as an angel and very well might be dead—gave you a key in your dreams?

Exactly.

As I crept down the dark classroom wing, I suddenly got a brilliant idea and changed my plans. Instead of spying more, I headed to a couple classrooms and collected a few things for my revenge plot.

And then I brought up the topic the next morning while we were getting ready for breakfast.

"So what do you think?" I asked as I took a pink-framed, pocket-sized mirror out of my desk drawer and held it up.

"Uh, w-why do you have a p-pink m-mirror?" Gil asked with his eyebrows raised.

"What's wrong with pink?"

Gil raised his eyebrows further.

"It's a gift for Tessa," I said.

If Gil could have lifted his eyebrows any more, they would have disappeared into his hairline. "Is there s-something you w-want to t-tell m-me?" he asked.

I laughed. "It's part of my revenge plan," I said.

"How's th-that a revenge p-plan?"

"I'm still working out the details," I said. "But I have a pretty good idea."

Actually, I knew exactly how it was going to be a revenge plan. We were going to turn the mirror into a locker mirror. And Tessa was going to stare at herself in it, and we were going to sneak up behind her, shove her in her locker, and lock the door. Simple and effective.

But I didn't want to tell Gil about the plan prematurely, in case he got cold feet.

"So w-where'd you get the m-mirror?" Gil asked.

"From the science lab. Painted the frame myself. You like it?"

"Guess s-so," said Gil, making a face. "Esp-pecially the p-purple hearts."

"Here. Help me stick these magnets on the back."

We peeled the waxy paper backing off the magnets and stuck them on the mirror. Then I wrapped the mirror in the pink tissue paper I'd "borrowed" from the art room.

"Now let's write a note to go with it. How should we start?" I'd never written a love note before.

"Dearest T-Tessa," said Gil. "You are the hot-test thing on the p-planet. I've b-been w-watching you from afar . . . "

I looked at Gil out of the corner of my eye. "Sure there isn't something you want to tell me?" I asked.

"Sh-shut up," he said. "You w-want m-my help or not?"

"Just buggin' ya. Keep going. You're on a roll."

We finished the note, folded it in half, and taped it to the front of the package. I wrote "To Tessa Tasselbaum" in a big heart on the front of it. I think girls like stuff like that.

"How are w-we gonna get it t-to her?" Gil asked.

"We push it through the slot in the mail room door late tonight, when Mr. Greer isn't there."

"Good enough," said Gil. "I'm s-starving. L-let's go eat b-before everything's gone."

I hid the package back in my desk. We grabbed our books and hurried to the Dining Hall.

"Who's on duty this morning?" I whispered as we grabbed our trays and joined the line. I picked up a bowl of what was supposed to be oatmeal, I think. I put it back.

We scanned the room. "It's only P-Professor Hester," said Gil, breathing a sigh of relief.

I spotted Professor Hester leaning against his walker by the kitchen door. His leg was bandaged from thigh to ankle thanks to Marion Bates.

"Th-thank God it isn't M-Mr. Ratsw-worth," whispered Gil.

I answered with a nod.

"Hey, do you mind moving on?" asked the person behind us in line. "They're closing up and I'd like to get some of that oatmeal."

We grabbed some food and took our trays to a table. We sat down just as a crowd was forming at another table on the other side of the Dining Hall.

"What's going on over there?" I asked.

"W-who knows? W-who cares? I'm eating," said Gil as he took a bite of his toast.

"I'm going to go check it out," I said.

"B-but I w-wanted to t-talk ab-bout the details of the T-Tessa p-plan," Gil said, spraying toast crumbs out of his mouth.

"When I get back," I said, eyeing the crowd, "I somehow have a feeling there'll be more motivation for it then."

As I made my way to the back of the crowd I heard a familiar voice speaking from within the middle of the swarm—an annoyingly familiar voice.

"So the next time they decide to pull even the slightest stunt—they're dead, so help me . . . "

I caught a glimpse of Tessa through the crowd of heads. She was sitting on the table, flipping her hair.

"Mr. Ratsworth always listens to me," she said. "I could tell him anything I wanted and he would believe me. Just wait and see. One of these days, they'll end up in . . . " her voice lowered to a whisper, "Detention Hall."

The crowd gasped.

"She said the 'D' word," someone whispered.

"And why shouldn't I?" Tessa said. "Mr. Ratsworth and I are super-tight." To drive home the point, she raised her hand and crossed her fingers. "After all, I am his favorite student since he and my daddy are *best* friends."

"So, Tessa," I called out. "What exactly are you planning on telling him about us?"

Everyone turned and looked at me.

"Yeah, Tessa," someone said.

Everyone turned back to Tessa.

"Oh, well . . . um . . . you'll never know!" she said, flipping her hair at me.

Everyone looked at me again.

"Well, I guess I can't tell you what we've got planned for you then," I said.

I heard a few snickers from the crowd as everyone looked back at Tessa. She squirmed and shifted her position, crossing one leg over the other.

"Oh yeah?" she said. "Well, let's . . . let's just see who gets to it first then."

"You're on!" I said, challenging her to the duel. And believe me, I was going to make sure I was the one to shoot first.

A murmur of excitement ran through the crowd.

"What's g-going on here?" asked Gil with his mouth full. He had brought along his plate of scrambled eggs. There wasn't much that could separate him from his food.

I cleared my throat. "Uh, they're all just saying how great it is that we pulled that prank in primeval history. And how great we are for getting away with it," I said, aiming for a reaction from Tessa.

"Oh, w-well, w-we haven't really gotten away w-with m-much," said Gil. "He just asked m-me to . . . "

He stopped and just stared at me blankly.

Actually, when I looked closer, I realized he was staring *past* me blankly. Then he dropped his fork on the floor.

Gil gulped. "Marion," he whispered and then slapped his hand over his mouth.

"Marion?" I repeated loudly.

Everyone gasped.

"What'd you call me?!"

11 Mad Dog

The crowd parted. Through it walked the biggest, meanest-looking kid ever. And his big, mean friends were right behind him. It looked like they had just finished lifting weights.

"What'd you call me?" Marion said again as he stepped towards me.

I was so caught off guard that every word I'd ever learned just seemed to grow wings and fly right out of my head.

"I asked you something, punk."

Everyone's eyes were on me.

Gil whispered something, but I couldn't hear it.

"Hey, it's the loser that tripped us up in the hallway," said one of Marion's friends when he got a good look at me.

"So it is," said Marion. "This loser thinks he can go around calling people whatever he feels like. Isn't that right?"

The room started spinning. It felt like the floor was shifting under my feet.

"D'you wanna call me that again?"

I swallowed hard.

"Didn't think so. Looks to me like you're not as tough as you wanna be, loser."

Marion's goons all laughed.

Everyone's eyes were still on me.

"Last time we were too busy stepping over you to give you a proper welcome," he said as he rolled up his sleeve, exposing a tattoo of a skull and crossbones on his forearm. "But it looks like we've got lots of time now. Since you don't even know my name yet, I'll take it slow. Let me first introduce you to my fist!"

Gil elbowed me in the ribs. He whispered something, but in my terror, I didn't get it. I wished I had gotten it when Marion grabbed my shirt and raised his fist. I wished I had gotten it when he came so close I could see up his nostrils and smell his morning breath. But I didn't get it. My brain had just stopped working.

Gil whispered, again louder this time. "He p-prefers M-Mad Dog."

"Mad Dog," I said, finally snapping to it just as Marion . . . er, Mad Dog lowered his fist and turned his head towards Gil. I noticed the bloody dagger tattooed on the side of his neck. "I . . . I called you Mad Dog," I said louder.

"Helping out your new little friend, are you?" Mad Dog sneered to Gil as he let go of my shirt. It took every ounce of the strength I had left to keep from melting right to the floor in a puddle.

"I . . . I—" stuttered Gil.

"You weren't thinking, were you, idiot?" He cuffed Gil up the side of his head.

Gil gulped again. He was sweating tubloads.

"And you weren't watching what you were saying! Were you, idiot?" Mad Dog demanded.

"S-s-sorry, M-Mad D-Dog," stuttered Gil.

"You're a stuttering idiot!" said Mad Dog, laughing. His friends laughed, too.

Mad Dog knocked the plate out of Gil's hands. It shattered as scrambled eggs and ketchup landed all over the floor. As Gil crouched down to pick up the plate, Mad Dog put his black-booted foot on Gil's back and pushed him down.

I looked towards the kitchen door, hoping to see Professor Hester limping in our direction. But he was gone. I quickly scanned the room. He was nowhere to be seen.

Mad Dog stuck his foot in front of Gil's face. "You got ketchup all over my boot!" he shouted. "Clean it off!"

Gil pulled his sleeve down over his hand and wiped the ketchup off the black leather.

Everyone, except Mad Dog's goons, stepped about five paces backwards and looked on quietly from outside the firing range. Tessa was still sitting on a table, at the back of the crowd, alone.

"Tell ya what," said Mad Dog as he stomped his freshly scrubbed boot on the floor. "I'm in a good mood today, so I'll let you and your new little friend go . . . IF you can say 'Mad Dog rules' ten times fast."

You could have heard a pin drop. Gil just sat on the floor. I knew just as well as anyone that something like that would be impossible for him to do.

No one moved.

"M-M-Mad D-D-Dog r-r-r—"

Mad Dog knocked Gil's glasses off his face. "We'll be here all bloody day if we have to wait for you! Just pick up your glasses and get outta here!"

My palms were sweaty and my face burned. Gil was as good as blind without his glasses, and to expect him to locate them on the floor was like asking someone to pull a purple crayon out of a box in the dark. And to make it worse, whenever Gil's searching hand got close to them, Mad Dog kicked the glasses farther away.

Cowardly little imp, I thought. I'm a cowardly little imp.

I wished the ground would swallow me up.

Mad Dog continued mocking Gil. "You're useless! That's why your mom left you on the steps in the freezing cold. She hoped you would die!"

My heart beat wildly in my chest, and I felt anger rise from my toes all the way up to the top of my head like mercury in an overheated thermometer.

I should have exploded right then and there.

I should have marched right up to Mad Dog and kicked him between the legs.

I should have helped my friend.

I should have had his back.

I should have.

But I didn't.

Because Mad Dog was standing there with his foot on Gil's hand and his fists clenched at his side, staring at me with his black outlined eyes, daring me to make a move.

When he realized he didn't have a taker, he knocked Gil to the ground again with one swift kick.

"That's so you never forget who's boss," he said. Then he and his goons took off.

The crowd slowly broke up, like chunks of ice off a melting river. I heard a snort of disrespect behind me, and, without even looking, I knew right away it was Tessa.

"You are pathetic," she said in my ear before she walked away.

Gil lay on the floor, and I felt lower than the dust bunnies under his body.

"Y-you know, S-Smudge, I'd s-sell my soul if I c-could only get r-rid of this s-stupid s-stutter," he said in a barely there whisper as I handed him his glasses and helped him up.

I was furious with myself.

Cowardly little imp.

"Sorry, Gil," I said.

"I know."

We walked to class in silence.

12 Maximillian

After everything that had happened in the Dining Hall, Tessa took it upon herself to make the rest of my day extra miserable. She continually made loud comments about how pathetic and moronic I was. I was feeling stupid enough about the things I had said and what happened afterwards, without having her rub it in. If I was planning on getting her before, it was nothing compared to what I wanted to do to her now.

I wasted no time in launching my plan of revenge. Gil was still wrecked from his encounter with Mad Dog and didn't want to leave the safety of our room that night, so I did it myself. At the stroke of midnight, I crept out of our dorm and made the drop-off at the mail room to make sure she got her "gift" bright and early the next morning.

As I had expected, she did. As an added bonus, Tessa put the mirror up in her locker right away. So I didn't even have to wait long for my chance.

Tessa was always the last one in the classroom wing at the end of the day, usually because she was sucking up to The Rat somehow, erasing the boards or sharpening pencils. Luckily for us, she decided to worship at her new mirror altar one last time before going to dinner. Gil and I hid around the corner and watched as Tessa fixed, refixed, and then fixed her hair again.

"I'm absolutely parched," she said as she tied a pink ribbon around one of her annoyingly bouncy pigtails. (They're called "pigtails" for a reason, you know. Think about it.) "I need a mineral water with lime."

I had no idea who she was talking to. I think she just liked the sound of her own voice. Either that or she had an imaginary friend, like Grampa.

"S-Smudge," whispered Gil. "I j-just thought of s-something. How are w-we going t-to s-sneak up b-behind her? She's going t-to s-see us in the m-mirror."

Aw geez! I never thought of that!

"Uh, we duck down, out of the line of sight, and move quickly," I said off the top of my head, trying to sound like I'd thought that angle through, like ducking out of sight was part of the plan all along.

Gil raised his eyebrows at me and made a face as if to say, "If you think so."

Luckily Tessa was admiring herself so closely that my half-baked plan actually worked. She wasn't at all aware of us sneaking up on her. Before she had time to bat another curled eyelash, we stuffed her into her locker and locked the door.

"Let me out! I'll scream 'murder'!"

Ah, yes, Tessa Tasselbaum in all her glory.

I smothered my laugh. No need to get traced back to this one. Gil used his sleeve to wipe our fingerprints off the metal door and lock.

"LET ME OUT!" Tessa screamed again as she pounded on the door. "I'm dying of asphyxiation!"

Asphyxiation. She spent way too much time trying to impress The Rat.

"M-maybe w-we should l-let her out," Gil whispered.

"Then she'd know it was us for sure," I whispered back. "She'll be fine." I pointed to the vents at the top of the locker door.

"Who are you?" Tessa screamed. "Sludge, is that you?"

"W-we should g-get out of here," Gil whispered. "Before s-someone hears her."

"You won't get away with this!" she screeched. "Whoever you are! Especially if your name is Sluuuuuudge!"

The way her whiny voice extended the "uuuuuu" made me want to turn myself inside out. I resisted the urge to block the locker door vents with the very shirt off my back.

"AAAAHHHHH!" Tessa screamed, her voice getting hoarse as she continued to pound on the door. "When my daddy comes to take me home, he'll bring his lawyer to prosecute you!"

That day can't come soon enough, I thought.

"S-Smudge, she's getting really l-loud," Gil whispered. "W-we should g-go."

"AAAAHHHHH!" she shrieked again. "This slipshod behavior will cost you some serious time!"

Hmmmmm . . . slipshod. I'd definitely have to check out a dictionary for that one.

I grabbed Gil by the arm and we ran off to dinner, leaving Tessa screaming and pounding behind us.

• • •

I excused myself from dinner that night because I suddenly didn't feel very well. It could have had something to do with all the stress from the last couple of days. Or it could have had something to do with the chicken livers and onions they were serving. Whatever the reason, I had to lie down.

As I walked into my room, I stopped just inside the doorway and looked at the mirror Grampa had sent me. It was still on my desk, leaning against the wall. I walked to the mirror and put my hand on the cold metal frame. "Where are you, Grampa?" I asked.

My head was throbbing and my eyes felt like they were on fire. I had to get to bed.

Just as I took my hand off the mirror and was about to turn and close my bedroom door, out of the corner of my eye I picked up something in the glass that had changed. I blinked hard because my image became really blurry. I leaned in close. I shook my head and blinked some more, but instead of clearing up, the edges of the mirror wavered and started to swim. It looked like the glass was liquefying.

"I've got to get to bed," I said. I wiped off the beads of sweat forming on my forehead.

Just then I heard a faint voice. "Help me out . . . I'm a little stuck here."

"Oh, great," I mumbled. "Now I'm hearing voices." I turned to flop down on my bed, but my T-shirt was caught on something. As I reached back to unhook myself, my heart jumped into my throat.

A hand had come out of the glass and had grabbed my sleeve! It was tugging me towards the mirror!

I screamed as I tried to pull the hand away. "Let go of me! Let go of me!"

"Just wait!" the voice pleaded. "I'm almost there!"

The voice was much louder. The hand still gripped my T-shirt, and I was horrified to see something else emerging from the mirror. It was a face, morphing and forming out of the liquid glass, as if being molded out of clay. It pushed its way through the mirror, blinked excess liquid out of its eyes, and stared right at me.

The second the face made eye contact with me, a flash of white light blinded me. That hadn't happened since the day I arrived at the school. This flash was long and intense, with a major sense of déjà vu. If the hand hadn't had such a firm hold of my shirt, I would have fallen to the floor.

When my eyes refocused I saw the face was that of a guy who looked a few years older than I was. I thought I knew him from somewhere. His voice sounded familiar, too.

"You all right?" he asked.

I shook my head. "Are you . . . a memory?" I asked.

He looked stunned. "Are you serious?"

I just stared back, probably looking as stunned as he did. Probably more.

"Who are you?" I cried.

"It's worse than I'd thought," he said, his grip tightening.

"What do you want?! Let go of me!" I wailed as I slapped his hand.

"If you really don't know, then you've got to promise to listen!" the face replied desperately. "If I let go of you, you've got to promise not to run off. And pay close attention!"

"Okay, okay," I said. "I promise! Just let go!"

"Mmmm, I don't think so," he said, smiling, his grip tightening even more.

"Who are you?" I asked again.

He shook his head and looked at me like I should already know his answer. "My name is Maximillian Snute."

Holy crow! I couldn't believe my ears! My mind flashed back to the story Gil had told me. That story had haunted me since I'd heard it.

But, as the story goes, the boy was never seen again.

Not until now, that is.

"*The* Maximillian Snute?"

"I'm the only one I know of," he said.

"Okay. I must be really, really sick. I'm going to close my eyes and count to three, and this will all go away." I covered my eyes. "One, two, three!"

When I opened my eyes, Maximillian's face was still staring back at me from the mirror, and he was still holding on to my shirt.

"Are you finished?" Maximillian asked as he nervously looked over his shoulder.

"How are you doing this?" I asked.

Maximillian rolled his eyes impatiently. "You couldn't have eaten the roots!" he said. "The short version is that this mirror is a portal from another realm. I'm using it to contact you."

"Are you serious?" I asked.

He nodded.

My skin prickled all over my body as I suddenly knew where I'd heard his voice before.

"Was . . . Grampa talking to you? In the attic?" I asked.

"Yes," he said. "Are you ready to cooperate now?"

This is nuts, I thought. The story of Maximillian Snute combined with my fever must have really messed my head up.

"Are you ready to cooperate?" he asked again.

"Uh, yeah, sure," I said, even though I actually felt like being sick. Maybe I should just let myself pass out, and then when I wake up he'll be gone, I thought.

"Good. It's time for you to bring the Key," said Maximillian as he looked over his shoulder again.

The key? How'd he know I had a key?

"What are you talking about?" I cried. That did it. The room starting spinning.

The expression on Maximillian's face turned to terror, and he lowered his voice so I could hardly hear him. "I can't . . . not now. I think he's found me."

I could hear footsteps coming down the hallway.

I looked at Maximillian. My eyes burned with fever. I tried to concentrate through the fog clouding my head. I put my hand in my pocket and held the key tightly.

The room spun faster.

"Just come, please!" He held his other hand out to me. "I'll answer your questions after I pull you through."

"I don't know what you're talking about!" I shouted.

Without saying another word, Maximillian pulled both his hands back.

I was free! But I didn't run. I just stared at the mirror, watching Maximillian's face melt back into the glass. He was saying something as he disappeared, but the words only came out as bubbles on the liquefied mirror.

I reached into my back pocket and pulled out my sketchbook. I flipped through the pages until I found the sketch that had changed: a face. A guy's face. Maximillian's face. The angles of his chin and cheekbones were sharper than I had drawn them, and his hair was longer and pulled back into a ponytail.

I suddenly heard voices chanting in the distance.

"The theventh thun, the theventh thun . . . "

" . . . ancient foretelling . . . "

"He's needed . . . "

I let the voices take me under. My eyes rolled back into my head and I passed out.

• • •

The next thing I knew, Gil was standing above me, tapping my cheek with his fingers.

"S-S-Smudge! S-S-Smudge! W-wake up! Are y-y-you okay? S-Smudge!"

I groaned as I held my head. "What happened?"

Gil wedged his shoulder under my armpit and helped me up. "I d-don't know. I j-just found you lying h-here on the f-floor." He half-carried me to my bed. "J-Jeepers C-Creepers! Y-y-you must b-be really s-s-sick."

I just grunted.

Sick, I thought. My head . . . my stomach . . . MY KEY! My hot skin prickled again at the thought. Got to keep my key safe. How—?

"I'm g-going to get the n-n-nurse," said Gil over his shoulder as he ran out of the room.

My whole body ached. It hurt my skin just to have the sheets covering me. I was sweating, but I had goose bumps all over my body at the same time. My hands and feet felt like blocks of ice. I couldn't make the room stop spinning. I felt like I was on a turbo-boosted merry-go-round.

And then I drifted away.

• • •

I opened my eyes but closed them again right away. The light from the night-light in our room felt like glowing knives cutting through my pupils. I must have groaned or something because Gil shushed me.

"Shhhh. It's okay. I'm h-here, S-Smudge. Lie b-back. Relax. You need t-to rest. It's l-late."

"What time is it?" I asked.

"Around m-midnight."

I must have fallen asleep. I couldn't remember.

"What happened?" I asked. My memory was like scattered pieces of a jigsaw puzzle lying face down.

Gil told me that when he returned to my bed with the nurse, I was hot and delirious. She gave me a shot so I could sleep.

"You've b-been s-saying lots of w-weird things," said Gil. "B-but the w-worst p-part of it all is that you w-were t-talking ab-bout M-Maximillian S-Snute." He said Maximillian's name in a whisper.

"What?" I croaked. "I was talking about . . . Maximillian?"

"Yeah, b-but don't w-worry. The nurse just s-said you w-were t-talking nonsense b-because you're s-sick w-with fever. She just b-blamed it on the flu."

Suddenly the vivid memory of the episode with the mirror assaulted my senses like bad perfume. I bolted up and felt my back pocket for my sketchbook.

"Is this w-what you're l-looking for?" asked Gil, holding my book up.

I nodded with a sigh of relief.

"It w-was on the floor b-beside you. You're r-really good," he said as he gave the book to me.

"Thanks," I said as I took the book and shoved it into my pocket before collapsing back on the bed. "Uh, Gil?"

"Yeah?"

"Uh, could you take that mirror down and put it in the closet for me?"

Gil looked at me with pity. "Yeah, s-sure," he said.

He probably thought I still had a thread of deliriousness wrapped around my head.

Trust me, if I had it my way, I would've wrapped a whole scarf of deliriousness around my head and skipped right into the land of insanity. Anything to forget the face and voice of Maximillian Snute.

13 Footprints in Gravel

I was feeling better by dinnertime the next night, just in time for calfbrains and scrambled eggs. I decided to pass. Again.

Where did they get that chef from, anyways?

Just as Gil and I were about to leave the Dining Hall (Gil took his dinner to go in a doggie bag. I swear, that kid will eat *anything*), The Rat came in through the main doors.

"Gil, look," I whispered, elbowing him in the ribs.

"Yeah, I s-see him," he said. He was already starting to wheeze.

The Rat stood in the doorway, scanning the hall.

"Do you think he's looking for us?" I asked as I put up my hood, hoping it would disguise me at least a little bit.

Gil gasped. "D-do you think Tessa . . . ?"

"Let's not wait to find out," I said. "This way. We'll sneak through the kitchen."

We slipped out the doorway at the back of the hall that led to the kitchen. As soon as we passed through the swinging double doors, the chef spotted us from behind his massive butcher block. He was wielding his butcher knife, as usual.

"Reporting for kitchen duties?" he asked in his gruff voice as he chopped the head off a chicken. A live chicken. Gil and I watched in horror as the poor headless thing ran a few laps around the butcher block, fell to the floor, and ran a few more laps around the chef's feet before it completely died. The chef picked it up by the legs and held it out to us. The blood drained out the neck and onto the floor.

"You can start by plucking this," he said.

Gil groaned.

"And take that hood off when you're in my kitchen."

"Uh, no. Actually, we're not here for kitchen duty," I said, pulling my hood off. "Not today, anyways. We're . . . uh, just, uh, late for our night class and thought we'd . . . uh, take a shortcut through here." I pointed across the kitchen to the door at the opposite side, the door that would lead us to freedom.

"Didn't know there were night classes," said the chef, scratching his tattooed arm with the bloody blade of his knife.

"Well, just 'specially for us," I said, digging myself into a deeper hole. "We . . . uh, need tutoring."

The chef tossed the dead, headless chicken into a container that, by the look of it, was full of other dead, headless chickens.

Gil put his doggie bag on the counter.

"Tutoring, eh?" the chef said.

"Yes," I said.

He eyed me suspiciously. "Go on then." He pulled another live chicken out of a cage and chopped its head off, too.

We hurried past him, and just as we went through the door, I heard The Rat enter the kitchen from the other side.

"Ah, Chef Brutus. I've been needing to speak to you."

"S-Smudge," whispered Gil when we were in the hallway. "The s-school doesn't have t-tutoring classes."

"So? Would you rather stay and pluck and gut those chickens?"

"No," he said, looking like he was going to be sick.

We ended up in a dark corridor that led to the classroom hallway. The floor-to-ceiling windows in the hallway looked out to the courtyard garden, just like the windows in the classrooms. I stopped in front of one of the windows and pressed my nose to the cold glass.

"What are y-you d-doing?" asked Gil.

Something was different outside; something seemed to be missing.

"Look!" I said, tapping on the window as it suddenly dawned on me. "It's gone."

The center of the courtyard was empty.

"Wh-what are you t-talking about?" Gil asked, pressing his nose on the glass, too.

"The dragon," I said. "The stone dragon is gone."

"Yeah, it is," he said, looking out at the empty spot left behind by the dragon. "L-look!" Now he was tapping on the window.

I followed his eyes and saw what he was seeing: an iron cuff dangling off the side of the platform the dragon had been standing on. It was the kind of cuff you'd imagine would be on a prisoner's ankle, attaching him to a heavy iron ball so he couldn't run off.

"And there!" he said, pointing off to the right of the platform.

Although they were barely visible, there was what looked like deep footprints in the gravel pathway. And they led to what looked like a root-cellar door in the ground.

"B-but that dragon m-must w-weigh a t-ton. No one w-would b-be able t-to lift it and carry it off."

"Maybe no one needed to lift it," I said.

Gil looked at me. "W-what are you t-talking ab-bout?"

I pointed back at the iron cuff. "Why'd it need to be chained down?"

We thought about that for a while.

"When do you think it went missing?" I asked.

"I d-don't know," said Gil.

"Do you remember seeing it today?" I'd missed all my classes for the day because of the flu.

Gil thought for a minute. "I d-don't remember," he said. "C-come to think of it, th-that's strange 'cause I a-always f-feel it s-staring."

I'll bet if I had been in classes I would have noticed for sure.

Weird that I saw Maximillian last night, I thought, and that the dragon is missing now. Could the two things be connected?

Gil sighed and said, "C-Creepers." He pulled me away from the window. "L-let's get b-back to our room."

"Gil, that's the first place The Rat will come looking for us after Chef Brutus tells him we've gone for tutoring!"

Gil gulped. "Yeah," he said. "So where sh-should we g-go then?"

"How about the root cellar?" I said, pointing out the window. I really wanted to find out what happened to that dragon.

Gil rolled his eyes. "I'll t-take my chances g-going back to our r-room," he said.

"Fine. Maybe we can just hide out somewhere else for a while. You know, in one of the deserted hallways or something."

"W-which one?" Gil asked.

"Let's try . . . this one." I walked farther down the hall and pushed in a telltale stone sticking out of the wall. An area of the wall, about two feet wide, silently slid down and disappeared into the floor.

"How'd you d-do th-that?" Gil asked.

"When you sneak around a place as much as I do, you get to know some of the clues about where hidden entryways are, really fast."

We walked along a passageway and then up a couple stairwells until we ended up in one of the vacant dorm wings.

"S-Smudge, have you ever b-been here b-before?" asked Gil, brushing dust off his shirt.

"Uh, no, I haven't."

Just as I spoke those words, the sound of music—loud music—started up from somewhere inside the dorm. And that struck me as really weird because only one wing was open for boys and one for girls to live in; the other two boys' and girls' dorm wings were closed. Vacant. Out of business.

But what was even weirder than hearing music in a vacant dorm was that Gil started walking right towards it.

14 Psycho-Conductor

"Gil, where are you going?" I asked, trying to keep up with his quick pace. "Do you hear the music, too?"

He didn't respond. He just kept walking.

I shrugged. "Good plan, Gil." I patted him on the back as I followed, amazed at his sudden impulse. "You're catching on."

We followed the sound of the music down a dark hallway until we came to the room the music was coming from. There was a dim orangish light seeping out from under the door.

Gil reached for the doorknob.

"What are you doing?" I hissed, grabbing his wrist.

A terrible screech came from behind the door. The music stopped, and Gil pulled his hand away.

"Smudge?" he asked, blinking furiously. "W-what are w-we doing?"

"What do you mean?" I asked. "We're about to find out who's making the music."

"W-what m-music?" he asked. "W-where are w-we?"

"We will try this once again!" came an angry voice from behind the door. "And this time you will cooperate!"

Gil's eyes widened as he stared at the door. "I . . . I don't know w-what you're t-talking ab-bout," he whispered.

"Are you serious?" I whispered back. "You were following the music!"

Just then the music started again. Gil put his hands on the door and leaned in until his ear was touching the wood.

What's up with him? I thought, shaking my head.

Suddenly the door clicked and creaked open a bit. I pulled Gil away and pushed him against the wall. I flattened my body against the wall, too.

But no one came through the doorway.

After a few seconds, I slowly leaned forward and peeked through the open crack.

"Gil, check this out," I whispered.

We had front-row seats to what probably should have been a very private show. The dim room was filled with tons of candles and different kinds of art. It was really creepy, but it was the perfect setting for the Psycho-conductor in the room to lead his orchestra.

Except there wasn't an orchestra.

But there was a big, potted plant in front of Psycho-conductor. Its brown leaves were drooping to the floor.

Classical music filled the room and leaked out the open door as he swayed his head back and forth and stabbed his white-gloved hands into the air. His long stringy hair hung out from under the hood of his black cape and flung around to the rhythm.

"Now can you hear the music?" I whispered to Gil.

He didn't respond. He just stared straight ahead with wide, watery eyes. I don't think he blinked even once.

Psycho-conductor paused, panting, and looked at the plant through the greasy hair that had fallen in front of his face.

"Do something!" he shouted. "Do something, curse you! This is an outrage!" Psycho-conductor knocked a sculpture of a head off a table with his baton. It shattered on the floor and the music stopped again. "Is this how you show your gratitude to me? I slave endless hours writing and composing incomparable works of art, and you have the gall not to respond! How can I work my magic if you won't cooperate in this wretched place?"

It looked like he was shouting at the plant. He paced back and forth across the room like a caged animal, so furiously that I thought the carpet might catch fire, if not from the friction of his feet then from the sparks that flew out of his mouth. He used words that I can't possibly repeat without giving this chapter an R-rating.

"Uh, S-Smudge?" I heard Gil say behind me.

"Shhh!" I whispered.

"This is unacceptable!" the man in the room shouted. "An artiste such as I should be respected! I can't work under these conditions!" And with a flick of his cape he headed for the door.

"Holy crow, Gil!" I blurted as I pulled him away from the door.

We barely had time to hide in an old (and luckily empty) wardrobe in the hallway before Psycho-conductor bolted through the door. The gaps between the wardrobe hinges were just wide enough for me to see what he was doing. He stopped just a few feet away from us and turned back to face the door he'd just flown out of. He was so angry that he was trembling.

"I'm going to set things right!" he shouted. "And when I do, you will have no choice but to respond!" He looked up and down the hallway, but I still couldn't see his face because of the hood and the hair in front of his face. He shot another glance at the room he'd been in.

"In fact," he said, "I shan't waste another moment. I'm going to rectify this unfortunate situation straightaway." With a flick of his cape, he turned away and charged down the hall.

When he was out of sight I creaked open the wardrobe door and stepped out. "Come on. Let's follow him."

"Are you c-c-crazy?" said Gil. "Have you g-g-got a death w-wish or s-s-something? Rememb-ber, w-we're s-s-supposed to b-be hiding!"

"Gil, come on. You wanted to find out who was making the music just as much as I did," I said as I tugged him along by his sleeve. "Besides, I want to find out what that 'unfortunate situation' is he's talking about."

"I d-don't know w-what you're t-talking ab-bout," Gil said, trying to keep up with me. "I'm s-sorry, S-Smudge, b-but I really didn't hear any m-music."

I stopped walking and looked him in the eye. He wasn't pulling my leg.

"Okay," I said as I let go of his sleeve. I believed him, but it didn't make any sense. Why was I the only one who heard it? And if he didn't hear it, why did he follow it to the exact place it was coming from?

"Let's keep going before we lose him," I said. I turned back around and continued walking.

"J-jeepers c-creepers, S-Smudge," he said. But he followed anyways.

We kept to the shadows and snuck back down the hallway, out of the vacant boys' dorm and into the hallway that connected the boys' and girls' wings. By the light of the candles on the walls, I caught the tail end of Psycho-conductor's cape disappearing around a corner halfway down the hallway. That corner led to the main staircase that wound down to the school's foyer. We hurried to the corner and peeked around it like two cops on a stakeout.

"L-look," said Gil, pointing to the landing at the bottom of the stairs.

There, in a crumpled heap, lay a black silk cape with red lining.

"It must have slipped off in his hurry," I said.

We snuck down the right side of the double staircase and stepped around the cape, careful not to touch it. Making sure we stayed more than a few paces behind, we followed Psycho-conductor through a hidden doorway and down another staircase, a narrow, spiraling one. My shoulders bumped the sides of the walls and brushed against the dried-out vines on the stones as I walked. Not much could be said for the headroom either.

At the bottom of the staircase there was a door. An eerie reddish-orange light seeped out from underneath it—the same kind of orangish light that had come from inside Psycho-conductor's room. As I reached for the doorknob, the floor beneath my feet creaked. I froze like that woolly mammoth they found from the Ice Age.

I looked at Gil and he stared back at me, shaking his head over and over and over.

I went ahead and cracked the door open. I held my breath, hoping that would somehow make me lighter, and stepped into an empty hallway.

Just as I did, I heard the echo of a door click shut.

A giant door stood at the very end of the narrow hall. A huge metallic snake was coiled around a large hook above the door. Its forked tongue stuck out of its mouth and its tail hung over the corner of the doorframe.

"I think it's okay, Gil," I whispered as I motioned for him to follow me. "It's a hallway, and it's empty. I just heard a door shut."

Gil held his breath, too, and sidestepped the creaky part of the floor. But he froze the second he saw the door and the snake at the end of the hallway.

"I . . . I don't know ab-bout this," he said.

I must admit, I was a bit freaked out, too. And the candles that were hanging on the walls, sending dark orange splotches of light bleeding onto the stone floor, weren't helping. The whole hallway glowed red. The walls were wet, and in the dim red light, it looked like there were streams of blood dripping down the stones.

But before I thought any further about exactly how freaked out I was, something else caught my attention: a drawing on the wall just above the snake's head. It was a black circle with something scratched into it: a three-point star.

"Come on, Gil," I said, taking a few cautious steps. "We'll just take a peek."

"J-jeepers creepers," he said and then followed. But about three-quarters of the way down the hallway, Gil suddenly stopped. "I . . . I can't g-go any farther."

I believed him. It looked like he was literally rooted to the floor, like he had been petrified to the spot.

"Tell you what," I said. "I'll go down and see if it's safe, and then I'll motion for you to come if it is, okay?"

Gil just nodded. He took a couple of puffs from his inhaler. He'd gotten into the habit of carrying it around with him ever since he started hanging out with me.

When I got to the door, I suddenly noticed that it was boarded up where a window used to be. There was no glass. I started to sweat as I imagined the scene of Maximillian shattering the glass into The Rat's eye.

I held my breath and bent down. I peeked through the keyhole, but all I saw was flickering orange light.

I pressed my ear to the wood, but I couldn't hear anything, probably because by that time my heart was thumping so loudly in my chest.

"S-S-Smudge?" I heard Gil say, interrupting my concentration.

"Don't come yet," I whispered as I waved over my shoulder at him to stay put. "Let me listen first."

"S-S-Smudge!"

"SSSHHHH! I think I hear something!" I pressed my ear to the door so hard that it hurt.

My whisper bounced off the wooden door, hissed its way down the hallway behind me, and came back as if to bite me as it rebounded off the far wall.

Only the voice that came back wasn't mine.

"Indeed you should," it said.

15 The "D" Word

A shiver went up my spine as I turned around to see The Rat holding Gil by the scruff of the neck. He was holding a narrow black stick across Gil's throat like a knife, and his greasy hair was hanging in his eyes, like thin, dead worms.

I blurted out a curse word and slapped my hand over my mouth. As if I wasn't in enough trouble already.

"Indeed," The Rat said again through gritted teeth. "Is this how you spend your free time: creeping around the school where you are not welcome?"

I figured that was what you call a rhetorical question. So I just stood quietly and didn't offer an answer.

"Evidently you have too much free time," he said as he flicked his stick across Gil's backside. Gil winced. "Perhaps it is time to redirect your energies elsewhere." His uncovered wandering eye flickered with a muscle spasm. "Coincidentally, I have been looking for you to rectify other such mismanagements of your time. So how fortunate that you should come to me. Should I assume your consciences are leading you to seek me out for confession?"

He stepped past Gil and towards me. He tilted his head and leaned in close, lifting his eyeglass on its hinge, something I'd never, ever seen him do. He didn't even flinch when the flesh around the hinge pulled at the edges of the scab, cracking it. A slight bit of dark blood oozed from the crack.

And then he stared me in the eye with that eye. Or should I say, that socket. There was no eye there. Only a strange, ghostly green light flickering inside the hollow.

The Rat never laid a hand on me, but the stare of his mangled, bare socket combined with the eerie green light was almost enough to do me in; it pulled me right close to him. He sniffed me like he had done many times before. Then I heard him say, "Confess if you will; however, I regret that my capacity for tolerance has been worn thin by the likes of you."

Or at least I thought I heard him say it. The only problem was that I didn't remember seeing his mouth move.

Man, this place must have me more freaked out than I'd thought, I thought to myself as I blinked hard and shook my head. I'm starting to hallucinate.

The Rat wiped away the small trickle of blood that had crept its way into his eye socket, lowered the eyeglass, and, with a slight smile, stood straight. "This has superseded any other transgression you have committed, including the locker stunt you pulled the other day."

Gil and I shot quick, discreet looks at each other.

But The Rat didn't miss it.

"Ah, yes. The ever so subtle confirmation of guilt," he said, tapping Gil on the shoulder with his stick. Gil squinted his eyes shut. "Mr. Lurch discovered her after dinner, during his cleaning shift," The Rat continued and then gave Gil a firm flick on his arm. "Lucky for you, she was still breathing." He narrowed his uncovered eye at me. "And luckier still, you came down with that nasty bout of the flu and the nurse insisted you not be disturbed."

How did he know it was us? I thought. As far as I knew, we hadn't made a sound the whole time. Tessa didn't even know it was . . .

Right. Tessa. She would have told him it was us even if she knew it wasn't.

As if he could read my thoughts, The Rat said, "Honestly, who else would display such an obscene lack of judgment? And so, I am pleased, er, sorry to say that you have just earned yourselves one week's detention—in Detention Hall."

Gil let out a high-pitched squeak.

"And, oh, look. How handy. We're already here!"

"What? This is Detention Hall?" Geez, talk about going from the frying pan into the fire in about a microsecond flat.

"It looks like your luck has finally expired," continued The Rat. "And the timing is absolutely impeccable."

Speaking of timing, when you're standing with your executioner in silence in a cold, empty hallway, everything happens in slow motion.

"Right this way," he said, turning towards the door. The sharp tinkle of keys echoed as The Rat reached his hand out towards the lock.

My heart pounded in my ears. I could faintly hear Gil's voice from the other side of The Rat, repeating,

"Oh, b-b-boy, oh, b-boy, oh, b-b-b-boy, n-now we've d-done it." By the way he was breathing, it sounded like he was headed for an asthma attack.

Everything continued to move in slow motion as The Rat inserted a large brass key into the lock.

The key turned. A loud click. The door opened. Dark room. Musty smell.

Sure enough, Gil sneezed.

"Allergic, are you? That's a shame," said The Rat in an almost caring voice as he took out his handkerchief and buffed his eyeglass. "We should have thought about that before." He put his handkerchief back in his pocket. "Don't worry, you'll survive."

The Rat turned to me. "I will explain the details of your punishment when we enter, and I will send Mr. Lurch to set up cots for you. We wouldn't want the rodents to nibble your ears off while you slept on the floor, now, would we?"

Gil squeaked again and put his hands on his ears.

"And I want to make it very clear to you that you are to complete the job in the time allotted," he said, "or something . . . unfortunate may befall you."

He pushed Gil inside and motioned for me to follow.

16 Under the Floorboards

The stories of the detention room horrors were true.

Well, not exactly the way we thought they'd be true— not in the Maximillian Snute kind of way.

But we quickly realized that there are different ways of inflicting horror, depending on your viewpoint.

See, from our viewpoint, the horror of our punishment wasn't the realization that we were in any form of life-threatening danger.

We weren't being mauled by lions.

We weren't being tortured with bamboo shoots shoved under our fingernails.

No Chinese water torture.

No burning at the stake.

We weren't even being interrogated under bright lights.

If only.

No, what we endured was a special kind of torture, designed especially for us by The Rat, that made me wish for a bamboo manicure.

We had to clean out the storage room.

Oh, don't be so quick to shrug and say, "Is that all?" We wouldn't have thought it was a big deal either, if we hadn't seen it.

Yes, our horror was the realization that the dreaded Detention Hall was really the storage room, a place where we would be forced into manual labor. Disgusting manual labor.

The storage room was full of junk and a few things in various stages of rot. We couldn't even decide between the two of us what exactly those things were. It looked and smelled like there hadn't been any spring cleaning done in the place since the original owners moved out.

So The Rat kindly brought us cleaning supplies and instructed us to clean the entire place. "And don't forget to mop the floor!" he said. And with that, he closed the door behind him, leaving us staring at the disaster.

There were crates of books, bits of broken furniture, easels, desks, old musical instruments, dusty sheets and tarps on the floor, a huge stack of boxes filled with who-knows-what in the center of the room, and, of course, the mass of cleaning supplies.

"So much for the rumor about Mr. Lurch taking weeks to scrub out stains after the Maximillian Snute episode," I said. "He obviously hasn't ever set foot in here."

"W-where does he exp-pect us to p-put all this junk while w-we m-mop the floor?" asked Gil.

"No idea."

"A-a-a-achoooooooo! I'm s-starting to get all s-stuffed up again," Gil whined as he wiped his nose in his sleeve. He took a couple of puffs from his inhaler and then sneezed again.

And again.

You have no idea how cruel this punishment was—for me. All the dust sent Gil into massive sneezing fits, and whenever Gil sneezes, he puts his whole body into it. And I mean his whole body. Most times there are noises that come out the other end that make breathing for the innocent bystander a difficult, if not impossible, thing to do.

"I swear, Gil . . . "

"B-But I'm allergic!" Gil sniffed.

"I know you are. I'm the one who has to deal with the nasty outcomes of all your sneezing," I said, fanning the wretched air.

I took a couple of steps backwards and accidentally knocked over the stack of boxes that were in the middle of the room. I cringed as I expected to hear them crash to the floor. But the strange thing was that instead of a crash, there was a loud crinkling sound and then nothing. Nothing for a few seconds anyways. Then there was a hollow thud, thud, thud.

"W-what the . . . " Gil said with his eyes wide, his mouth open, and his finger pointing over my shoulder.

I turned around. All the boxes, except for the one I assumed had been at the bottom of the stack, had disappeared.

"The . . . the b-boxes f-fell on a t-tarp that w-was crumpled on the f-floor, and the t-tarp—" Gil jabbed his finger downwards a few times.

"Huh?" I nudged the remaining box with the toe of my shoe. It slid and then teetered. And then disappeared into a black hole in the floor.

"Why the heck was there a tarp covering a huge hole in the floor?" I asked.

Gil shook his head and lifted his shoulders to his ears. "M-maybe s-someone's t-trying to hide it."

"Or maybe *someone* didn't want us to see it until *after* we fell in!"

"D-do you think?" asked Gil, taking a step farther away from the hole.

"I wouldn't put it past him."

I walked towards the hole. "Hey, there's a ladder," I said as I knelt down. A knotted rope ladder hung from the edge of the hole and disappeared into the darkness. I sat on the floor and swung my legs into the hole. "Coming?"

"Y-you're going in?" Gil asked. His face turned as white and pasty as . . . well . . . paste. Between you and me, white's not his color at all.

"Gil, get a grip! It's a hole. What do you think it's going to do? Eat me?"

"M-maybe."

I started climbing down.

"W-wait!" Gil shouted.

I looked up at him.

"W-what if . . . w-what if M-Maximillian's b-body's down th-there?" Now he was whispering.

I tried to hide the shiver that went down my spine. What if it is? I thought. I peered into the darkness below.

"We'll never know if we don't go," I said. I started moving downwards again.

I heard Gil say, "J-jeepers c-creepers!" just before I saw his foot slide onto the top rung.

It was really dark at the bottom of the hole, and we both stumbled over the boxes that had fallen in.

At least that was all we stumbled over. No dead body.

At least not that I could see.

As I shoved the boxes out of the way, I noticed there was a bit of light coming through a slit in the ceiling. I walked towards the light and tripped again. But it wasn't on boxes this time.

"Hey, there are steps going up here," I said as I started climbing.

I reached the slit of light and stuck my finger through. The ceiling gave a bit, so I pushed. And it opened.

"This is the root cellar!" I exclaimed when I realized that what I'd thought was the ceiling was actually a door. I pushed it all the way open and stepped up into the courtyard.

"Get b-back down here!" shouted Gil. "Are you nuts? S-someone'll s-see you!"

I turned around to go back down the steps and saw something on the root cellar floor.

"Look at that!" I said, taking the stairs two at a time. "It's no stone dragon, but it sure is something!"

It was a large mosaic made of what looked like shattered bits of colored glass. It was pressed into the floor and was designed in the shape of a semicircle. The colors glittered in the light from the open door.

Gil was breathing heavily. "Okay, s-so now you've s-seen your root c-cellar, and there's no dragon in here. Can w-we go b-back up now?"

"I wonder what it is," I said as I tapped my toe on the mosaic.

"Don't s-step on it!" exclaimed Gil as he came and stood beside me. "It m-might b-break!"

But it didn't break. It exploded into a bright, firey kaleidoscope of color that shot in every direction around the root cellar. Gil and I shielded our eyes from the lights that flashed and blinked and twinkled up from the floor through the multicolored bits of glass.

"W-what's g-going on?" Gil shouted.

That's when the root cellar door slammed shut and the walls started spinning. The floor stood still, but the walls spun around, faster and faster.

And then the lights went out. It was suddenly dark. Pitch dark.

The colors combined with the spinning walls had made me so dizzy that I was totally disoriented when the lights went out. I fell backwards. But as I put my hands behind me to catch myself, they only met air. The floor wasn't there anymore.

17 Bizarre Message

I was falling; no doubt about it. And in total darkness.

But it wasn't like a dead-drop, lose-your-lunch kind of a fall. It was like I just tumbled and twisted and floated downwards like a leaf falling from a tree. When I finally landed, though, it was hard. I felt like I'd been tackled to the ground by an entire football team.

My ears were ringing. The air around me felt cool. And I realized I was getting wet. All over.

What I didn't notice was that my eyes were shut tight—so tight that I was beginning to get a headache.

I slowly opened them. My sense of hearing suddenly returned with my sight as I realized I was lying flat on my back behind a roaring waterfall. On a really narrow, slippery ledge.

"I knew I'd regret f-following you one day," Gil shouted from his sprawled-out position beside me as he rubbed his head. "I just hoped it w-wouldn't b-be t-today!"

I sat up and crawled against the rocks. A deep-grey mist covered me. It was hard to breathe.

Gil crawled over beside me. "W-where are w-we? W-what happened? How do w-we get out of here?" he gasped. I guess the mist was getting to him, too.

I stood up and stumbled along the ledge, landing on all fours on the rocks at the edge of the waterfall. I looked down and saw just how enormous the waterfall was; the drop must have been a hundred feet or more, and the water was mercilessly pounding the rocks at its base.

"Gil!" I shouted over the roar. "We've got to go down!"

Even though the sound of the rushing water was deafening, I heard Gil groan.

We slowly inched our way down the slippery rocks and it wasn't until we came to the bottom that it struck me.

The waterfall, I thought. In my dream there had been a waterfall.

The adrenaline started rushing through my body as I reached into my hoodie pocket for my sketchbook. I flipped to the sketch of the waterfall. It was exactly like this one.

I put my book in my pocket and started back up the rocks.

"W-what are you doing?" Gil called after me.

The eagle had nudged me along a ledge to the entrance of a cave.

"S-Smudge?"

But I don't remember seeing an entrance when I got here. Did I just miss it in the shock of it all?

I kept climbing.

"Are you nuts?" Gil shouted. "Why are you going b-back up there?"

I didn't answer. I just continued up to the ledge. Then I crawled my way across the wet ridge, looking for the entrance to the cave.

But I just ended up coming out the other side of the waterfall.

I crawled back again, certain that I'd just missed it. But I hadn't. It really wasn't there.

"Where is it?" I shouted into the roaring water.

"P-please don't t-tell me I've got t-to climb b-back up th-there," Gil called up to me.

I climbed down.

"Did . . . did you happen to see a cave?" I asked. "An entrance to a cave? When you were up there?"

Gil shook his head. "B-but then again, I w-wasn't really l-looking for one," he shouted. "I just w-wanted to get down as quickly as p-possible."

I looked back up to the ledge.

"S-Smudge? P-pleeeeease don't," Gil said, shaking his head.

I crawled across that thing twice, I thought. I would have seen an entrance to a cave for sure, if it was there.

"C'mon, Gil. Let's walk."

All along the river stood towering pine trees, the kind you see in nature magazines. The kind that make the person standing beside them look like a dwarf. Vines had grown up and twisted themselves up and down the trunks and branches of the trees, completely covering the bark in green, leafy ropes. Some of the trees had lost all their leaves, needles, and pinecones and were just basically vine statues. Others were completely dead, trunks stripped of their bark and no vines on them at all.

We made our way downstream and sat on the rocky bank. It was far enough from the falls that we could hear each other speak without shouting.

"W-what are you l-l-looking for, S-Smudge?" asked Gil as he followed my gaze upwards.

"The eagle," I whispered as I scanned the sky. Maybe I didn't find the entrance to the cave because I need the eagle to guide me, I thought.

"Have you b-been here b-before?"

"Maybe. I think so. I don't know."

We stared at the sky for quite some time.

I waited.

And watched.

And waited some more.

But the eagle never came.

"Where are we?" I asked.

Gil suddenly had a terrified look on his face. "Do . . . do you think w-we're d-d-dead?" he asked in a whisper.

Maybe, I thought. Maybe we are. But I kept that thought to myself.

"No, of course not," I said.

"Whew," said Gil, swiping his hand over his forehead. "I w-was s-starting to think that m-maybe . . . Hey! W-what's that? Over th-there!" he exclaimed, looking over my shoulder and pointing downriver towards a huge tree stump. The air around the stump seemed to be moving and looked strangely colorful—sort of like pictures I'd seen of the Aurora Borealis.

"I don't know. Let's find out," I said, standing.

Gil jumped to his feet. "Oh, no," he said, grabbing my sleeve. "I just read ab-bout s-something like this this m-morning. L-looks l-like it could b-be s-some kind of extraterrestrial l-life form calling to its m-mother ship. L-look here," he said as he pulled a mystery magazine from seemingly out of nowhere. "In issue 179 of M-Mysteriously M-Mystifying M-Mysteries, there's a s-story called 'M-Murder on Venus.'" He flipped through the pages with shaky hands and stopped about halfway through. "Th-there's this extraterrestrial—s-see?—w-with t-transparent s-skin. Its evil p-pulsing heart l-looks just exactly l-like . . . " He looked back at the colors. "I think w-we should go the other w-way." He snapped his magazine shut and pulled on my arm. "You w-wouldn't w-want to see how those th-things kill their uns-suspecting p-prey."

Evil, pulsing-hearted extraterrestrials or not, curiosity got the better of me—especially since it seemed those colors had just shown up out of the blue. So I headed in the direction of the lights, making sure to stay well hidden behind the dying trees, though, just in case Murder on Venus was actually written by someone who'd been here before and mistakenly thought he was on Venus.

And of course, Gil just said, "Aw, c'mon, S-Smudge," and followed.

As we snuck closer, much to Gil's relief, we saw the pulsing colors fade and then disappear. But the tree stump was still there, and we found that it was hollow.

Well, it would have been hollow if it wasn't stuffed full with the best food in the world: candy! I had to laugh as I watched Gil immediately dive in and devour the treats. So much for caution! He was a candyholic if there ever was one.

There was every kind of candy you could think of in that tree stump: chocolate bars, lollipops, licorice, jujubes, peppermint sticks, gummy worms...

And pink bubble gum.

Suddenly I wasn't in the mood to eat anymore. I decided to just put a few of the treats in my pocket for later.

Just as Gil reached for another jumbo chocolate bar, he stopped dead in his tracks.

"S-Smudge, l-look at this."

"What?"

"L-look at this note."

Tacked onto the side of the stump was a handwritten note. It was written in strange-looking letters with black ink on thick paper that was burnt around the edges.

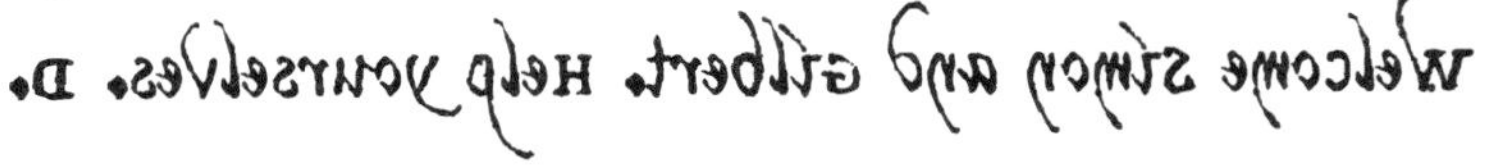

I pulled the note off. As I looked at it again, the letters seemed to quiver and blur a bit. I blinked a few times to clear my eyes. Suddenly the letters stopped moving. And I could read it! It said:

Welcome Simon and Gilbert . . .

Gil grabbed the note out of my hands before I could finish. "Th-this is creepy! Oh! I've read ab-bout this b-before . . . in one of the first issues of M-Mysteriously M-Mystifying M-Mysteries. Do you have a m-mirror?"

"Oh, yeah, sure thing. I just happen to have one in my back pocket," I said sarcastically. "Who do you think I am? Tessa? Why would I have a mirror?"

"I don't know. I need a m-mirror. Do you have anything l-like a m-mirror?"

"What does a mirror have to do with anything?"

"Just . . . I just need one!" he shouted at me. "Oh, here," he said as he slid down the river bank. He held the note face down above some calm water that had collected in a rocky pool.

I slid down beside him. The toe of my shoe landed in the water.

"Don't!" he shouted. "You w-wrecked it!"

"Wrecked what?" I asked. He wasn't making any sense.

"The w-water's all ripply now! Just w-wait." He sighed and then after a few seconds he said, "Ok-kay. Now l-look. At the w-water under the p-paper," he added before I could ask him where exactly he wanted me to look.

The reflection of the note was floating on top of the water. The water was acting like a mirror.

"W-Welcome Simon and Gilbert. Help yourselves. D," Gil read.

"Geez . . . good job, Gil," I said. "But I could have told you what it said without all that bother."

Gil's jaw dropped. "W-what do you m-mean?"

"I was in the middle of reading what it said before you grabbed it out of my hand."

His jaw dropped wider. "You . . . you could read it?"

I nodded.

"How?"

I shrugged and took the note back from him. "I don't know."

And I really didn't.

Gil looked at me sideways. "M-maybe you're an uns-suspected genius," he said. Then he tapped the note. "M-mirror w-writing. DaVinci w-wrote l-like this, t-too."

"Who?"

"L-Leonardo DaVinci. The famous artist. He w-was a genius."

"Do you think he wrote it?" I asked, pointing to the *D*.

Gil slapped his forehead. "And I s-suggested you m-might b-be a genius! DaVinci's d-dead."

How was I supposed to know that?

"How do you th-think this *D* guy knew w-we w-were coming here?" asked Gil. He dropped his fistful of gummy worms and they plop, plop, plopped into the pool. "I m-mean, w-we didn't even know! W-we didn't even know this p-place existed . . . w-wherever it is that w-we are." He looked around slowly, his eyes wide behind his glasses.

Even I was at a loss.

I scanned the landscape, looking to the right, to the left, and behind us. Directly in front of us was the river, with the waterfall to the right. To the left were trees. Behind us were trees. And the farther away the trees were from the waterfall, the sicker they looked. Most of the trees downriver had all their bark stripped. Some even farther down had their trunks splintered and their branches dangling.

"Hey, Gil. Look over there." A little farther downstream, on the other side of the river, was a patch of dark-green trees. "Someone must live there; there's smoke rising from the middle of the trees. Let's go see."

Suddenly a strange sound hung in the branches above our heads. It was almost like a radio playing with a bad, staticky reception.

"Do you hear that?" I asked.

But Gil didn't respond. He just turned his back on me and started walking into the dark, dead woods.

18 Place of the Wild Vines

"Where are you going?" I called and jogged up beside him. "Do you hear it this time, too?"

But Gil still didn't respond. He just kept walking. His eyes were unmoving, staring straight ahead.

I looked up into the treetops as I followed Gil. The vines I'd seen on some of the trees before were now everywhere, hanging from the branches and climbing up the trunks. And it looked like they were growing out of the ground right before my eyes. I thought of the vines that used to pop out through the stone walls at the academy, only those vines withered and died almost faster than they grew. These were showing no signs of doing either.

"Gil, we should head back to the river and see if we can cross to the other side. To see . . . "

The music suddenly picked up its volume.

Gil picked up his pace. He wasn't listening to me.

The half-dead flowers scattered randomly on the ground seemed to perk up and nod at us as we passed by them. The vine-smothered trees even moved aside to make a clear path for us.

We entered a marsh, and soon we were up to our knees in mucky water.

Suddenly the bass tone in the music swelled and held a steady note, vibrating the grass and water around our legs.

"Let's get out of here," I said. I was actually afraid we'd get a shock from the sound waves pulsing through the water. The vibrations rattled my bones and made my teeth chatter.

But Gil kept on walking—sloshing—through the marsh. It didn't look like he'd heard a word I'd said.

I squished and squashed through the wet grasses, trying to keep up with him. Just as I reached out to pull him back to find out what the heck was going on with him, one of his shoes got stuck in the muck. No sooner had that happened that a vine began climbing up his leg.

"Gil!" I shouted as the vine tripped him and seemed to pull him down. But he was totally oblivious to what was happening.

I grabbed and pulled at the vine. But it fought back! It nipped at me with its jagged leaves and continued to climb even more quickly than before. Soon it was around Gil's waist. Then another vine popped out of the ground and wrapped itself around Gil's other foot. I kept pulling and tearing, but doing that only seemed to make them grow faster! They began sprouting new shoots where I tore the leaves off. I was no match to the strength and speed of the growing vines. Gil was almost completely swallowed.

I stood, frozen, deafened by the music and totally powerless to do anything for him. How could this happen again? What kind of a person can never think of the right thing to do to get his best friend out of trouble?

"I'm going to . . . " I tried yelling over the sound of the music so Gil could hear me, but my voice got lost in the pulse of the bass.

I tried again. "I'm going to find help!" I shouted as my words got swallowed.

And then I ran.

I ran and ran and ran, but didn't have a clue where to go, where to turn.

The woods had changed. The trees stopped making a path for me. Instead I had to force my way through their low, thorny branches as they cut my face and arms. The vines had stopped growing, too, and they dangled from the trees like twisted dreadlocks. The flowers drooped their heads and snapped off at the stems as I ran past them. My lungs were on fire and felt like they were going to come out of my throat, but I had to keep running. There was nothing else I could do.

19 Terrible and Beautiful Colors

I somehow made it back to the river. I saw the smoke again, rising from the middle of the trees on the other side. I stood, panting, with my hands on my knees.

I've got to cross, I thought, to get to those trees.

But the water was rushing like rapids, foaming at rocks and drowning the unlucky leaves and sticks that had fallen in. There was no way I could swim it.

I ran upstream towards the waterfall and climbed the rocks. I skidded down the other side and fell the last few feet, landing hard and twisting my ankle. Pain shot up my leg, but I couldn't stop. I scrambled to my feet and kept running.

I ran downstream and finally made it into the green branches of the trees. I ended up in a clearing and fell to the ground.

"Help me!" I wheezed.

There was a man sitting by a fire. When I tumbled into the clearing, he let out a screech and nearly jumped into the burning pit.

"Oh, me soul!" he said as he picked up the stick that he'd dropped and steadied himself on it. He wore a dark brown, ground-length hooded cloak over what looked a lot like a long potato sack tied at the waist with a rope. He brushed off his clothes. "What's da meanin' of startlin' a poor, old, defenseless man? Who are you? What are you doin' here?"

"I need help!" I said. I stood up the best I could. It felt like there were hot needles in my ankle. I tried to catch my breath as I spoke. "Please . . . my friend . . . needs help."

"It's you! Great goblets of gumdrops!" said the man as he hobbled towards me. "How'd you . . . ?" He looked behind him and then back at me. "You're really here!" Then he dropped his stick and knelt in front of me. He put a hand on top of one of mine.

"My name is Smudge, er, Simon," I said, sure he must have had me confused with someone else. "Simon Mugford. And . . . and my friend needs help."

"Yes, yes, I know who you are. Greasy goose giblets," he said quietly, patting my hand. "You said dere's a friend wit' you? Where is he?"

"He's . . . he's . . . on the other side . . . of the river," I said, motioning towards the trees with my head.

"I needs to help him, I do," the man said as he stood up and wrapped his cloak around his body. He picked up his walking stick.

"But I'll never find . . . my way back to where he is!" I said.

"Where were you?" he asked.

My mind was scattered. "Grass . . . there was grass. Tall grass. And music! The music was so loud!"

"Music," he said in a half whisper. "You heard music?"

"Yeah, but I don't think Gil did," I said. "He never hears it!"

"I'm not surprised by dat. Did you see anyt'ing besides grass?"

"Trees . . . and vines! Growing right before my eyes! And . . . water! Mucky water, like a . . ."

"Marsh!" the man finished my sentence. "Da Brackish Marshes." He pointed at me with his cane. "You stay here. I'll go finds your friend. I knows where he is."

"But I need to come with you!" I said.

"No!" the man shouted. "You needs to stay here. It's too dangerous fer you to be out dere. You should never have been wandering around."

"But I have to come with you! I . . . I should never have left him alone! I have to go back to him!"

The man sighed loudly, grabbing my hood, and pulled me back just before I could duck under the branches of the trees. "Den at least put dis on." He handed me a stone that was hanging from a piece of twine. It didn't look any different from a smooth, flat rock that you would skip on the water at the beach.

"What's . . .?"

"Jes put it on and let's go!" he said as he tightened the belt around his waist and rushed past me into the woods.

I tied the twine around my neck and ran after him. My ankle was throbbing and burning hot; just trying to keep up with the man's quick pace was a killer, never mind reclimbing the waterfall to get back to the other side of the river. But I had no choice.

"Gil! Gil!" I barked through gritted teeth as I speed-limped through the trees.

I actually expected to find him suffocated to death where I had left him, but, miraculously, I heard him call back to me.

"I-I'm here, S-Smudge!"

There Gil was, sitting against the trunk of an enormous tree, pulling dead leaves out from under his shirt and pant legs. He seemed really calm, considering he was up to his eyeballs in vicious vines not even fifteen minutes ago. When he saw me, he forced his mouth into a smile.

"How the heck did you get out of the vines?" I shouted.

"W-Well, there w-was this . . . " He stopped speaking and turned his head, as if he had heard something. Then he continued, "Um, I d-don't exactly know w-w-what happened," he said. "The v-vines just . . . um . . . fell off m-me. M-must have decided they w-weren't hungry anymore."

"Did you hear the music?" I asked wondering if the music had had something to do with it.

"No."

"Well, no matter. I'm just glad to see you're not compost," I said.

The old man humphed. "We must head back," he said and he brushed past without looking at either one of us.

Gil just sat there, looking at the ground. I pulled him up and we followed.

The man walked quickly again. He took long steps with his cane at his side. He didn't say a word the whole way back. Neither did Gil.

When we finally reached the clearing, the man sat on a tree stump and pulled something out of his cloak. He held it in his hands and began chanting. I couldn't make out the words he was saying.

I sat on a rock by the fire and took my shoe off. My ankle wasn't swollen or anything, but it was red and it still really hurt.

As I sat there rubbing my ankle and listening to the drone of the man's chanting, I looked around the clearing. It was set up like a campsite, only there were no tents. But there were different blankets spread out on the ground. One was piled with pots and pans, kettles and cauldrons. One was covered with baskets and dried leaves and roots. One blanket was piled high with twigs, branches, and logs, and one had two chests on it: a huge wooden one with black, metal hinges and another smaller one beside it. The small chest looked like it was made of bronze and had a lock that was way too big for the size of the chest.

After some time had passed, the man stood up. I put my sock and shoe back on.

"You needs one of dese, too," he said to Gil. He held out the object he was holding. It was a stone that looked just like the one he'd given to me. Gil took it.

"You boys needs to wear dese Eart' Stones," he said. "Dey is livin' Stones. Dey'll protect you. Dey'll guide you. And dey'll help you make good decisions. But you've gots to wear dem 'round your neck. Never takes dem off! Da moment you takes dem off you'll be openin' yourself up to bein' led astray, jes like you was out dere," he said to Gil as he motioned towards the trees. Gil looked at his feet.

"Who . . . who are you?" I asked.

"Gruesome Goliat'! Considerin' da circumstances, I should be askin' you, what wit' da way you came chargin' into me clearin'," he said as he hobbled to the blanket that was piled with cauldrons and kettles. He pulled a large kettle out from underneath the pile, which made the rest of the pots and things sink and clang loudly. He filled the kettle with water from the river and set it down on the flaming logs.

"You didn' arrive at all like I'd expected you to."

I think my heart stopped beating. "We didn't? I mean, you were expecting us?"

"Grudges in gingham! 'Course I was!"

"Are you *D*?" I blurted out, remembering the signature on the note Gil and I had found with the candy.

Gil gave a little wheeze.

The man looked at me like I was nuts. "Grapes 'n' ginger! 'Course I am! M'name's Drofgum."

"Drofgum," I repeated. "So you wrote the note on the tree stump?"

"What note? What tree stump?"

"The note we found with the candy," I said.

"Candy . . ." He nodded as he looked at Gil. Then his face fell. "Did you eat any?" he asked me.

"No," I said as I pulled my stash of lollipops and jujubes out of my pocket.

"Give me dose."

I dumped them into his hands.

"You gots any more of dose?" he asked Gil.

Gil reached into his pockets and pulled out gummy bears, lollipops, chocolate bars, licorice, bubble gum, jelly beans, rock candy, and even a small bag of chips. By the time he was done, it looked like he could have opened a candy store of his own.

How'd he fit all that in there?

Drofgum threw my few candies into the fire. And then he shoveled Gil's hoard into the flames with a plank of wood. The fire exploded with multicolored sparks and sent toxic fumes into the air as the candies fizzled and sizzled on the burning logs.

"Dem terrible and beautiful colors," said Drofgum, watching the sparks. "Sure sign of Da Powers of Darkness."

"The portal we came through was full of colors, just like those," I said.

"Grizzly goat's guts!" Drofgum exclaimed. "Dat sure wasn't how you was supposed to get here! Well, no matter. Yer here now." He looked at me sideways. "You sure you didn't eat none of dose candies? Didn't even lick one?"

"I'm sure," I said, staring up at the colorful fumes.

He looked at Gil. "How're you feelin'?"

"Uh, fine," said Gil, putting his hand on his stomach. "I think."

"You t'ink," repeated Drofgum. He made his way to the big wooden chest, rummaged through it, and pulled out a small green bottle.

"My bet is dose candies was what gots you into trouble out dere. Here, drink dis," he said as he uncorked the bottle and held it out to Gil. "It'll help dissolve what's left in your stomach before you digest it any furdder. Hope it's not too late."

Gil looked at me as if he wanted my permission to drink it.

I shrugged my shoulders. "Go ahead," I said. "You want to digest enchanted candies?"

Gil shook his head double-time and took the bottle. Wrinkling up his nose, he drank a bit.

"More," said Drofgum.

Gil took another swig. He coughed and wiped his mouth. "It t-tastes like milk," he said, sounding surprised.

"Do you likes milk?" asked Drofgum.

Gil nodded. "It's my favorite."

"Let me see your tongue," said Drofgum.

Gil stuck out his tongue. It had turned as green as the bottle.

"Well, at least we knows it's workin'," said Drofgum as he took the bottle back. "How're you feelin' now?"

Gil rubbed his stomach. "Great," he said. "Never felt b-better. Can I have s-some m-more?"

"No, dat's 'nuf fer now. But you start feelin' sick or light-headed or anyt'ing, you let me knows right away, you hear me?"

Gil nodded again.

"So . . . if you're not the *D* who wrote the note," I said after Drofgum recorked the bottle and put it back in the chest, "then who is?"

"Demlock."

"Demlock?"

Drofgum looked at me with a sad smile. "Do you knows where you are?"

I shook my head. "I'm guessing this isn't Grimstown."

"Well, if you was still in your own realm you'd be in Grimstown."

"Huh? What do you mean, 'realm'?"

Drofgum took in a slow, deep breath. "Now, how do I explain dis wit'out makin' you more confused den you already are? Let's jes makes it simple fer now. Hmmm . . . Let's see . . . bare bones . . . bare bones . . . Okay. Here it is: A realm is a sphere; a dimension. And da realm you came from—da realm of Eart'— well, dat realm is very closely connected to dis one. In fact, once, when da two realms was united, dey occupied da same space. But dey ain't united no more, and as a result Eart' is only an incomplete reflection of da realm you is in now."

"That's the simple explanation?" I asked.

"Simple as it gets," Drofgum replied. "'Course dere's a lot more to it, but if I starts in wit' diggin' back into da history of da whole t'ing, we'd be up all night." He rummaged through the chest and pulled out a small brown sack, tied at the top with twine. "Leaves, fer our tea," he said with a wink.

"But . . . if you're saying we're not on Earth anymore," I said, looking around the clearing, "You at least have to tell us where we are."

"You're in da realm of Emogen."

"The realm of Emogen?"

Drofgum sighed, closed the chest lid, and hobbled back to where we were sitting. "You two have so much to learn—too much to be startin' in on it now; it's gettin' late. No needs to be fillin' your heads wit' stories before you goes to sleep. Besides, you'll be safe so long as you stay in dis clearin' and keep dose Stones on," he said, eyeing Gil.

Gil nodded and looked at his feet again.

"I'll clue you boys in on some details in da mornin'."

When the kettle boiled, Drofgum made us some tea and passed us some bread and cheese. I've never really been a cheese person, so I kind of had to psych myself up to eat it. It smelled rank to me. But I didn't want to be rude (and I wasn't guaranteed anything else to eat), so I buried the cheese the best I could in between the crusts of bread and ate it anyways. I was thankful for the tea to wash it down with—leaves and all.

"Yer not s'posed to swallow dem," Drofgum said, chuckling, as I choked and coughed some up. For the first time I noticed his two front teeth were silver—pure, shining silver.

When we finished, Drofgum pointed to the big wooden chest. "Help yourselves to some of da blankets in dat chest over dere."

I limped over to the chest and creaked open the heavy lid. Other than blankets, the chest was full of all kinds of old tools and gadgets and pottery and things. A round bronzed case caught my eye. It had interesting engravings on it and looked like something from a hundred years ago. I lifted it out.

"This looks really old," I said. "What is it? A pocket-watch?"

"Nope. It's me compass," said Drofgum, "but it don't work. Open it and see fer yourself."

I clicked the case open. The needle swayed back and forth, back and forth, and then finally landed on the *W*.

"It points *West*!"

"Yep, dat it does," said Drofgum.

"Too bad." I clicked the compass shut and put it back in the chest. I got a few blankets out. "Here," I said to Gil as I tossed him a couple.

Gil put one blanket under his arm and unrolled the other. He suddenly screamed and tossed both blankets to the side.

"Oh, me soul! What was dat all about?" Drofgum asked.

"S-S-Spider!" Gil said, flapping his hands.

I rolled my eyes and picked up the blanket and shook it out for him. "Here. No more spiders."

He looked at the other blanket that was still rolled up on the ground, as if a hoard of spiders were waiting inside, ready to swarm him the second he touched it. I shook that one out for him, too.

He carefully inspected both blankets and then spread one of them out on the ground and lay down. He put his glasses on the ground beside him and used the other blanket to cover up with, rolling himself up like a mummy so only his nose was poking out.

"What are you doing?" I asked.

"Keeping the s-spiders out," he said from inside his cocoon.

I wrapped a blanket around my shoulders and lay down beside him.

Gil was really restless. He kept tossing and turning and peeking at the sky from the slit in his blanket as if he expected something to fall from it. The moon shone bright and full. It was the biggest full moon I'd ever seen.

"Gil?"

"Yeah?"

"How are you feeling?"

"Fine."

"So what exactly happened today, after I left? Do you remember?"

"Aw, I don't w-want t-to t-talk ab-bout it. Can I t-tell you s-some other t-time?"

"Uh, okay," I said. I guess I probably wouldn't have wanted to talk about it either, if it had been me. "Well, g'night." I tried to make myself comfortable.

"G'night."

I don't know if I was between sleep and awake or if I was already asleep, but suddenly the voice of the angel spoke to me, like it had in my dream, and echoed in my head.

"You must keep it safe."

My eyes flew open because it sounded like she was right beside me, whispering in my ear. I looked around, thinking maybe Drofgum had said something and I just mistook it for the angel's voice. But he was fast asleep, his head on a rock pillow.

Then I heard it again.

"You must keep it safe."

"Isn't it safe?" I whispered.

But there was no answer.

I wasn't sure who I was supposed to keep it safe from. Drofgum? Or Gil? As far as I knew, neither of them knew anything about it.

But why would the voice tell me to keep it safe if it already was?

Maybe it wasn't safe *enough*, since I was in a different realm now.

A different realm, I thought. Emogen. That's nuts.

I waited for a few minutes and made sure Gil's breathing was slow and steady before I took the key out of my pocket and pushed it down into the earth under my blanket.

20 What Gil Did

It was almost dawn when I woke up, and the little clearing was lit by a faint bluish light. A few glowing embers in the fire pit sent whisps of smoke circling into the air.

As I stretched and yawned, I was struck by the sudden memory of what had happened the day before.

I rolled over to see how Gil was, but he wasn't there.

"Gil!" I shouted as I bolted to my feet.

"You must let him go, boy," Drofgum said from behind me.

My skin prickled from my head to my toes.

"What do you mean? Where's Gil?" I exclaimed as I turned to see Drofgum hobbling around the clearing, putting things into two sacks.

He mumbled, "I was afraid dis was goin' to happen."

"What? You were afraid what was going to happen?"

He stopped and turned to me. "Dat da tonic was goin' to be futile. I tried—even gave his Stone an extra blessing. But it was all in vain, 'specially since he's not even wearin' da Stone." Drofgum nodded towards Gil's blanket. There was his Stone.

Drofgum put down the sacks and sat me down on the rock. "Now, you needs to listen to me," he said urgently as he took my chin in his hand and turned my face so he could look me in the eyes. "And listen to me good. Your friend made a contract wit' Demlock in da woods yesterday, Simon. And no one who makes a contract, 'specially one wit' Demlock, can ever get out of it."

Demlock . . . the guy who had left us the candy . . .

"What . . . what kind of a contract?"

"A blood contract," said Drofgum. "When an individual gives of deir blood, dey are symbolically bound to da individual dey gives it to. It is usually done as payment fer a significant deed—life fer life type of t'ing. Your friend now belongs to Demlock."

"Why? Why would Gil do something like that?"

Drofgum shrugged and let go of my chin. "People sign deir life away fer all kinds of reasons. Demlock most likely promised your friend somet'ing he t'ought he'd never get udderwise."

Then, as if I were smacked in the head with an unexpected foul ball, Gil's words from the day Mad Dog humiliated him suddenly hit me hard: "You know, S-Smudge, I'd s-sell my soul if I c-could only get r-rid of this s-stupid s-stutter!"

What has he done? I thought.

"Da contract can only be broken when da Elements have been released," continued Drofgum. "Only den can what's been done begin to be undone, t'roughout all Emogen."

"The Elements? What are you talking about? You need to tell me what's going on!" I shouted. "And start by telling me about this Demlock and why he's taken Gil!"

Drofgum sighed. It wasn't an annoyed type of sigh, though; it was more of a sad-sounding one. "Demlock's a born Emogenite. But somet'ing went terribly wrong wit' him, so much so dat he tried to overt'row da Sustainer."

"But what does that have to do with Gil?" I asked.

"I'm gettin' to dat."

"Fine," I said impatiently. "Who's the Sustainer?"

"Da one who sustains Emogen. Sort of like a king would be on Eart'. Da four Elements of creation—Eart', Air, Water, and Fire—are cared for by da Sustainer. Demlock tried to gets possession of dem, but da law states dat only da Sustainer and his bloodline are aut'orized to have possession of dem. So because of Demlock's rebellion against dat law, da Elements disappeared into deir silver Chalice and were locked up in a Casket, deep in an underground Crypt to be kept safe. But as a result, Emogen's slowly dyin' wit'out da Elements. Jes look around outside me clearin' and you can sees da consequences of Demlock's idiocy. Goes right t'roo all four regions and beyond, it does; right on t'roo to da realm of Eart'. See, since da two realms are so closely connected, we share da same Elements. So da effects of dis will also be evident on Eart' but, luckily, in a radder diluted manner. And me compass, da one dat your friend ran off wit' in da night, is furdder proof dat dis whole realm is completely off its hinges: nut'tin's workin' like it should. Everyt'ing's a mess."

"Gil took your compass?" I asked. "What would he want with a broken compass?"

"Not exactly sure, but rumor has it dat Demlock's taken up residence in da mountains of da western region of Tor. Could be dat's where he wanted your friend to bring da Key."

The Key!

My heart skipped a wild beat as I jumped up and whipped my blankets back. The Key was still there, stuck in the ground. I pulled it out.

"So dat's where you hid it!" Drofgum exclaimed. His face instantly relaxed. "Gruesome gargoyles! Good t'inkin'! But I must say, you must sleep like a sack of rocks! He was rootin' t'roo your pockets like dere was no tomorrow. And you didn't even twitch."

How the heck did Gil know I had a key in my pocket? How did Drofgum know I had a key in my pocket?

"You mean you saw him?" I asked, stunned.

"Yep. 'Course he didn't sees me watchin' him, so when I asked him what he was lookin' fer, he pretty near keeled over in fright. Den he jes ran off."

"Why does Demlock want this key?" I asked, looking at the key that was still in my hand.

"Dat's da Key dat's meant to unlock da Casket to set da Elements free. And unless da right person unlocks dem and resummons dem into da environment, every-t'ing will remain under Demlock's curse. Includin' your friend. And da longer da Elements is gone, da worse t'ings will gets until Emogen becomes so messed up it will basically self-destruct. But t'ings could get worse, too, in da meantime if Demlock manages to get his hands on da Elements. So dat dere is probably da most important Key in all of history," said Drofgum, pointing at it with his pinky finger.

"So are you saying this key has something to do with getting Gil back?"

"I'm sayin' it has everyt'ing to do wit' gettin' your friend back."

"And you're saying that until the Elements are set free, Demlock's curse can't be broken?"

"Dat's exactly what I'm sayin'."

"Then it needs to unlock the Elements! Now!"

"Yes, it does. But it hasn't yet been reunited wit' its udder half," Drofgum said. "Won't do much good like dat, will it?"

I took my sketchbook out of my pocket and flipped it open to the page that the sketch of the half key was on. "Well, it's my job to find it," I said. "The twencil told me so."

"Da twencil?"

I took it out of the coil book spine.

"Ah," said Drofgum. "I see." He smiled and nodded, exposing his glittery, silver teeth.

He held his hand out for the key. I put it in his palm. Then he took my sketchbook. "Let's see what else dat smart pencil can tells us."

He slid the Key on top of the drawing, just like I had done the night I got it. The shape still fit perfectly.

"Reveal to me da location of da Key," Drofgum said.

The paper around the sketch suddenly caught fire, and a dragon's head leaped from the flames like a jack-in-the-box. A horrible roar escaped from its firey mouth. I covered my ears. Drofgum looked horrified.

"What has he done?" he whispered, his hands trembling. He dropped the Key and the book. The fire went out and the roaring stopped. The sketchbook looked like it hadn't been touched.

"What has who done?" I asked, searching Drofgum's face. "What's happened?"

"Da Key . . . is . . . in da belly of a Beast—a great and terrible Stone Dragon. Millian!" Drofgum cried as he fell to his knees.

21 This'll Only Hurt a Little

The horror on Drofgum's face gripped me.

"Did . . . did you say the Key is in the belly of a Dragon? A Stone Dragon?"

Drofgum's expression suddenly turned to one of anger. He picked up my sketchbook, stood up, and handed it to me. "Now Demlock's stepped way over da line. He should'a left Millian out of it. He's gonna pay for dis, I can tells you dat!"

He gave the Key back to me and hurried back to the sacks he'd been packing when I woke up. He shoved some brown packages and a couple blankets into each one and then buckled them tightly. He tossed one to me and slung the other one over his shoulder.

"Are you going with me?"

"No. I must go somewheres else. I've gots to finds someone. Jes waitin' fer Melchior to arrive."

"Melchior?"

Drofgum didn't answer. "Da bloody bugger! I swear if he . . ." His voice trailed off. "Now, get your friend's Stone, tie it around your neck, and take bot' of dem in your hands."

I did what he said, and when I was holding the Stones, Drofgum put his hands under mine and the Stones began to transform. A deep pomegranate-colored glow spread out from the center of my Stone. The hue pulsed to a slow rhythm and continually changed shape, resembling something like lava or really thick blood. A blazing-bronze inscription was written in the middle of the pulse point. It was written from right to left, just like the note Gil and I found with the candy.

It said:

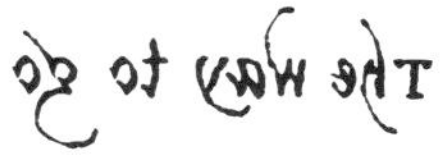

(The way to go)

Then I noticed the other Stone also glowed with the same intense light. But it read:

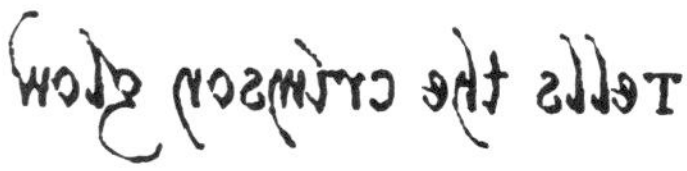

(Tells the crimson glow)

I still didn't know how I could read this kind of writing so easily.

"Follow dem exactly," said Drofgum. "Dey'll makes da way clearer to you as you go. And dey'll help heighten da sound of da music, too. Remember, never takes dese Stones off, 'specially when you're out dere. And dey'll tell you what to do when you face dat dastardly Dragon."

The Dragon . . .

"And dere's somet'ing else you'll be needin'," he said. "Sit down on dat blanket while I gets it." I sat down as he hobbled over to the wooden chest, leaned his walking stick against it, and creaked the lid open. He took something out and came back to me. There was a knife lying across the palms of his outstretched hands. He sat cross-legged on the blanket, facing me.

"Where's dat pencil?"

I took the twencil out of the coil spine of the sketchbook and put the book back into my hoodie pocket.

"Hold dis." He held the knife out to me. I picked it up by the handle.

"Let me have dat pencil." I gave it to him. "Dis here pencil is no ordinary pencil, as I'm sure you've already noticed. It's a very powerful tool: da writin' implement of Mudder Yegra herself."

"Mother Yegra?"

"Da Creator of Emogen. She used it to record and advance da events of creation. Its powers bring t'oughts to life, and it refines and increases da purpose of da t'ings it marks. And so I will use it to refine and increase da purpose of dis here Knife.

"Lay da Knife flat across your palms."

As I did, I noticed there was writing on the blade. But it was dull and parts of it had been worn off, so I couldn't read what it said.

Drofgum held the twencil up in his palms like he had held the knife. He said, "Wood feeds fire, fire refines metal." Then he rolled the twencil between his palms. The lead inside the twig seemed to melt, and it dripped to the ground. As it dripped, the liquid lead at the tip of the twencil turned to fire and shot out like a mini blowtorch.

Drofgum used the fire to trace the words on the silver blade of the knife, melting the letters right into the metal. He wrote from right to left, and as he wrote he said, "Be refined and tune your ear to da needs of your secondary master."

I was worried, thinking the letters would melt right through the blade and scorch my hand. But the blade itself never got hot. It stayed cool.

When Drofgum had finished writing, the twencil turned to dust in his fingers and the powder sprinkled into his lap.

"You won't be needin' dat no more. Now read dis," he said, pointing at the blade.

"From beginning to end, life is in your hands." As I read them, the engraved words shone from the blade like a beam of sunlight.

Drofgum picked up the knife, kissed the blade, and said, "Give me your hand."

I held it out and before I could think twice about it, Drofgum grabbed it and turned it over so my palm was facing up. He held it tightly. "Dis'll only hurt a little," he said as he pressed the tip of the knife blade into my palm.

Never believe anyone who tells you, "This'll only hurt a little." It hurt like an army of red ants doing the conga on my flesh. Drofgum carved a spiral into my palm just as easily as if he was decorating icing on a cake. I couldn't help but scream.

"Dere. Dat does it." He placed the knife in a sheath and snapped it onto my belt. "And dis is da proper way of carryin' it, by da ways. It deserves its own special place, not t'rown into a pocket wit' lint and dirty tissues."

Then he held my bleeding hand in his, and I felt an intense heat pulsing between our palms. After a few seconds, he let go.

I looked at my palm. The spiral cut had turned into a shiny black scar.

"How'd you . . .? What's this for?" I asked.

"How doesn't matter," he said. "But da what . . . you'll be findin' dat out when da time comes. Now listen, dat Knife on your belt possesses special powers—powers to create. Ever since da Elements vanished, I've been protectin' as much of Emogen as I can. Every now and den I sticks it into da ground and into da trees around da perimeter here. Doin' dat protects me little clearin' from da influences of Demlock's evil enterin' in. Dat's why dis is da only safe place around. And now, me boy, all da powers of da Knife are yours."

Suddenly a familiar squawk rang through the trees. I craned my neck to see through the branches and my heart stopped cold. There, swooping in for a landing, was the biggest, coolest looking eagle I'd ever seen.

That I'd ever seen in real life, that is.

He landed in the clearing without a sound.

"My dear friend Melchior," said Drofgum.

Melchior. The eagle. My mom's guardian.

Melchior stepped towards us, gave Drofgum a friendly peck on the shoulder, and nudged my arm. I put my hand on his head.

"Hi, Melchior," I said. Melchior's eyes were just as dark and intense as they had been in my dream. Maybe even more intense.

Melchior squawked and clawed at the ground. He nudged me again before looking at Drofgum.

I was just about to ask Drofgum if he knew anything about my mom, seeing how he knew Melchior, when Drofgum reached out and hugged me so tight I thought he'd squeeze all the air right out of my lungs. "Da Son of da Sevent' has returned, Melchior," he said as he released me.

Those words left an imprint in my mind, as if they had been pressed into dough. Son of the Seventh . . . Son of the . . . Seventh . . . Grampa's rhyme!

The seventh sun, the seventh sun
Lives so pie in the sky
Unawares he is
Of the job that's his
To do lest we all die

The seventh sun . . . The seventh *son*! It's son, not sun! And I have a job to do before everything dies! Grampa knew!

"Now you must takes your Key and journey nort'," said Drofgum. "I wish your friend hadn't pilfered me compass. At least you could have figured out nort' from where it was pointin'. But regardless, you needs to head to da nort'ern region of Ur da best you can. Follow da mosses on da trees. Granted, dey is dyin' and barely clingin' on, but what little's left of dem is on da nort' side of da trees. In da region of Ur in the village of Tezema Raha, you will find da Beast who's . . ." he paused and choked back a tear, " . . . who's swallowed da udder half of da Key. Remember, follow da Stones; dey'll tell you what to do."

Melchior squawked.

"Yes, my friend. Da time has come," Drofgum said. He turned to me. "Do you t'ink you can do it?"

"Uh . . . well . . ."

"Good," said Drofgum. "Now I've gots to go." He put his hand on my shoulder and squeezed. "And so must you. Jes remember all I've told you and you'll find what you're lookin' fer."

Then with a heave and a ho, Drofgum climbed up on Melchior's back.

"Oh!" I cried. "What should I do once I get the other half of the Key?"

"Do you remember where you landed when you gots here?"

"At the back of a waterfall," I said.

"Dat's where you needs to go. Wit' da completed Key. Da Sustainer'll be waitin' fer you dere to takes you t'roo da Labyrint' to da Crypt where da Elements are."

"The Sustainer?" I exclaimed.

"Yes, of course," said Drofgum. "How else do you expect to finds your way to da Crypt? Da Labyrint' is pretty confusin'— so many tunnels and all. It's a wonder da Sustainer himself don't get lost down dere. He'll be at da waterfall, waitin' fer you."

"Will you be there, too?" I asked.

Drofgum nodded. "I sure hope so. Up, Melchior."

Melchior gave my arm another nudge and then he lifted off, leaving me alone in Drofgum's clearing.

22 Unwelcome Guest

The moment I stepped out of Drofgum's little green clearing, I was plunged right back into the middle of the brown, dingy forest. For hours I shuffled through piles of dead leaves and pine needles and crawled under low-reaching branches, but the Stones had nothing to say. And I mean nothing. They were dark and cold and lifeless, like stones are supposed to be, I guess. But I'd seen with my own eyes that these Stones weren't like other stones. And I expected them to do what Drofgum had told me they'd do. But they weren't.

I held one of the Stones in my hands and rubbed it as if I expected a genie might pop out and show me the way. I was totally discouraged, almost to the point of finding my way back to the clearing and waiting for Drofgum to return. I seriously started doubting my part in all of this. I mean, the more I thought about it, who Emogen really needed on a Beast-slaying, evil-lord-defying mission like this was Spiderman or Superman, not Smudgeman.

I headed north the best I could without a compass. I had followed the river upstream and was already quite a distance past the waterfall, but the mosses had slowly disappeared the farther I got from the falls until I couldn't spot a trace of one anywhere. So for all I knew, I could have been way off track.

Wandering around in a wasteland with no one to talk to and nothing to do gives you a lot of time to think. And believe me, my mind didn't stop.

I replayed the scenes from my dream over and over again: the Key, the Stone statues, the eagle, the angel. The Key, the Stone statues, the eagle, the angel. The Key: the Key to the Casket. The Stone statues? Stone statues . . . stone statues—hair like fire, wind, water, and leaves . . . the four Elements of creation! The eagle: Melchior. The angel . . .

My mom.

The angel: my mom. I wished I had asked Drofgum about her. If only he hadn't been in such a hurry.

How's my mom connected to the Elements? I wondered. How'd she get the Key? And why did she give it to me? Had she meant to meet me here? Why did I have to lose my memory?

Then I did remember something: The image of the horrible creature that had torn into my dream sprang vividly to my mind like I'd just seen it yesterday. Demlock! Could he be the monster that took her from me?

"Where are you, Mom?" I asked as I stopped and looked up through the bare branches of the trees. The sky was grey and the woods were deathly quiet. Not a bird, not a woodland creature anywhere.

I rubbed the Stones again. I sure wished they would hurry up and say something.

I sat down with a grunt on a tree stump, rolling my eyes at them. If only Gil were here. He would think of something.

Then I heard a faint whimper nearby. It sounded like an injured animal. I took a few steps towards it and stopped. Through the trees I could see a girl sitting on a log. She was crying.

"Hello?" I called out as I walked towards her.

The girl screamed and jumped to her feet, turning around to face me.

I couldn't believe my eyes.

Tessa Tasselbaum.

She screamed again when she saw me. The sound of her voice and the sight of her standing there made me want to stuff my ears full of pine needles and gouge my eyes out.

"What are you doing here?" we both asked at the same time.

"I said, what are you doing here?" Tessa demanded again. "Why are you following me?"

"What? I'm not following you! You're following me," I said.

"As if I would follow you. Get real! I've got better things to do with my time than follow you!" she said, pushing her hair out of her face. Her hair and clothes were damp. I guess she had landed behind the waterfall, too.

"Oh, yeah? Then how did you get here?"

"I just appeared," she said, as if it happened to her on a regular basis.

"Oh, really?"

"Yeah."

Silence.

More silence.

"Okay! So I wanted to taunt you because you got sent to detention," she blubbered as she pushed her damp hair out of her face again.

"We didn't actually get sent there," I said. I sure didn't want her getting any satisfaction thinking we were sent to detention, especially if she thought it had anything to do with her.

Her face fell. "What do you mean? Of course you were. As soon as I heard you guys didn't return to your dorm after dinner, I thought for sure . . . and then rumor of it spread like wildfire."

I'll bet I know who started that rumor, I thought.

"What does that have to do with you being here?" I said.

"Well, this morning, I thought I'd pay you a short visit . . ."

"What? You came to visit us?" I asked, interrupting her. "Haven't you heard the stories about that place?"

"Sure, but I wanted to witness your torture first-hand. I thought the risk was worth it. Besides, I'm not stupid. I wasn't planning on just walking in. I listened at the door first."

"Man, you really are sadistic, aren't you?"

"Only where you're concerned," she said.

"How did you get in? I thought the door was locked."

Tessa rolled her eyes. "You don't always need a *key* to open a locked door, you know."

"So you mean you actually went into Detention Hall and climbed down the hole in the floor?" I asked, stunned, remembering how I got here.

"Of, course! Do you think only boys are adventurous?"

"Well, uh . . . no . . . but . . ."

"When I saw there was a ladder leading below the floor, I just knew you two were up to something. So I grabbed a candle and headed down myself. And before I knew it there were these bright lights and I was falling. And it's all your fault!"

"It's my fault you followed us?"

Tessa squared her shoulders, flipped her hair, and stood tall. "Of course. If you morons hadn't gotten a detention in the first place, then I wouldn't have had to taunt you about it."

"I already told you, we weren't sent there with a detention!"

"Yeah, whatever." She put her hands on her hips and looked around. "So where is loser number two?"

"He could be dead, okay?"

"WHAT?" Tessa screeched. "How could you even say such a ghastly thing?" she screamed and slugged me in the arm.

"Hey!" I shouted. She had quite the right arm on her. But I didn't want to admit it by giving in to the painful urge to rub my arm, so I just gritted my teeth and sucked it up.

Tessa stood there, huffing, with her hands in tight fists, looking like she would strike again at any second.

"I said it because he could be!" I shouted back at her. "You have no idea what we've been through! So for all I know, he could be dead. But for now I'd like to just think he's missing."

"What do you mean, 'missing'?" she demanded.

"Missing—means he's nowhere to be found, not here, gone."

"I know what it means!" she shouted.

"Then why'd you ask? He's just missing, okay?"

Tessa huffed again. "Just so you know, I almost died!" she said. "I was in quite a state when Mr. Lurch found me in my locker!"

"I have no idea what you're talking about," I lied.

"I know it was you! That's why I told Mr. Ratsw—where do you think you're going?" Tessa suddenly sounded more nervous than angry as I turned to leave. She quickly sniffled back the last traces of her tantrum.

"I'm leaving," I said.

She tried to hide the look of horror that leapt from her eyes. She cleared her throat and flipped her hair. "Oh, and I suppose you know where you're going."

"Yup," I lied again as I started to walk away. Now, which way was I headed before Miss Annoying showed up? I thought as I discretely tried to get my bearings.

"Oh, yeah? Well . . . well, don't think you're going to get away with this one," Tessa threatened as she followed me. "Just wait until Mr. Ratsworth finds out about this!"

Once a Tattlebaum, always a Tattlebaum.

I kept walking.

She followed me. Very closely.

"Are you listening to me? I'm speaking to you! Sludge Mugford, don't ignore me! And don't think that you can abscond just like that!"

I turned around so quickly—and Tessa was following so closely—that we collided.

"Abscond off!" I said as I grabbed her by the elbows. "Shut up! Do you hear me? Shut up! I've had enough of you and your whining. If you don't quit complaining, I'll . . . I'll feed you to the wild vines. And believe me, they're really hungry." I pointed to where vines aggressively choked the trunk of a tree.

Luckily the vines were all she needed to see. She didn't make another sound for a really long time.

And she stuck so close as we walked that she stepped on my heels a few times.

"So . . . so, where are you going?" she finally asked.

I just kept walking.

"I'm talking to you," she said.

"And I'm ignoring you," I replied.

Tessa huffed.

We walked on.

Tessa suddenly grabbed my arm and pulled me back. "I demand you explain what's going on, this instant!"

"You demand it, do you? Demand all you want. It won't get you any answers."

Tessa huffed again and kept following me.

After a few minutes of silence, she asked through gritted teeth, "Smudge, could you please explain what's going on?"

At least it was an improvement.

"We're in a place called Emogen," I said.

"And?"

"And nothing."

"You're impossible, you know that? I'm trying to have a civil conversation, and you're . . . you're being so . . . so . . . moronic!" Tessa's face was red and she was shouting really loudly.

"Remember the vines," I said.

"Ugh!" She crossed her arms and stomped along behind me. "You're so . . ."

"Okay, okay," I interrupted her, putting my hand up. "Here it is. Well, here's what I know." I took a deep breath. "We're in a realm called Emogen that's really closely connected to our realm, Earth. How it's connected, I don't have a clue, but everything that happens here affects Earth. And there's this guy named Demlock who got greedy and wanted to control everything, so he decided he was going to try to get control of the Elements. They're the forces that control the environment—you know: Earth, Air, Water, and Fire. Anyways, Demlock messed everything up, and because of him the Elements are now locked away in some secret Casket in a Crypt, and Gil's in huge life-threatening trouble, and I've got this half of a Key—see?—and these Stones that I got from an old man named Drofgum, and I'm supposed to use the Stones to find the other half of the Key so I can put the two halves together and unlock the Casket that the Elements are locked up in so Emogen, Earth, and Gil can be freed from Demlock's curse. Got it?"

Tessa blinked a few times. Then she flipped her hair and said, "So you mean to tell me *you* are *important* here?"

Leave it to Tessa. *Two entire realms* are being destroyed because of an evil thirst for power, and all she's concerned about is status. *Classic.*

I just nodded.

"I'll believe it when I see it. Now, enough about you. I've got some questions."

Great, the exact thing I was trying to avoid.

And away she went. She asked if I thought Gil was mad at me for something and why I figured he left if he wasn't. She asked about the weather (because her hair doesn't do well if it's too humid), if the Elements were male or female, and even what Drofgum was wearing when I met him.

"How am I supposed to remember that?" I asked.

She looked at me, an expression of complete disgust on her face. "How could you not remember that?"

I just rolled my eyes. It wasn't even worth a response.

"And so what do you know about what happened to Gil?" she finally asked just seconds before I was going to tell her to put a sock in it.

I paused. "Not much," I said. I didn't know what to tell her. I sure didn't want to tell her about the candy or that he'd tried to take my Key.

"That's just like you, isn't it?" she said. "You don't seem to know much about anything."

"Well, there is one thing that I do know for sure. Are you interested?" Even though I would have endured brain surgery without anesthetic if it meant getting rid of her, I knew I had to help her. If I didn't she'd probably go missing, too. And I sure didn't need that on my conscience on top of everything else.

"Is it something intelligent?" she asked with a swivel of her head.

I took one of the Stones off and held it out to her. "You need to wear this."

"You call that intelligent?" she said, making a face at the grey Stone.

"Just take it! Who knows what kind of trouble you'll land us in if you don't."

Tessa took it and turned it over in her hand. "It's not very pretty," she said.

"Just put it on!"

Geez, trying to save a snooty girl's life isn't as easy as it sounds.

"Drofgum gave me these Stones and told me to wear them," I said. "They're meant to guide and protect us."

"Protect us from what?" asked Tessa.

"From Demlock's music," I replied. "Gil didn't have his on the night he disappeared."

"So have they really been telling you where to go?" she asked as she looked at the Stone and then held it to her ear.

Aw geez. "Uh, well, not yet. But . . . they will."

She handed the Stone back to me, brushed off her skirt and said, "As exciting as this is, I've given it some thought and . . . I've come to the conclusion that this quest doesn't suit me. Besides, I can feel my hair frizzing as we speak. So I'll just be heading back now."

"Doesn't suit you? You'll be heading back?" I snorted back a laugh. "To what? Your *daddy*? Is he finally going to spare us all and take you home?"

Tessa straightened her shoulders and flipped her ponytail. "Yes. So if you don't mind showing me the way . . . What are you laughing at? I don't see anything funny about this at all. Now, as I was saying, if you don't mind showing me the way, I'll just . . ."

"You're not going anywhere," I interrupted.

"Excuse me?"

"I said, you're not going anywhere."

"Oh yes I am!" she screeched. "Tell the portal to open now!" Missiles flew from her eyes.

"I can't just tell a portal to open! Besides, it was opened with Dark Magic."

Tessa's eyes filled with tears. "What do you mean, 'Dark Magic'? I don't believe in magic!"

"Well, whether you believe in magic or not, that's what got you here. How else do you think portals operate? By pushing a button?"

"This truly is asinine!" Tessa was pretty much screaming by now. "Make the portal open and take me back! I don't care how you do it! Push a button! Pull a cord! Clap your hands! I don't care! Just do it! I demand it!"

"You know what I said about how effective your demands are," I said as I turned to walk away.

"You told me about your supposed purpose in being here!" she shouted after me. "Well, my purpose just so happens to be back at the academy! My purpose is there, not here, looking for some old key bits and a stuttering fool who doesn't know any better than to wander off by himself in the middle of the night in a strange place!"

I turned and shouted back at her. "And what better purpose do you have back at that prison that's more important than finding Key bits and a stuttering fool in order to help save an entire realm?"

Was Tessa at a loss for words? She just stood there staring at me.

"So? What've you got that's more important than that?" I repeated.

Tessa looked at her feet. "Making the honor roll," she whispered, wiping her eyes.

"Figures," I said as I turned around and kept walking.

Tessa followed in silence for quite a long time before she said, "Okay, I'll help you."

I spun around on my heels. "What did you say?"

"I said, I'll help you," she repeated as she stepped closer to me. "But don't think I'm liking this. Not even one bit." She flipped her ponytail in my face as she stepped past me, grabbing the Stone and tying it around her neck.

I caught up to her and planted my feet in front of her, blocking her way. "Just don't get the wrong idea and think we're partners," I said.

"No worries there," she said. She stuck her tongue out at me.

"You will always be stuck-up," I said.

"And you will always be a moron."

"We will never be friends."

"Agreed."

23 Broken Glass

As usual, Tessa couldn't keep quiet. She kept telling me what to do with our Stones, what not to do with our Stones and what we probably should be doing with our Stones.

And, as usual, I got really annoyed with her.

She shook her Stone like it was a can of whipping cream. She glared at it and growled. "Useless."

"They're not the only things," I muttered.

"*Excuse me?*"

"Nothing."

"It'd *better* have been nothing!"

"Yeah, yeah," I said, kicking the ground with my foot.

"I'm starving. Have you got anything to eat in there?"

I hadn't really noticed up until then, but it was dark and I was pretty hungry myself. So I lifted the shoulder strap over my head and dropped the sack on the ground under the nearest tree. I opened it and pulled out a small loaf of bread, a water skin, and something wrapped in brown paper and string.

"What's in the paper?" asked Tessa as she took the water. She popped off the cap and took a long drink.

I unwrapped it. It was a whole fish—tail, head, eyeballs, and all. Well, I guess it wasn't exactly a whole fish; there was a slit down its belly and the guts were gone.

"Ew! Gross!" screamed Tessa. "If you think I'm going to eat that, you can think again!" She grabbed the loaf of bread.

"I think it's cooked," I said as I picked at the dried scales. "Or smoked or something."

"I don't care! I refuse to eat something that's looking at me! Anything else in there?"

"Just some more water, about three more loaves of bread, and about the same number of brown paper packages," I said as I poked around in the sack.

Tessa rolled her eyes. "Great. Looks like it's bread and water for me. I feel like I'm in prison!"

"Well, then you should feel like you're right back where you want to be: at the school," I said. I looked up. "Hey, Tessa, have you ever seen a full moon that big before?"

"Don't try to change the subject," she said. "It won't make me feel any better about this whole horridly unacceptable diet we've got to survive off of."

"Holy crow, look at that!" I said, cutting Tessa off. I stood and pointed at the moon.

"Excuse me, but I was talking about this whole horridly—gosh!" she said as she followed my gaze upwards. She stood next to me.

The gigantic moon was suddenly being covered over by a black shadow.

"It's a half . . . now a quarter . . . now it's gone!" said Tessa in disbelief.

I hadn't realized before, but the brightness of the moon had actually given us enough light that we could see each other fairly clearly. But now that it had been covered over, the woods were completely and totally dark. There wasn't a speck of light anywhere, not even from the stars. They seemed to have been covered over, too.

"What's going on?" I asked.

"Most likely a lunar eclipse," said Tessa. "That's when the moon gets covered over by the planet's shadow," she added, probably getting the feeling I was going to ask her anyways.

We stood for what seemed like an hour before the moon finally started reappearing. It probably wasn't really an hour, but when you're standing in the middle of the woods in pitch darkness, even thirty seconds can feel like an hour.

"Look! There it is again," said Tessa. "Quarter . . . half . . . full."

The little area around the tree lit up again with pale light.

"Whoa. What's that?" I asked as something on the ground strangely reflected the dull light and caught my attention with a rainbow of color.

Without giving it a second thought, I bent down and grabbed the thing, shouting out as a sudden sharpness ripped across my thumb. I let go and flapped my hand in the air.

"What are you doing?" yelled Tessa.

I held my hand close to my eyes to check the damage. I was surprised by the amount of blood I saw. There was a small but deep gash on the pad of my thumb. I tightened my grip on my wrist and held my throbbing hand.

"I said, what are you doing?" demanded Tessa.

I paid no attention to her. I used the toe of my shoe to kick at the sharp, rainbow thing that was stuck in the ground.

Finally, I unearthed a jagged piece of glass that was attached with a wire to another shard of glass. I yanked it out of the ground by the wire.

Oh, great! A lousy pair of broken glasses!

"You nearly severed your hand for a pair of shattered glasses?"

"Well, I'd hardly call it severed," I said, but she wasn't listening.

"You really do need to be more careful, you know. Next time you go diving in before thinking, you should really consider—"

"Shhh!" I hissed. I spotted some interesting scratches on the side of the frame. I held the glasses closer to my eyes.

"What?" she snapped, probably annoyed that I'd cut her off.

"Shhh!" I hissed again.

Tessa folded her arms and huffed.

"It says 'G.M.' Holy crow! These are Gil's glasses!"

"Let me see those," Tessa said and grabbed the glasses out of my hand. "And you'd better do something about that before it gets infected," she said, pointing to my thumb.

"Yeah, whatever. Give me those back," I said, grabbing the glasses back from her.

"You really are stupid, you know," Tessa said, suddenly sounding a little nervous. "You're losing a lot of blood. All I need is for you to pass out and die from a loss of blood, leaving me stranded here, alone."

"Geez, thanks for your concern."

"We've got to tie it up," she said, pulling a ribbon out of her hair. She grabbed my arm and wrapped the ribbon around my wrist and tied it tight. The bleeding slowed down a bit. She took another ribbon and wrapped it—tightly—around my thumb.

I gritted my teeth. "I'm sure this gives you great pleasure."

She just smiled and tied a triple knot tight enough to completely cut off any circulation in that digit.

As I carefully picked the shattered pieces of glass out of the frames, trying to take my mind off the throbbing in my thumb, Tessa stepped out from under the battered branches of the tree and looked up at the sky.

"What do we do now?" she asked, raking her fingers through her now loose hair.

I hate to admit it, but that's a good question, I thought. We're way off course. We're supposed to be going north, but if Gil passed by this tree on his way to Demlock, then we're headed west. Stupid Stones!

I held my Stone and waited for an answer. Nothing.

"I didn't think so," I said to the Stone. "What good are you?"

"Maybe they need batteries."

I rolled my eyes. "Enchanted Stones don't need batteries," I said.

"Well, then why aren't they working, Mr. Know-it-all?"

I suddenly felt like I was going to faint. I dropped the frames and let go of the Stone as I leaned back against the tree.

"Are you all right?" Tessa asked, eyes wide.

"Yeah," I said. "Guess I just lost a lot of blood too fast." I reached over and picked the frames up and put them in my pocket.

"Told you so." Tessa crouched down beside me and felt my forehead. Then she said, "Oh!" and took my bandaged hand in hers. "We'd better take this off, now." She began undoing the ribbon she had tightly tied around my wrist. "Or else the lack of blood flow to your hand may cause permanent tissue damage and we'll be forced to do something hideous."

"Like what?" I asked.

"Amputate."

I wasn't sure if she was joking or not. I didn't ask.

She unwound the ribbon, and I felt a sudden rush of blood flow back into my hand. It felt like pins and needles. She left the other ribbon on my thumb.

"Why are you doing this?" I asked. "Why are you helping me?" Twenty-four hours ago she hated me and would rather have seen me tortured. Or amputated.

She shrugged.

"Well, it's too dark to go anywhere now, so I think I'm going to try to get some sleep," I said, forcing myself up on wobbly legs. I had to create some distance between us before she tried to be nice to me again. "It'll make the night pass faster."

I spread out one of the blankets Drofgum had packed in my sack and gave Tessa the other one.

"Uh, where are you going to be?" she asked.

"Right here," I said as I flopped down on my blanket. "Where else do you think I'm going to go?"

"Uh, sure you'll stay there?" she asked as she spread her blanket out, too.

"Yeah, are you scared, Tessa?" I asked, sort of in a teasing way. I didn't really want to sound like I was teasing too much, because if the truth be known (between you and me), I was kind of scared myself.

"No," she said. "Why are you asking?"

"Uh, because you practically put your blanket on top of mine."

24 Liquid Mercury

I woke up the next morning to music. It was eerie and distant but at the same time it sounded like it was hanging right above our heads from the tree we had slept under.

I looked over to where Tessa had been sleeping, but she wasn't there.

Not again! I thought.

"Tessa?" I called as I jumped to my feet.

"The trees are opening up a path for us," I heard her say.

She was standing on the other side of the huge tree, pointing towards the woods. I joined her.

Maybe it was only because we were both staring so quietly at the moving trees, but it seemed like when she said that, the eerie music got a speck louder. And it actually seemed to be the sound of the music that made the trees shift and move.

Just like the day Gil and I were in the Marsh.

Tessa took a step forward. I put my arm out in front of her. "No. Wait."

"Why?" she asked. Her eyes were glued to the trees. "This is obviously a sign. It must be the way we should go."

"Tessa, Drofgum warned me about this," I said. "Do you hear the music?"

"Hear what?" she said.

"The music!"

"All I see are trees doing a dance. And it's beautiful. It must be a sign!"

Don't tell me she can't hear the music.

"I don't trust it," I said as the music got a bit louder.

"It's amazing," whispered Tessa as if she were in a trance. She pushed my arm out of the way and darted towards the trees. They curled up and then bent forward, creating a sort of branchy entrance to a dense forest passageway.

"Tessa! Stop!" I shouted. But it was too late. She had run through the entryway.

I ran after her. I guess even though Tessa Tasselbaum was the last person on earth—or *Emogen* for that matter—I wanted to be with, I just didn't feel right about letting her take off on her own, especially if she really couldn't hear the music. Besides, I figured that if Demlock had set this whole dancing tree thing up, maybe it was worth the risk of entering. Maybe it would lead me to Gil.

Once I stepped through the archway of trees, I felt strangely anxious. The feeling of distrust I had earlier suddenly became more intense. I ran to catch up to Tessa and pull her back. But the moment I reached her, the air around us transformed into a colorful prism of dark, liquid mercury.

Colors—terrible and beautiful colors. That's what Drofgum said about the Powers of Darkness!

Drofgum, what do I do now? I thought.

Suddenly the archway closed up and there was a huge crash as the ground gave way directly beneath our feet.

Tessa grabbed my arm and dug her fingernails into my skin as we tumbled headfirst, rolling and bouncing downward.

When we finally stopped, I lay still, gasping for air. The place where we landed was really earthy and dry. The grass looked all burnt, and the trees were nothing but brittle-looking branches. I immediately noticed that the air was thinner. It was the regular oxygen-filled kind that was easy to breathe, not like the thick liquidy kind we were just in. But I still felt groggy, like I'd woken up from a deep sleep.

We both lay still for quite some time.

"What just happened?" Tessa asked as she suddenly sat up. "How did we get here?"

"The colors, the music! Don't you remember?" I said. "Did you hit your head on the way down or something?"

"What music?" she asked. "I don't remember hearing any music."

So she really didn't hear it, I thought. Just like Gil.

"Drofgum warned me about the music," I said. "It opened up an archway, and you went through it. Well, we both did. I thought it might lead us to Gil. That's the last time I do that!"

"Smudge," said Tessa with a look of panic on her face. "I don't remember any of that. Not even the colors."

"Tessa, where's your Stone?"

She reached up to her neck. It wasn't there. "Oh, here," she said, reaching into her pocket. "I took it off because the twine was scratching my neck. I thought it would still be safe enough to keep it in my pocket."

"Sheesh!" I cried. "You better put it back on! If you're not wearing the Stone, you won't be able to hear the music! Remember? Gil wasn't wearing his the night he disappeared."

She immediately tied it back around her neck.

"Don't ever take that Stone off," I said.

"Why, Smudge Mugford, do I detect a note of concern in your voice?"

Did she just smile at me?

"Huh? Uh, no. No, I don't think so," I stammered.

"How are you feeling?" asked Tessa as she started picking twigs out of her hair. "Did the music affect you at all?"

"Uh, no. Actually, it never does."

Tessa burst out laughing.

"What are you laughing at?" I asked, beginning to sense the familiar feeling of annoyance creeping in. "I'm serious. The music never affects me."

"No, no, I believe you," she said. "But I just can't hold it in any longer. Just look at yourself!" she exclaimed as she laughed and pointed at me.

"How am I supposed to do that?" I asked.

She pulled a little mirror out of her sweater pocket. A pink mirror with purple hearts. And magnets stuck on the back.

"Uh, where'd you get that?" I asked, trying to sound as innocent as possible as I took the mirror from her.

"From someone," she said with a little smirk. "A secret admirer."

"Any idea who?" I asked, cringing.

"It wouldn't be a secret then, would it?"

"Guess not."

I turned the mirror over and took a look to see if I really did look as hilarious as she seemed to think.

I did.

I was covered from head to toe in burrs and my hair was totally matted. I had dried mud stuck up my nose, and twigs popped up out of my snarled hair like antennae.

"Yeah, yeah, okay, okay. I guess I do look funny," I agreed as I pulled the antennae out and gave the mirror back to her.

But Tessa wasn't laughing anymore. She was on the verge of going ballistic.

There, with its head reared up in striking position, was a huge green snake. And it had its beady eyes focused on Tessa.

25 The Snake and the Eagle

"Shhhh," I said as calmly as I possibly could. "Don't move. And for Pete's sake, don't scream."

"Will the Stones protect us from that, too?" Tessa asked as she slowly put her hands behind her and shifted her weight away from the snake.

"I said, don't move," I whispered again.

The viper hissed and coiled its thick body around to look at me, its fangs dripping a murky, white liquid.

Tessa jutted her chin out towards me.

"What?" I whispered.

She mumbled something, but I couldn't hear her.

The viper rose up and arched its neck back in Tessa's direction.

She opened her eyes wide, looked at my side, and jutted her chin again.

What is she doing? I thought. I looked down at my side. Oh, the Knife.

"But it's supposed to be used for life!" I whispered, maybe too loudly. The viper hissed and spit its venom in my direction.

Tessa rolled her eyes. "Maybe try to use it to save mine!" she whispered back. "Stab it in the head!"

The snake raised its head higher towards her when she said "head," as if on cue.

"Do it!" she mouthed.

I slowly and quietly took Drofgum's Knife out of its sheath.

As the viper prepared to strike, the bright yellow stripe in the middle of its head suspended the suspense in midair. I squeezed the Knife's handle. My heart felt like it was pumping enough blood to quench the thirst of a thousand vampires as I started a mental countdown.

Ten, nine . . . before I even got to four, I flung myself at the viper and aimed the Knife right at its yellow-striped head. Just as my feet left the ground, the snake turned its dripping fangs on me, spitting some of its poison into my face. A few drops landed on my lips and I instinctively spit. It tasted awful.

The Knife got the snake right between the eyes, and it came out through the back of its neck. The snake's body struggled and thrashed about as I used all my strength to jam the Knife into the ground, trapping the viper upside down by its head.

It struggled and hissed for a few seconds longer and then lay lifeless in its own blood—blood that was a really thick yellow slime. It crystallized as it flowed out of the dead snake.

I slouched to the ground and crawled away from the dead reptile. I wiped my lips and spit on the ground over and over again to get the rest of the foul taste out of my mouth. It tasted really, really awful.

"Look!" exclaimed Tessa.

The snake's body had started trembling. And then its tail flopped from side to side, looking like it was trying to free itself from the Knife.

"It's coming back to life!" Tessa shrieked.

"I told you!" I cried.

But the snake gave a final violent thrash of its tail, and then its body deflated like a balloon. All that was left was its skin, as if it had just shed.

I wasn't feeling so hot all of a sudden. I slowly attempted to pull the sticky barbed balls from my hoodie, socks, and hair.

"I'm beginning to think that maybe you aren't that much of a moron after all," Tessa whispered.

"Well, don't worry about it," I said as I struggled to my feet and reclaimed the Knife from the snake's flattened head.

What was she trying to do to me? First she goes and bandages my hand up, and then she starts talking about how she thinks I might not even be as much of a moron as she'd thought. What was I supposed to do with that? I mean, we were supposed to be on strictly non-friendship terms. We had even made an agreement.

Besides, I'd already fallen for her once before and had nightmares of beautiful blonde-haired, blue-eyed praying mantises for a week after. I sure didn't do myself any favors by being so stupid.

"Hey, look at this. Sick, huh?" I said, trying to change the subject. I didn't want her turning to mush on me.

I held the yellow blood-encrusted Knife up and then quickly wiped the blade off on the ground before putting it back in the sheath.

"Well, I just wanted you to know," she said calmly, "that you don't seem quite so moronic anymore."

"Yeah, well, 'moronic' comes more naturally to me than 'non-moronic,'" I said, making little quotation marks with my fingers to emphasize the words. "So don't be disappointed if it doesn't last."

Aw, geez. "Moronic comes more naturally to me than non-moronic"? And did I really have to do the quotation marks? What's wrong with me? Can't I think of something intelligent to say?

And then I actually did have a suddenly intelligent thought. And it was good enough—luckily—to totally change the subject.

"We really need to start following the Stones."

"But the stupid things aren't working," Tessa said. "Look." She shook her Stone.

"But that's not the point. We need to wait. Drofgum said they would lead us, and we have to believe him."

"I guess you're right," she said.

"Did you just say I'm right?" I asked.

Tessa rolled her eyes. "Yeeessss."

I had to sit down. I wasn't sure if it was from the shock of Tessa saying I was right or if it was because that viper had spit stuff in my face. All I knew was that I was getting really super-dizzy.

"Are you all right?" asked Tessa. "You don't look too good."

"I . . . I really don't feel so—"

I was suddenly interrupted by a flutter of feathers and a loud familiar squawk as Melchior landed with a nearly soundless thud on the dry grass, right beside the dead snake.

"Are . . . are you seeing this, too?" I asked.

"Yeah," she said quietly. "I am." And then she shouted, "Smudge! Your Stone!"

Melchior squawked.

I looked down. My Stone was casting a serious red glow. As I held it in my hand, it gave off such a gleaming ruby shine that Tessa shielded her eyes.

Then I noticed that Tessa's Stone was shining too.

"They are working!" she shouted. She looked at her Stone. "What? What good are these? I can't even read what it says! It's in a different language!"

I looked at her Stone. It was backwards . . . well, to her at least. I could read it.

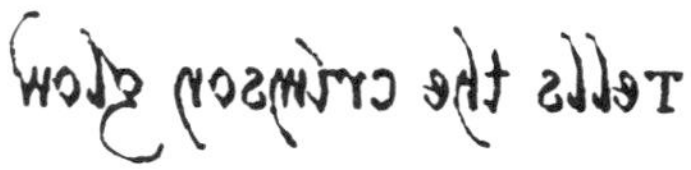

(Tells the crimson glow)

I grabbed my Stone. It read:

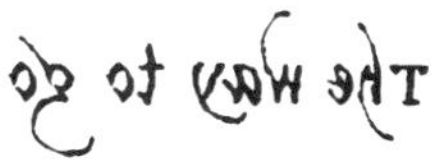

(The way to go)

"The way to go tells the crimson glow. That's what they said before," I said, disappointed.

"How are you reading them?" asked Tessa.

"Just look in your mirror. The words are backwards here."

Tessa took her mirror out of her pocket and held it in front of her. "Tells the crimson glow!" she exclaimed. "You're right. How did you figure that out?"

I shrugged.

Melchior squawked again.

"Melchior's trying to tell us something," I said.

"Who's Melchior?" asked Tessa.

I pointed to the eagle who was now circling around the snake. He eyed it and me as he squawked a few more times. Then he stepped towards me. I had to steady myself on a tree trunk as I looked up into the eagle's eyes. I was feeling really dizzy now.

The eagle stepped around in front of me and, with his wings stretched out on either side of his body, ruffled his feathers. I stood, staring, trying to focus through my dizziness.

Melchior nudged my Stone.

I held it in my hand. "There's a new word written on it!" I said. "Finally!"

"What does it say?" asked Tessa.

"'Go.'"

Tessa held her mirror to her Stone. "Mine says 'north'," she said.

"'Go north'?" I asked the eagle. "I know! But which way's north?"

"I thought you said you knew where you were going!" exclaimed Tessa, glaring at me with her hands on her hips.

Luckily for me, Melchior changed the subject as he squawked and nudged my hand with his beak. The hand he nudged was the one with the black spiral scar.

"Will I find out what this is in the north?" I asked.

Melchior squawked again, and as he did, another thought popped into my head.

"Is that where my mom is? Are you taking me to her?"

He didn't squawk this time. He was quiet.

After a few seconds, the eagle squawked again and knelt down.

"He wants us to get on," said Tessa.

I heaved myself onto his back and then pulled Tessa up. The eagle stood up. It was a lot higher up than it had been in my dream. We gripped the oily feathers at the back of his neck.

"I guess we're headed north," I said.

Tessa rolled her eyes. "Thank goodness someone knows the way."

Melchior stepped back, raised his head high, flapped his giant wings, and lifted off. He squawked loudly as he flew low, weaving his way through the trees.

26 Descending into Danger

During our flight north, we saw a bit more of the Emogenian landscape than we would have if we'd stayed on the ground. We flew along a craggy mountain range that had a village built right into the side of it and crossed a small area that looked like a dried out ocean with tall, random bits of shriveled seaweed sticking straight up out of the ground. Tessa didn't even start complaining until after we'd taken a sharp right and started covering an area of land that looked like a totally barren tundra.

"When are we going to land?" she shouted back at me. "My hands are cramping up!"

"I have no idea," I said. "But I hope it's soon." I was feeling even more light-headed and dizzy than I was before. My eyes were burning, and my throat was getting really dry.

As if Melchior took his cue from us, he started descending and landed in the middle of a dusty clearing right in the middle of the tundra. The only things in sight were rocks, dried mud, and a few brown plants poking up out of the cracks in the mud.

The eagle knelt. Tessa and I slipped off his back, and I walked around to the eagle's head.

"Now what?" I asked.

He squawked and nudged my Stone.

"Does it say anything?" Tessa asked.

I looked at it. "No," I said.

Melchior stood, ruffled his feathers, and lifted off again, leaving us standing in the middle of the wasteland.

"But the Stone doesn't say anything!" I shouted after the bird.

He flew around, circling us a few times, and then, about a hundred yards ahead of us where there was a ridge of huge jagged rocks, the eagle flew straight up, up, up.

And then he came straight down like a torpedo.

"What is he doing?" asked Tessa. "He's going to kill himself!"

We watched in horror as the eagle continued diving straight down.

"Pull up! Pull up!" I shouted.

Tessa screamed and closed her eyes seconds before it looked like he was going to splatter on the ground.

But he didn't.

He just disappeared behind the rocks.

"Is he . . . dead?" she whispered from behind her hands.

"I . . . I don't know," I said.

Tessa slowly lowered her hands. "Where'd he go?"

"I don't know," I said again.

I stood on my toes to see if the added height would give me a better view. I still couldn't see anything beyond the rocks.

"Here. Have a seat," I told Tessa, trying to find the most comfortable-looking rock I could. "Rest a bit while I go see what happened."

"You're going to leave me here?" she shrieked.

"I'm not going to leave you," I said. "And you can come if you want, but I'm not sure you really want to see it. Do you?"

"No, I guess not," she said as she sat down.

"I'll just go see," I said, pointing to the ridge. "And then I'll come right back."

"Well, just don't be gone too long. This rock is horribly uncomfortable."

As I made my way towards the ridge, my Stone started glowing again. With each step I took, the red got brighter and deeper. I looked at it to see if there was a new message.

There was:

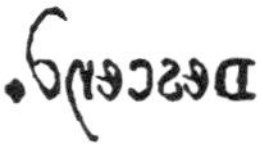

(Descend.)

Descend? Where?

As I got closer to the ridge of rocks that the eagle had "disappeared" into, I realized that it was actually the edge of a cliff. I inched my way closer and then lay flat on my belly and slithered like a skink to the rim and peered over the edge, expecting to see feathers, guts, and blood all over the place.

But I saw something totally different.

There, at the bottom of the cliff, lay a lonely village. But the position of the village was very strange. It was as if a huge round scoop had been taken out of the ground and the village had been built at the very bottom of the scooped-out land. An inky darkness encircled the outer perimeter of the village all along the scooped-out edges. It looked like a huge black sheet was suspended in midair, separating the outer perimeter of the village from the cliff. I looked straight down from where I was lying and saw there was actually a space between the rocks and the black sheet—a space that was wide enough for me to slip into. I looked over the black sheet into the village, and saw dirt roads, houses that looked like nothing more than upside-down clay bowls, and, in the middle of the village, a lake dotted with a small island.

There were also smoldering fires scattered throughout the village. The entire place looked like a hurricane had ripped through it.

Now my Stone was glowing so brightly I could actually feel heat coming from it. I was afraid it would burst into flames if it got any hotter.

Descend, it still said.

But then, the "escend" part of the word faded out and changed to "anger."

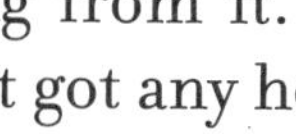

(Danger.)

Danger pulsed a couple of times and then changed back to Descend. And then it changed back to Danger again.

Danger . . . Danger . . . Descend . . . Danger . . . Danger . . . Descend . . .

If the Stone wasn't confused, I sure was. Did it want me to go down or not?

I really wanted to find Melchior, so I decided to chance it and go down quickly to see if I could find a sign of him and then go back to Tessa.

I began the steep climb downward, the whole time keeping my body close to the rocks. Even though I still felt dizzy and my eyes were burning, the ride with Melchior had cleared my head a little.

I continued my descent, straining my eyes to see below. When I reached the top edge of the black sheet, it suddenly got a lot darker. I paused before going any farther. I slowly reached out to touch the edge of the sheet, but my hand just swooshed through it, like there was nothing there. I kept climbing down between the rocks and the blackness, trying to keep my body close to the rocks so my back wouldn't touch the darkness. It kept getting darker the deeper I went until there was no noticeable space between the rocks and the darkness anymore. I had completely entered the darkness. But my Stone was lit so brightly that I was able to see, although it gave the darkness an eerie red tinge. I was concentrating so strongly on not slipping and killing myself that when I finally got to the bottom, it took me a few seconds to realize I was actually there.

What I also didn't realize right away was that a welcoming committee had been waiting for me: a dozen or so mangy wild dogs, all growling and glaring at me with glowing green eyes as they licked their drooling chops.

I quickly turned to climb back up the slope, but lost my footing as one of the beasts grabbed my pant leg. It shook me, pulling my legs out from under me. I fell and hit my forehead, hard, on a jagged bit of rock that stuck out of the ground like a spear. Blood immediately blinded me. I managed to scramble away, but only made it back up the wall a few feet before one of the dogs clamped its fangs onto my heel. I reached up to grab hold of a root that stuck out from the side of the cliff, but it was no use. The root gave way, causing me to skid back down the side of the gorge on my belly. Chunks of rock and splinters of wood scratched my bare stomach and cut deep into my skin.

When the dog loosened its grip, I scrambled along the ground and managed to grab a stick. I stood as best I could. I used the butt of the stick to try and fend off the dogs. The beasts growled, and it sounded like they had circled around me. They were snarling and biting the air in wild excitement.

My head throbbed as blood and sweat continued to run down my forehead and into my eyes. I stumbled and fell to the ground on my back.

I tried to open my swollen, stinging eyes, but only managed to peek through the puffy lids. I heard a long, low growl and smelled a wretched breath close to my face. I figured one of the dogs had straddled me.

Through my bleary eyes, I thought I saw the black outline of a human standing beside the beast. I heard a horrible wheezing sound. I tried desperately to stay conscious. Why was this guy just standing there while I was about to be made into dinner?

Help me! I screamed on the inside. Please help me!

But on the outside I was too weak to even make the slightest sound. I was barely even able to open my mouth.

The person bent down and leaned in close, making his outline a little clearer for a few seconds.

Gil? Gil, is that you? I wanted to ask out loud. I tried with all my strength to reach up to him, but my arms were dead weights. I tried to reach behind me to pull his glasses out of my back pocket so he could see them and know that I had been looking for him.

He whispered something to the beast and stood again, stepping back into the darkness, his image fading into the background.

Gil, no. Gil!

I fought hard to keep from passing out.

Gil, please help me!

The dog that was straddling me raised his head high and howled. He was going in for the kill.

The beast let out a horrible howl, and the glow from my Stone shone just enough red light that I saw it bare its fangs at me. It growled again, and just as it lunged for a chunk of my bare throat, a loud squawk ripped through the air. Or was that another growl?

Suddenly a deep groan came from the dog's gut as he was sent flying through the air, landing in a heap. Painful yelps and howls filled the air. I closed my eyes tightly, hoping they would somehow all just forget I was even there.

Before I knew it, everything went silent.

I thought that maybe I had finally passed out or maybe even died. But it sure felt like I was still in my body, lying on the ground.

I slowly opened my eyes and suddenly wished I was dead.

Through the red glow of my Stone I saw a different, much bigger creature straddling me. It was a massive, rust-colored, lynx-type cat. It was bigger than I'd imagined any lion could be.

I felt queasy as the lynx licked my cheek and then stepped around my body to stand by my feet. It clamped its jaws around my ankle and started dragging me away. My body bounced limply along as the cat pulled and jerked me down the dirt road.

Just when I thought I couldn't take the pain anymore, I passed out and everything went black.

27 Yegra Root

I woke up to warm liquid being poured down my throat and the sound of a soft, sweetly singing voice floating to my ears. I bolted upward and then crashed back down just as quickly because I'd knocked my head on a knobby wooden beam. I swiveled my head slowly and looked around. The room I found myself in was cramped and cluttered, and I was lying on a bed underneath what looked like a bench. There was hardly enough room for me to stretch out flat on my back without my nose brushing the underside of the rough wood, never mind sitting straight up.

And I had an excruciating pain in my head. I wasn't sure if I'd had it before I knocked myself on the beam or not.

In the warm orange glow of candlelight and through my grogginess I saw a beautiful woman sitting beside me. I was totally stunned.

"Mom? Mom? Is that you?" I croaked.

"Shhhhh . . . you must rest," said the woman as she gently sponged off my forehead. "Drink this." She dribbled some more of the warm liquid down my throat.

"Mom? I need to know if you're my mom," I protested as she gently held me down.

I could have sworn I smelled bubble gum.

I had no idea how long I went in and out of consciousness. Each time I woke up, I saw my mother. And each time, in my ever-so-brief moments of consciousness, she comforted me and told me that I was on the right track.

When I finally woke to full consciousness, my mother was gone. I called out for her, but it was Tessa who came.

"Where's my mom?" I asked, bolting up and whacking my head again. I had forgotten about the wooden beam.

"You'll never get better if you keep doing that," said Tessa, shaking her head.

"Yeah, thanks for the tip," I said, groaning, as I rubbed my head. I kicked down the covers so I could roll out of bed, even though it felt like my brain might pound right through my skull. "She was here. My mom. I fell asleep. Where is she?"

"Your mom? She wasn't here," Tessa said gently.

"I figured it was too good to be true," I said as I carefully rolled to the side of the bed and slid out from under the bench. All I could manage was to sit on the floor and rest my aching head against the hard bench seat.

"So what happened? Where are we?" I asked as I looked around. My eyes were still puffy and felt heavy.

The house we were in was made up of one main room and what looked to be a smaller room attached to it by an arched door frame. The main room had a dirt floor and a huge fire pit in the middle of it. The fire warmed the house, and the smoke drifted up and escaped through a hole in the roof. There was a bulky wooden butcher-block table with wooden stools around it, which stood next to the pit. A torch-holding chandelier hung from the ceiling above the table, dripping hot wax onto the mounds of weeds and roots that were spread out on the tabletop. A wooden cabinet stood against the wall behind it.

A short, wide woman stood at the table with her back to us.

"This is Rama's house," said Tessa nodding towards the woman who was busy picking through the weeds and wiping her hands on her apron. "We're in a place called Tezema Raha."

Tezema, I thought. This is the place Drofgum had mentioned. I made it.

"How long have we been here?" I asked.

"Oh, not long. Just a few hours."

"Ah, miracles upon miracles! That tonic always works wonders! I see the young man has awoken," said the woman as she turned around to look at me. She had a plump face and hands to match. She grabbed a bunch of gnarled roots, a bowl of water, and a cloth. "And how are you feeling? Better?"

"Yes, thank you," I said, making eyes at Tessa that meant I needed her to explain who this woman was.

"This is Rama," said Tessa as the woman came over to where I was sitting. "It was Rama's Cayenne that rescued you."

Rama knelt down beside me and put the bowl on the floor.

"Cayenne?"

All of a sudden, the same dark, rust-colored cat that had dragged me away from the wolves was sitting beside me, too. She had deep yellow eyes and black tufts of hair on her ears. She licked my cheek.

Rama laughed a deep belly laugh. "Yes, my baby Cayenne. You did a good job rescuing him," she said as she crumbled the dried roots into the bowl, dipped the cloth into it, and sponged off my forehead. The cloth smelled lemony. No, pepperminty. No, actually, the smell kept changing. From lemon to peppermint to . . . something kind of grassy. It was warm and felt really good.

"How did you find me?" I asked Tessa.

"Well, to make a long story short," she said, "I heard you screaming and I realized my Stone was blazing. I ran towards your voice and came to the edge of an enormous precipice. But I couldn't see you, even when I peered over the edge. There were howls and yelps and shrieks and all sorts of other noises. It was horrible. Then suddenly everything was quiet. I decided it was either go down to see what happened to you and risk my life to falling, or stay where I was and risk my life to who knows what! So, obviously, I chose to find you. Of course, I was furious with you that I had to climb down those murderous rocks into complete and utter darkness, but luckily my shining Stone helped me see. I got through the darkness, and I ended up on a dirt road, which I followed until I found you lying on the ground in the middle of a yard. Cayenne was licking your face. Of course, I didn't know that was her name at the time, but I guess she was trying to wake you up. Then Rama came out and we carried you inside."

That was making a long story short? I thought. Well, I'd asked.

Cayenne purred and licked my face again.

"Oh, yes, yes," said Rama. "Cayenne did a good job in saving you. And I could tell by the blaze in her eyes it was . . . he—or at least someone sent by him—who had you," she said with disgust in her voice. "His kind live in The Darkness, I tell you. They must have known you were voyaging through The Darkness; they must have been lying in wait for you. He and that hideous mutt of his."

"He? A boy?" I asked. "Was it a boy?"

"Oh, heavens. If only he were a boy. Then I could take my broom and shoo him off. I could . . . I could take him by the nape of his neck and send him on his way. I could pull him in here by his ears and . . . and teach him a lesson, I could. Oh, heavens no, he's no boy, not the one that's behind it all. Oh dear me."

"I guess it was just a vision then," I said, rubbing my head. I was starting to feel a headache coming on again.

"What are you talking about?" asked Tessa. "What vision?"

"I thought I saw Gil standing there with the wild dogs. But he didn't do anything to help. He just stood there and then disappeared."

"Must have been a vision," said Tessa. "By the look of it, you did get knocked on your skull pretty hard. And besides that, Rama said it looked like you had signs of ghex poisoning."

"Ghex poisoning?" I asked.

"Oh yes, dear," said Rama. "But don't worry; the Yegra Root has taken care of that, too."

"The Yegra Root?" I asked.

"Oh my. The poisoning must have done quite a number on you. Oh dear. Poor, poor boy. I should slow down now, shouldn't I? Well, let me see, the ghex is the deadliest viper in all of Emogen. A spot of its poison is enough to bring down a whole army of warriors—it's that deadly. It's a phenomenon you survived as long as you did, considering how far the poisoning had already gone."

"Yeah, your eyes were completely black," Tessa interrupted. "The white parts, I mean. The white parts were black!"

"Oh, yes, and your blood was actually crystallizing within your veins due to the amount of flesh wounds you had. The air was getting at it, and at a rapid pace," said Rama.

My mind flashed back to the snake's yellow, slimy blood. And how it had crystallized as it flowed out of its body.

"My blood was crystallizing?"

"Oh, yes, yes indeed. And had it reached your heart . . . oh dear. Yes. Crystallized blood. The most certain sign of ghex poisoning. Well, that and hallucinations."

"Hallucinations?" I asked.

"Oh, yes, yes. And to hear of your hallucinations doesn't surprise me at all; not at all," said Rama. "Ghex poisoning is well known for that. To the point—for some unfortunate souls—that it drives them to utter madness before death."

"So you think I was just hallucinating then?" I asked. "When I saw Gil?"

Rama cleared her throat. "Well . . . now, I really—"

"Of course you were," Tessa interrupted. "Gil would have certainly helped you if he saw you were in trouble. He's your best friend."

"Yeah, that's what I thought, too," I said.

"Strange thing about living in Emogen since the days of Demlock's Rebellion," Rama said as she poured some of the water from the bowl into a cup, "is that things aren't the way they should be. Everything has the ugly, mottled stains of evil on it. Oh, dear me. It's getting so it seems you can't even trust your own best friend anymore. Could have been a vision . . . could have been—"

"Could have been?" asked Tessa. "But you just said that hallucinations are a standard result of ghex poisoning."

"Oh, heavens," said Rama. "There I go, shooting off at the mouth when I should be helping you. Here. Drink this," she said as she offered the cup to me.

I lifted the cup to my lips but stopped to take a whiff before I took a gulp. The steam drifted up into my nostrils, and I automatically scrunched up my nose at the smell of it. It was putrid. It wasn't lemony, pepperminty, or even grassy anymore. It smelled a little like . . . well . . . cow dung.

And that's exactly the way Grampa's roots used to smell.

"Do I have to?" I asked, lowering the cup.

"Yes! And quickly, too. Oh my, quickly, before the full effect of the root wears off. See, I was busy talking when I should have been busy getting you to drink. Quickly, now," she said as she guided the cup back up to my lips with her chunky fingers.

I took a teeny-tiny sip.

"Oh, heavens no," she said. "More, much more. I could only manage to dribble a bit of it down your throat when you were unconscious, so you really must give it a good gulp now. Really, it doesn't taste that bad once it touches the back of your tongue. Actually, it will taste just like your favorite drink. Really, honestly. Oh dear, you don't believe me, do you?" She turned away from me and I saw her fingers crossed behind her back. "Oh, I do hope it works," she whispered, probably hoping I wouldn't hear.

I decided to plug my nose just in case and, not wanting to be rude, gulped down the whole cup in one shot. Surprisingly, when I let go of my nose, my tongue had the faint aftertaste of my favorite soda.

"Mmmmm . . . root beer," I said.

"Is that so?" Rama asked, sniffing the cup. "I didn't know the tonic could adopt malt qualities and taste like beer. Besides, aren't you too young for beer to be your favorite drink?" she asked with a confused look on her face.

I suddenly had a really strange tingling sensation that started on my tongue and rushed through my entire body. My headache disappeared. The gashes and scrapes and bruises I had all closed up and healed right before my eyes. Even the swelling around my eyes went down.

"I . . . I feel like going for a jog," I said, barely able to keep my feet from running away.

"Wonderful!" Rama clapped her hands. Then she took the cup from me and put it on the floor. She had me sit down as she held my bandaged hand in hers. "Now, let's see what we have under here." The ribbon Tessa had tied around my thumb when I cut it on Gil's glasses was soaked in blood. It was starting to turn brown. "Looks like it must have been a nasty cut," Rama said as she slowly undid the knot, unwrapped my thumb, and . . .

"There's nothing there!" exclaimed Tessa, grabbing my hand and turning it over. "Smudge, your cut—it's gone!"

"Properly so," said Rama with a smile as she tossed the bloody ribbon into the fire.

And it was gone. Totally gone. The gash hadn't even left a scratch.

"What is that stuff?" Tessa asked, taking the empty cup and sniffing it. She gagged and gave it back to Rama.

"Oh my. You really don't know much about this region, do you?" asked Rama.

Tessa glanced at me. "Uh, no," she said.

"Then I suppose I should tell you some things," she said as she glanced at the door. "Come closer."

28 Tezema Raha

Teşsa and I sat next to Rama on the floor. I really wanted to look like I was paying attention, but I just couldn't keep my feet from tapping. My insides felt like they were already halfway through completing a triathlon. That drink was nuts!

Rama didn't seem to mind my tapping. "What I have here, and what has healed you, dear boy, is the sacred Yegra Root," she said as she took a small, snarled root out of her apron pocket. "The Yegra Root was made by and named after Emogen's creator, Mother Yegra. It is a highly valued healer, for this medicine has the power to transform its patient's deepest desires into pure regenerating energy. The Yegra Root conjures up, from deep within one's untainted desires, the very force that heals and gives renewed strength. Without a doubt, dear boy, the healing powers of the Yegra Root were able to perform their magic because they were channeled through your most pure and fervent wish."

My mom. She had healed me. She was there, in a way.

"It just so happens that in my generation, I am the Herbal Healer in this village," she said as she fluttered her eyelashes and blushed. "And I am therefore the one who administers the Root to the hurt and dying."

"Wow," said Tessa. "That's quite an honor."

"Oh, it is my extreme honor to use my giftings to bless my people," Rama continued, "especially in a time such as this. The sacred Root's strong healing power is allowing the injured to recover from the wounds the Dragon has begun to inflict on us."

"There's a dragon here?" exclaimed Tessa. She flashed her wide, horrified eyes at me and squeezed her kneecaps until the tips of her fingers went white.

Oh no! I seriously considered laying myself back down on that bed and sitting up really fast again, to knock myself out real good. For two reasons: One—the Dragon. Two—Tessa. I'd forgotten to tell her about the dragon.

"It is a Stone Dragon," said Rama.

Tessa's grip on her kneecaps loosened a bit.

"Demlock set it in place a couple of weeks ago when he raided our village and took for himself some 'collateral,' as he calls it. Prisoners of war, as we call them. He . . . he captured some prominent villagers in a siege and has seen fit to curse the rest of us further by placing us under the tyranny of this Dragon. We had been unaware of its purpose when it first took its seat. But just last night . . ." Rama's voice cracked and she gritted her teeth. Cayenne nuzzled up to her and rested her head on Rama's lap. Rama absentmindedly stroked the back of Cayenne's neck. "Just last night, under the shadow of the Lunar Eclipse, the Dragon turned to flesh and awoke."

"It awoke?" screeched Tessa. "It turned to flesh? Last night? We saw that eclipse, Smudge! We saw it!"

"Yes, all of Emogen saw it," said Rama. "And on any other given night the eclipse is a stunning, truly extraordinary occurrence. But last night, the magnificence was overshadowed by the Powers of Darkness."

"That's horrible," said Tessa.

"Oh yes, and that's only one-twelfth of it," said Rama. "Emogen has three moons that are each on a quadmonthly rotation. Oh, dear me. My dear children, last night was only the first of many. The Dragon will awake three days in a row, four times each year."

"Three days in a row four times each year? That's horrendous!" screeched Tessa.

"Oh, yes. That it is," said Rama, slowly nodding.

"It's even worse than I'd thought," I whispered.

Tessa stood up and looked down at me through slit eyelids. "You mean to tell me you've heard of it?"

Cayenne lifted her head and her ears perked up. She made a strange gurgling sound in her throat as she stood up and padded away. She made herself comfortable under the table.

"Oh dear," said Rama, "Cayenne senses you are not pleased. Oh, I knew I shouldn't have said anything. I should have stopped when the voice inside said, 'Rama, you're saying too much. You need to stop now.' Oh, heavens above, why do I never listen to that voice? I know it's there for a reason. Oh dear, I've said too much, far too much and it's only going to make you want to leave . . . but of course the eclipse cycle has begun, so there's really no chance of that, for the next couple of nights anyhow, and—"

Rama stopped short and clapped her hand over her mouth. And then, as if she wanted us to forget we were just in the middle of a conversation, she changed the subject. "Oh, I really must bake that bloodberry pie Quar was asking for the other day. Have you ever had a bloodberry pie? Oh, you must stay and have some of mine. Bloodberry pies are simply to die for! Although I do hope we all live long enough to have some of—" She stopped again and slapped her hand back over her mouth. "Will you two excuse me so I can get started on that pie?" she mumbled through her fingers as she stood up.

"Uh, sure," I said.

"Certainly," Tessa said at the same time, without taking her eyes off me.

Rama picked up the cup, bowl, and cloth that were still on the floor beside us and put them on the table in the kitchen, all while keeping one hand firmly planted on her mouth.

How bizarre.

I heard Rama scolding herself silently in a low whisper as she opened and closed cupboard doors.

I looked at Tessa and saw she was still staring at me with narrowed eyes.

"Uh, Tessa, sit down. There's one other little thing you should know . . . "

29 Bloodberry Pies and Other Diversions

"What?" whispered Tessa so loudly that it could hardly be called a whisper. Not surprisingly, the sound of her voice attracted Rama's and Cayenne's attention.

"Is everything all right, dears?" Rama asked. Cayenne gurgled again and put her head back down on her paws.

"Yeah, yeah. Everything's okay," I said.

"Oh, all right, then," said Rama. "Carry on. Don't mind me. I'm just going to boil the bloodberries. Pretend I'm not even here."

Tessa continued in her loud whisper. "How could you leave out that little bit of information? How could telling me about a Stone Dragon that has swallowed the other half of the Key we happen to be looking for just slip your mind? Have you got soggy noodles for brains? How could you be so—"

"Just calm down, will you?" I put my hand over her mouth. I think she really was trying her best to whisper, considering the information that was just dumped on her. I motioned with my head towards Rama, who had begun whistling. "I don't want her to hear. Don't you see, Tessa? This is it. This is what we've been looking for. And this is why my Stone had told me to descend even though there was danger."

"Your Stone told you to descend?" Tessa asked when I removed my hand from her mouth.

"Why else do you think I'd climb down a killer cliff?"

"You've done stupid things before," she said.

"Yeah, I know. But this time I had to do it."

"So you could be eaten by a Stone Dragon that comes alive during eclipses?"

I slapped my hand over her mouth again.

"No, to kill it and get the Key," I said as I took the Knife out of the sheath with my free hand and showed it to her.

Tessa pulled my hand away from her face. "Oh, kill it before it makes us into hors d'ouvres for lunch. Now, why didn't you tell me that before I got so upset?" she asked, rolling her eyes.

Rama stopped whistling and looked at us. "Oh dear, is—"

"Yes, thank you," I said before she could finish. "Everything is still all right. Tessa was just saying how she's craving hors d'ouvres, that's all."

"Excellent," said Rama, sounding relieved. "I'll make us some." She started whistling again as she wiped her hands on her apron.

Tessa glared at me.

Just then Rama's front door swung open and a large muscular man filled the entrance.

"Good day, Rama. Have you got the tonic ready? There isn't much time."

"Oh dear, is it that time already? Oh, heavens, I've been so busy . . . er . . . boiling bloodberries for your pie, and then there were the hors d'ouvres, and, of course, I was just having a friendly chat with my guests," she said, throwing us a desperate look.

"Rama, really now. Boiling bloodberries when there is so much to do? And hors d'ouvres? The niceties must wait, dear sister."

"Yes, of course," said Rama.

"And chatting . . . well, you know that isn't always a good—"

"Uh, Smudge," Rama said, interrupting the man. "This is my brother, Quar. Quar, this is Smudge. And you've already met Tessa, and—oh look! I've completely lost track of the time. Oh heavens, not good, not good at all," she rambled as she fumbled around, clearing off the tabletop. She pulled a boiling cauldron off the fire and placed it on the table. "And yes, actually, the tonic is ready, my dear, dear brother. Please do not assume I would let a little pie and some niceties get in the way of accomplishing my task. As a matter of fact, I was busy brewing the tonic when my honored guest woke up."

"Ah, yes," said Quar, turning his attention to me. "And he is looking much better, I must say. Hopefully Rama has spared your ears some, boy," he said as he gave her a quick, sharp glance and then turned back to me.

"So I trust the Yegra has done its work? Show me your tongue," Quar said to me.

"Oh, yes, yes, it's green as it should be," said Rama pleased with herself.

Green? I stuck my tongue out as far as I could so I could see it, but I couldn't get it out far enough.

"It is green!" squealed Tessa.

"Oh, yes," said Rama clapping her hands, turning back around to face Quar. "It's green. I saw it changing color while we were talking about the St—" she stopped, her eyes flashing quickly towards Quar's eyes and then down to the floor. He glanced at her with a sideways look.

"The St...?" he asked, crossing his arms.

Rama quickly put her head down. She turned her back to Quar and busied herself at the table again as if he hadn't asked her a question.

"Rama?" he demanded.

She put her hands on the table and turned her head to look at him.

"We'll talk later," he said firmly.

Rama blushed several shades of pink and turned back away from him.

The tone of Quar's voice made it clear to me there was probably a really good reason she had suddenly changed the subject to bloodberry pies earlier on.

"Now, let me take a close look at your tongue, boy. I always love to see the Yegra at work." He took a few steps towards me and stopped, raising his hand to shield his eyes as a flash of light caught him in the eye. The firelight had reflected off the blade of the Knife I was still holding. I didn't think to put it away before anyone else saw it.

"Is that what I think . . . " said Quar slowly, as if he thought finishing the sentence might make the Knife disappear.

Rama turned back around. She gasped as she pointed to my hand.

Quar blinked and rubbed his eyes. He took slow, steady steps towards me.

"Can it be? Is it? Yes," he said when he'd come close enough to see the Knife up close. "It is. This is the Knife of Creation."

Tessa looked at me with wide eyes.

Quar looked at Rama.

"And they have Stones!" Rama said to him.

"Yes, yes, of course they do," said Quar, nodding. "I knew they had them the moment you told me they had arrived. No one else, other than Demlock, the Dragon, and the Priestess, has ever emerged from the other side of The Darkness of the Unknown."

"No one?" asked Tessa.

"No. Of course not," said Rama. "It's impossible! Why, once . . ."

"Rama . . ." Quar warned. "The Priestess forbids us to speak of such things."

"The Priestess?" I asked.

"She lives in the House of Sacred Writings," Rama said. "She arrived shortly after the Dragon, and she has warned us not to speak of The Darkness."

"Why not?" I asked.

"Well because The Darkness is—"

"Rama," Quar said again, with more than a slight tinge of warning in his voice.

He grunted and crossed his arms, not taking his eyes off her.

"Where did your Priestess come from?" Tessa asked after a short silence. I thought it was pretty brave of her, considering Quar's body language. But then again, she did need to know everything about everything.

"She announced that she had been sent by Yegra," said Rama, eyeing Quar. "Yegra sent her to protect us from the Stone Dragon."

"And did she?" Tessa asked. "Did she protect you last night?"

"We must cease this conversation. Now!" roared Quar. Literally. The "ow" from his "Now!" was long and drawn out, like a lion's roar.

"Oh, yes, yes," said Rama. "No more talk of the Priestess. Or The Darkness. Actually, if it weren't for you being here and asking these questions, I wouldn't have mentioned them at all. Quar forbids any questioning of such things in this home."

Quar made his way to the front door.

"Quar always has done things by the book," Rama whispered to us so he couldn't hear. "He likes to keep—and enforce—the rules of the village, although I myself would rather discuss the—"

"Come!" Quar suddenly said to me as he turned in the doorway. Rama snapped her mouth shut. "We must go directly to Helyas the metalsmith. He must see this Knife you have. He has been waiting a lifetime to behold its legendary craftsmanship."

30 The Metalsmith

Quar and I left Tessa and Rama in the kitchen. We walked down the pathway that led us from Rama's door to her front gate. It was just as dark outside as I'd remembered it had been when I descended into the gorge. If it hadn't been for the many torches and the full moon, there wouldn't have been any light. Quar opened the latch to the gate, and we entered the dusty common area. The entire village was in the shape of a huge circle with many pie-shaped lots, but most of them had been destroyed by the Dragon's rampage the night before.

As we walked through the torch-lit trampled village, I saw that some people were in their shops (if they were lucky enough to still have a shop), but most others were rushing around the common area. Everyone looked busy—and exhausted. Some people were bringing wagonloads of wood and other wreckage from one place to another; some people were sweeping and rebuilding. A few men were quickly herding cows and goats. It looked like they were separating them into smaller groups and taking the groups to different parts of the village. I saw one woman sitting in the dust beside a destroyed shop, sewing what looked like thick leather undershirts, and she was crying. A splintered sign dangled from a post above her head. It said, "Tailor."

Then we came to a cemetery. There were many fresh mounds of dirt on the ground with small groups of people gathered around them. A few women were going from grave to grave, planting flowers. And I heard singing.

Strange, I thought. Why would someone be singing in the cemetery?

But as we walked on, I realized the voice wasn't coming from the cemetery. It came from the building next to it. Standing on the porch of a raised clay structure—that had "House of Sacred Writings" painted on a sign above the door—was a woman in a flowing blue robe. She wore strings of beads around her neck and a thick golden band around the top of each arm. She also had a clunky ring on every finger. Her long blonde and red dreadlocks twisted and coiled around her face as if they were snakes.

This was the woman who was singing.

When she saw me, she narrowed her eyes. She was either squinting because her eyesight was bad or she didn't approve of me being with Quar. Somehow I got the feeling that it was the second reason.

"That's Aldusa, our village Priestess. She arrived a few weeks ago, at the time of the Stone Dragon's inauguration. She is singing a blessing onto our village. She is a highly regarded woman," Quar said as he bowed his head in respect towards her as we passed by.

I did the same.

Aldusa narrowed her eyes further and then nodded her head to Quar in acknowledgement.

"Do you think she doesn't want me here?" I asked when we were past the House of Sacred Writings.

"Who?"

"The Priestess."

"No, oh no. The moment I reported that outsiders had emerged through The Darkness, she blessed my household. She is thrilled."

She has a strange way of showing it, I thought.

Quar looked up at the sky and stopped walking. "We must go directly across to the other side of the village," he said. "And we must take the shortest route." He pointed. "There isn't much time."

I looked to where he was pointing: right at the lake.

On the bare island, floating in the middle of the inky, black, churning water, sat the Stone Dragon.

I have to slay that thing to get the Key, I thought as my heart started racing. My Stone shone brightly at the thought of it.

Courage, it said. I squeezed the Stone and then quickly tucked it under my shirt.

"He's harmless at the moment," said Quar. "It is safe to approach the shoreline."

"Right," I said.

I couldn't take my eyes off the Dragon the whole time we walked along the shoreline. How the heck am

I going to get the Key out of that body? I suddenly, and very seriously, hoped the Stones wouldn't be silent when the time came.

The Dragon looked awfully familiar to me, sitting there, its red eyes glaring across the village. I got the feeling I had seen it somewhere before.

And then in a split second I knew where: He was exactly like the statue that had gone missing from the academy.

Demlock must have made that portal in the academy and taken the statue through there, I thought. But why? Just to bring it here to have it swallow the other half of the Key? Why didn't he just take the Key himself? And why would he take the trouble to get into the academy but not even try to steal my half of the Key while he was there?

With these thoughts churning in my mind, we reached the opposite side of the village. Quar greeted a few of the villagers before we entered the metalsmith's shop. This shop was one of the few buildings that were still standing. A bell tinkled from above as we opened the door.

"Good evening, Helyas," Quar said to a wiry man bent over a fire.

"Quar!" said Helyas as he fumbled with what was in his hand, dropping it into the burning pit. The cluttered room would have been completely dark if it weren't for the orange light that baked us in waves of heat that ballooned from the flames.

"My apologies. I didn't mean to startle you," said Quar.

"Oh no, no worries. What a pleasant surprise," Helyas said, wiping his hands on his smock and bowing his head in greeting. His deep-set eyeballs looked too small for the wrinkly sockets that held them in. They looked more like two black marbles that had been deeply pressed into partially dried dough. "'Tis always a pleasure meeting you. And yes, let's hope it turns out to be a good evening, as you say."

"Oh, I believe it will," said Quar.

Helyas laughed, still wiping his hands. His eyes wrinkled deeper into his thin face, and the grey scruff on his chin glittered in the firelight like coarse salt. "Oh, the eternal optimist, you are. 'Tis the eve of the Second Eclipse, and we know what the Dragon shall do, yet still you are an idealist."

I looked around the room and saw half-finished windows leaning against table legs, chairs, and walls. The glass shone and gleamed in the flickering firelight.

Funny, I thought. I don't remember seeing that any of the buildings had glass in the windows.

"The Knife has arrived," Quar said, plainly, as if he had just informed Helyas that he was breathing air.

Helyas stopped wiping his hands. There was a long moment of stunned silence. I heard the sound of bubbling liquid coming from a large beaker-type thing that was hanging over a small fire in the far corner of the room.

"The Knife, you say? The Knife of Creation? Where? Where is it?" Helyas took a step towards Quar, kicking something that crashed to the floor like a stack of pots and pans. He didn't even seem to notice.

Neither did Quar. He held out his hand to me. I took the Knife out of its sheath and laid it on his palm. Quar turned towards Helyas. "I had thought you might like to see this . . . with your very own eyes."

"Oh . . . my . . . " sighed Helyas, barely able to speak. As his hand trembled towards the Knife, veins bulging underneath the thin skin, he shuffled right through the clanging mess on the floor. "Yes, yes, the Knife it is. The Knife . . . so beautiful." He couldn't even control his hand enough to touch it as his fingers were shaking and bouncing so wildly.

"So it is . . . ?" said Quar. But it sounded almost like a question, like he wasn't really sure if it was what he thought or not.

"Yessssss . . . " hissed Helyas.

"So the Second Essential has truly come to us," said Quar.

Helyas looked up at Quar as if Quar had just shouted a curse word.

"But what of the First?" Helyas whispered. "And the Third?"

"The First, yes," said Quar. "Surely he would not have made it through The Darkness of the Unknown without it. The Third, however," he said, eyeing me carefully, "is yet to be seen."

"Come now," Helyas said, his eyes flashing. "Show us the Third Essential; show us . . . the Key!"

"Helyas!" Quar interrupted, shouting and raising his hand to stop Helyas's hand.

In the darkness of the shop's rafters, I heard a flustered rustling and sharp cawing. I strained my eyes, but I couldn't see what had made the noise.

Quar gently closed his fingers around Helyas's bony wrist and softened his voice. "Helyas, my friend, there is no hurry. All in good time."

Helyas cleared his throat and tried to steady the trembling hand that was in Quar's grasp with his other hand. "Yes, yes, of course. All in good time," he said.

"Helyas, as you can see, is overwhelmed to have the Knife back in Tezema Raha," Quar said to me, letting go of Helyas. "And rightly so, for the metal used to craft this blade was harvested from the Caverns of Mettle, deep within the core of Emogen. Helyas is an extremely rare and highly esteemed Tezeman metalsmith. The crafting of metal is what our people are renowned for, and the Knife you possess was fashioned of a magnificent steel alloy combined with precious silver by the Original Master Metalsmith himself."

Helyas was still as dumbstruck as ever—and even more so when Quar mentioned the Original Master Metalsmith. Helyas swayed and almost keeled over at the sound of that name.

"The Master consecrated this Knife with the Elemental powers to create," Quar continued, "and even to regenerate a wasted life. Not even our exceptionally sanctified Yegra Root has that power."

"You mean it can bring someone back to life?" I asked, stunned, eyeballing the blade.

Helyas suddenly snapped out of his daze and laughed. "Bring someone back to life?" He looked at Quar and put a wiry hand on his shoulder. "Surely the boy jests! Have you ever heard such a thing?" He laughed again.

Quar shook his head. "No. Once a life has crossed the line, there is no reawakening it to its old, former self. The Knife can, however, draw someone back from the brink of death, if that soul is willing."

Just as suddenly as Helyas snapped out of his daze, he snapped right back in. "Yes, that it can do. And to think it is here, in my shop." He put one hand on his forehead and one hand on the wall to help him cope with another dizzy spell. His eyes were glassy and fixed on the blade. "If only I had metal such as this to work with—"

"Helyas," Quar interrupted again. But this time his interruption sounded more like a warning, kind of like the way The Rat would say my name to wake me from a daydream in the middle of class. "You know such a thing can never, and should never, be duplicated."

And Helyas responded quite the same way I would have at the sound of that tone of voice. "Uh, oh yes, yes, of course," he said, shaking his head as if he was trying to shake out the thoughts that were stuck inside. "May I . . . may I hold it?" he asked.

But before Quar could respond, a terrible, deafening sound came from outside; it was like the blast of a thousand rusted-out trumpets. I heard the rustling and cawing in the rafters again.

"The occurrence is within reach. Not now," Quar said to Helyas as he gave the Knife back to me. "Quickly. Put it away. We must make haste."

If Helyas could have plucked his marble eyes out and put them right into the sheath along with the Knife, I'm sure he would have.

"I pray your optimism makes good at long last," said Helyas as he pried his gaze off the Knife and looked back at Quar.

"Protect yourself nonetheless," said Quar. "Yegra's speed."

"And to you," said Helyas.

"Come on then," Quar said to me. "Let's go."

I rushed past—and had to be careful not to knock over—some of the windows resting on the floor of the shop. I noticed that most of them were being made with stained glass.

As we stepped out of the shop, I saw that the full moon already had a crescent-shaped sliver missing.

"We must hurry," said Quar.

As we rushed back across the common area to Rama's house, it didn't take me long to detect that the village had changed. Dramatically. All the shutters in the shops had been closed, and all the activities had been replaced with people gathering weapons, lighting torches, and sharpening swords and axes. Catapults were being dragged out of their hiding places, and marksmen were taking their places, along the water's edge, facing the island.

"Uh, Quar?" I asked, trying to keep up with his pace.

"The Second Eclipse is at hand. The Dragon is about to awake."

31 The Second Eclipse

"There is no time to waste," said Quar, quickening his steps. "We must be single-minded and get back to Rama's house immediately."

We walked past the House of Sacred Writings. The Priestess wasn't singing anymore. She was gone. And the front door was closed. There was red paint splattered on her doorframe.

"Keep walking," said Quar. "And let not the absolute chaos distract you."

Let not the absolute chaos distract me? The words struck me in a funny way. Not in a funny "Ha! Ha!" kind of way, but in a funny "odd" kind of way. And that was because it wasn't at all the way I'd expect "absolute chaos" to look and sound and feel like. The odd thing about this "chaos" was that it was going on in complete silence. No one was screaming. Even though it was only the second time this had ever happened in the village, it seemed people knew exactly what was expected of them and exactly where they were supposed to go. I figured that must have been thanks to The Priestess.

Tessa and Rama were busy scurrying around the kitchen and Cayenne was sitting near the fire, licking her paw, when Quar walked through the front door. I stopped in the doorway.

As soon as Rama saw us, she rushed over to the totem-pole cabinet that stood next to the door and opened it for Quar. It was crammed with weapons, some wooden, some metal. Quar hooked a wooden crossbow onto his left shoulder and chose a massive sword and guard before slamming the cabinet door shut. "Rama, you must take them, before the moon is completely covered over. The spheres will soon reach full alignment."

I turned around and looked at the sky. The moon was slowly disappearing into Emogen's shadow.

"No questions now," he said to me as he kissed Rama on the forehead. "Take care of her, Cayenne," he said to the huge cat. Cayenne's ears perked up and she padded across the room and stood beside Rama.

Quar put his hand on my shoulder as he gently pulled me out of the doorway and into the room. He ran off, leaving us standing in Rama's great room.

"Tessa, help me, dear," Rama said as she hurried to the wooden table.

As Rama and Tessa rushed around, gathering all of the Yegra Root and dropping it into the cauldron, I stepped back outside to see where Quar had gone. I felt like I should have followed him, but by the time I got out in the yard the moon was more than half covered and there was almost no natural light. It was impossible to see.

"You mustn't stand out in the open like that! Come!" Rama shouted at me from her front door.

I rushed back into the house.

"Take those torches," Rama said, motioning to the wall in her kitchen.

I lifted two torches out of their brackets.

"We must hurry!" Rama shouted as she and Tessa ran out the door. They each had bundles of roots and weeds in one arm and the cauldron swung, hanging from their hands, between the two of them. Cayenne was still at Rama's side.

I quickly followed.

A flood of bodies rushed in our direction, sweeping us away towards the right side of the village. Towards a mound of large boulders.

We squeezed through a gap in the rocks and climbed through a secret doorway in the ground that led to a cave. No one spoke a word, but we all panted to catch the breath that escaped our mouths in warm, misty puffs.

"Put the torches over there," Rama said, pointing to a crevice in the cave wall.

I shoved the ends of the wooden sticks down into the cracks. I noticed some other people were doing the same thing with their torches.

I also noticed that the other people were kids. They were all kids. The cave was full of children. Young children. I suddenly felt really out of place.

"Why are we down here with all these little kids?" I asked.

"The Second Eclipse is about to take place," Rama said as she and Tessa put the cauldron down on the stone floor of the cave.

"Yes, Quar told me, but, Rama, shouldn't I have gone with him? Everyone down here . . . they're all . . . little kids," I whispered.

I heard a sudden, sharp cough from a dark crevice in the rock, and I squinted in the torchlight to make out the shape of the person who was huddled there, seemingly trying not to make himself noticeable.

It was an adult.

The only adult besides Rama.

And a male adult, at that.

"Well, they're all kids except . . . " I whispered again and motioned with a slight twitch of my head towards the coughing man.

It was Helyas.

And his beady little black eyes were glued to me.

"Oh, yes," replied Rama in a whisper. "Yes, well, dear old Helyas is an extremely exceptional metalsmith." Rama gazed at Helyas who was in the middle of a terribly phlemy coughing fit. "The Chalice that houses the Elements was fashioned by the Sustainer of the purest of all silver; its magnificent beauty and brilliance is rivaled by no other creation of such precious metal." Rama peeled her admiring eyes away from Helyas and leaned in close to us. "It is believed that Helyas's gifted hands are second only to the Sustainer's own hand. Such an extraordinary individual must be protected."

Helyas slowly made his way over to us.

"Helyas," said Rama, her voice thick with admiration.

"Rama, children," he said in an "I-just-had-a-coughing-fit" voice. He seemed to stand extra close to me. Too close for my comfort.

I stepped aside.

He stepped closer.

Then I could have sworn I felt him trying to reach into my pocket. But I wasn't totally sure because the next thing I knew, he suddenly jerked back and was flapping his hand in the air.

"Dear Helyas," said Rama with concern. "Are you feeling all right?"

He wrapped his cloak around his hand. "Yes, yes. No worries," he said. "Just a bug bite, I'm sure."

Yeah, bug bite I'm sure, I thought as I realized what had happened. He was trying to take my Key. Are the zaps coming from the Key? This zap and the other ones The Rat got?

"As long as you're sure you're okay," said Rama.

"Yes, yes. I'm fine. Just peachy," he said, his black eyes narrowing as they stared at my pocket. When he realized I was watching him, he coughed again and looked at Rama. "I'll just head back to my spot. I don't want to spread my germs." He coughed really loudly for added effect.

When he was out of earshot, Rama said, "Dear, dear Helyas. Always so concerned for the well being of others."

Right, I thought.

"Rama, Smudge is right. We should have stayed up above to help," said Tessa. "After all, we are much older than they are." She motioned to the kids who were all beginning to huddle together into small groups.

"No, no, darling children. For now, you must be protected, too," said Rama. "For you are extraordinary individuals yourselves. You must be kept safe."

"But I should be . . ." I felt I had to finally tell Rama the real reason I stumbled into Tezema Raha: I had to fight the Dragon.

"Yes?" Rama asked.

"Rama, I think—no, I know I should be up there battling that Dragon. That's why I'm here. That's why we're here," I added, nodding to Tessa. She kind of gave a half smile, enough to acknowledge that, yes, she was here for the same reason, but not enough to suggest she was happy about it.

"Yes, I know," Rama said.

"You know? Then why did you bring us down here?"

"The Priestess told Quar this morning that we are to wait for the Third Eclipse before sending you onto the battlefield."

"But why? Why not tonight? Why wait until more people are killed?" I asked. That just didn't make sense to me. If you have a cure for something, use it. Why wait until things get worse?

"The Priestess said the timing isn't right yet."

"What do you mean?" I asked. "How can the timing

not be right? People are going to die tonight. The more manpower up there, the better!"

"I suppose. But the Priestess has said that your efforts will be strongest at the end of the first cycle. The odds of defeating and annihilating the Dragon completely will weigh most heavily in your favor on the Third night, the night of the Blue Moon."

"The Blue Moon?" asked Tessa.

"Yes. The Blue Moon is a very rare and special moon. It is an extra full moon that appears blue in the night sky. The Priestess has said that the overshadowing of such a moon during an eclipse will bring good luck to those in its shadow. The Priestess prefers you wait until then. Oh, dear me. She says you will need all the luck you can get."

"I see," said Tessa.

"But I, on the other hand . . . oh, sometimes I feel so guilty and useless indeed, Blue Moon or no Blue Moon," she said as she began stirring the tonic bubbling in the cauldron.

"Why, Rama?" asked Tessa.

"Because besides the children, Helyas, and the Priestess, I am the only one who must be protected during the Eclipse. Being the village Herbal Healer, Quar has said I am needed after the devastation, and cannot afford the risk of being injured in battle."

"But the Priestess isn't in the cave with us, is she?" I asked, looking around.

"No, no she isn't. She must stay with the Sacred Writings. It is her duty to protect them and ensure they are not destroyed."

"What are the Sacred Writings?" Tessa asked.

"No common villager has had the privilege of seeing them yet," said Rama. "For the time being, they are only for the Priestess's eyes. They are prophecies sent directly to her by Yegra herself, by way of the stars. The Priestess charts the stars by night and transposes the messages in the Inner Sanctuary of the House by day. She spends many long hours of each day in the Inner Sanctuary."

"Any idea what these prophecies say?" asked Tessa.

"Oh, no," said Rama. "No. And the Priestess has advised against questioning. She has said it will only anger Yegra if her creatures begin to question."

"How is that fair?" asked Tessa. "I think everyone should have the right to that kind of information, don't you?" she asked me.

"I . . . I guess," I said.

"Will anyone else ever see them?" Tessa asked.

"Shhh," said Rama. "Not so loud. The Priestess knows best, and we must not question her authority. But to answer your question, yes. Helyas has been commissioned to engrave the prophecies on a silver tablet. He is the only one, other than the Priestess herself, who has been granted permission to enter the Inner Sanctuary. He is the only other person who has seen them—another reason he must be protected during the Eclipse. And then when the tablet is completed, it will be displayed in the Outer Sanctuary of the House. The Outer Sanctuary is open to all villagers. It is our place of worship."

"How does the Priestess escape the Dragon's destruction, then, if she doesn't hide?" Tessa asked.

"She must place spatterings of her own blood on her door frame," Rama said.

"Her own blood?" Tessa asked, putting her hand over her mouth.

And I had thought it was red paint.

"Yes," said Rama. "It is the only thing that deters the Dragon. Since she has been created and sent by Mother Yegra herself to oversee the spiritual direction and well-being of the village, the Dragon is repulsed by her blood. He will not go near her."

Rama was suddenly interrupted by a ferocious rumbling—a rumbling that seemed to come from the very center of the earth. The walls of the cave shook and cracked. Rocks fell from the ceiling.

"The Dragon has awoken," whispered Rama as she pulled us close. All the children held in their cries as they clung tightly to each other.

The rumble up above was deafening, and it was followed by more horrifying sounds. The whole nightmare seemed to take the entire night, but in reality it only lasted about fifteen minutes from start to finish. I had no idea what was happening above us.

And I wasn't prepared for what I saw when we came out.

32 Back from the Brink

We made our way out of the tunnel and reached ground level. It was even darker than it had been before, because most of the street torches had been destroyed or had gone out. But the moon was full and bright again, casting its pale, deathly glow on the village.

The destruction was endless. Even more houses were crushed and the land was torn up, like it had been scratched with a thousand claws. There were patches of burning and smoking wood everywhere. The only-building that was untouched this time was the House of Sacred Writings. Oh, and the metalsmith's shop.

But the Dragon looked like it hadn't even moved. It was stone once again, and was sitting in its chair as if it were watching a game of football on TV on a lazy Sunday afternoon.

But the worst part of it all by far was that the ground was littered with the bodies of Tezeman warriors.

"Quar," Tessa whispered.

Rama placed a hand on her shoulder. "He is fine," she said as if she really believed what she was saying. "He has the power of the Root in his blood."

The children exploded from the cave behind us, carrying their small torches and calling out the names of their parents and older brothers and sisters.

Rama set the cauldron on the ground and stirred the brew that was still bubbling inside.

"Now, quickly, both of you must help me administer the Yegra to the people while its powers are at their peak," Rama said as she tapped the huge wooden spoon on the rim of the cauldron. The smell of lemon, then peppermint, and then finally grass floated in the air.

I knew all too well what smell came next.

Tessa took a cupful of the Yegra tonic to a man lying face down in the mud.

"Sir? Sir? Please let me help you," she said as she knelt beside him and tried to sit him up. Tessa gasped and then screamed as the weight of the man's lifeless body slumped back with a thud, his unmoving eyes staring up at her.

Rama and I rushed to her side.

"Oh my! Poor, poor Leofwin!" Rama said as she recognized the man lying there. Rama stroked Tessa's hair as Tessa buried her face in Rama's shoulder. "I'm so sorry, my darling. Oh dear, forgive me. In the heat of the moment I neglected to advise you to only approach those who call out. The Yegra is powerful indeed, but despite all its magnificent glory it is unable to bring back a life that has crossed the line."

It was then that I saw the man's eyelid flutter. Very, very slightly.

"I . . . I don't think he's exactly crossed the line yet, Rama," I said.

Suddenly the words Quar had spoken in Helyas's shop echoed in my head.

"The Knife can, however, draw someone back from the brink of death, if that soul is willing."

My adrenaline started pumping as I knelt beside the man Tessa had tried to help. "Let's see if you're willing," I said as my shaky hands unclipped the sheath. I pulled the Knife out and held it above the gaping wound in the guy's chest. I took a deep breath as I slowly lowered the blade.

"What are you doing?" Rama asked, sounding slightly horrified as she put her hand around my wrist and pushed my arm away from the man's body.

"Quar told me this Knife has the power to bring a life back from the brink of death, if the person's soul is willing. I just wanted to see—"

"Yes, yes, of course!" exclaimed Rama, interrupting me. She quickly raised my hand, and the Knife, back into position. "Yes! Do it! Stab him!"

Clutching the Knife firmly, I sunk the blade deep into the wound on his chest. Besides breaking out into a cold sweat and having a massive wave of queasiness wash over me, I have no other words to describe how nasty it felt to do that. Tessa's breath caught in her throat and she turned her head.

Rama gasped and her hand flew to her mouth. She stood with her eyes wide as a deep golden glow pulsed from the middle of the blade and the torn flesh started to close up around it. I slowly pulled the blade out, and the gash, which was nothing more than a slit at that point, closed up completely.

"I have never . . . " said Rama in a whisper, her hand still over her mouth. "In all my life . . . "

Just then the man groaned and coughed and sat up, rubbing his chest. "I keeb tellin' Isolda: that lentil stew of hers is jus' too darn spicy," he said in a slow drawl. "Gibs me awful heartburn and gas pains eberytime. It gonna kill me one'a these days."

"Dear, dear Leofwin," said Rama with tears in her eyes. "Welcome back." She hugged him and giggled at the look of confusion on his face.

"Where'b I been?" he asked.

"Don't worry, dear. It will all come back to you," she said, patting his arm. "Now, if you'll excuse us, we've got some more work to do."

We left Leofwin sitting there, burping up the air that had probably gotten trapped in his system as the gash was closing up. And he thought it was because of spicy stew!

Rama, Tessa, and I made our way around the village, sinking the blade deep into people's wounds. And just as it had done with Leofwin, the Knife worked its magic, restoring and healing everyone it pierced.

"Amazing," said Rama with her hand over her mouth again as we watched while yet another horribly injured man was woken up and healed.

Once every warrior was healed and together with their family, I suddenly felt really queasy again. When

I actually stopped to think about what I'd just done, all the images of blood and gore were enough to flatten me. I needed to walk. I needed a drink.

"Come with me?" I asked Tessa before I headed off to the village well.

After I pulled up the water bucket and we both took a long, deep drink, I crouched down next to the low stone wall and balanced on my heels. Tessa crouched beside me.

"I can't believe the knife killed that snake . . . but also brings these people back to life," said Tessa. "How can that be?"

I showed her the words engraved on the blade of the Knife and said them out loud.

"From beginning to end, life is in your hands."

Each of the words glowed when I spoke them, as if they were carving themselves into the blade, exactly like they'd done the first time I read them.

"Wow . . . " Tessa breathed.

As I looked around at the wreckage all around me, something Drofgum had said suddenly popped into my head—how he had talked about protecting the clearing with his Knife. I let my knees fall to the ground and then I leaned forward until I was on all fours, like a dog.

"Smudge, what are you doing?" Tessa whispered. "Are you okay?"

But I didn't answer. Not with words, anyways.

With a hefty shove, I sunk the blazing words of the Knife deep into the ground. From that spot, the ground shook and an explosion of water shot up, out of the well. It fell back down to the ground like a heavy rain, spreading out across the entire village, soaking, coloring, and restoring everything it touched. Incredibly, the land leveled, houses were built up, and gardens sprouted fresh new leaves. Villagers shouted and cried. Some laughed. But most just stood in awe, letting themselves get drenched in the water, until there was only the sound of a few remaining droplets falling from tree branches.

The village Priestess reappeared in the doorway of the House of Sacred Writings. She had a scroll in her hands and she raised it high above her head as she sang a song. Slowly, all the villagers joined her, and soon everyone was singing: men, women and children. It got louder and louder by the second. The song filled the air and shook the leaves on the newly grown trees.

After quite some time of watching what was going on, I realized I was still kneeling with the Knife stuck in the ground. I finally stood and pulled the Knife out.

Every single person stopped singing all at once, and it was silent.

Completely silent.

The whole crowd faced me.

"Well done," said Quar as he stepped out of the crowd. He had a long gash across his cheek, right from his ear to his chin. "We can never repay you for what you have done for us."

"What *we* have done," I said as I pulled Tessa beside me, "doesn't need any payment. We're just happy to help."

Quar turned to the people. "He is the One. The One we've awaited," he shouted.

All at once a cheer rose up from the crowd.

Quar turned his attention towards the Priestess. Everyone else followed his lead. She unrolled the scroll and read:

"Sleeping by day
In the old stone chair
Eclipse the night
So you'd better beware!
No axe, no club
No rich man's bow
Can free the land
Of this tyrant's blow
Brought from the South,
The Stones, Knife, Key
Up to the North,
To set them free."

The Priestess stepped down from her porch and stood beside Quar.

"You have proven to have two of the Three Essentials mentioned in the Sacred Writing: the Stone and the Knife," she said to me. "But there is still the Third Essential you must possess, that I must see."

Helyas appeared as if out of thin air, and stood next to the Priestess. Her robe fluttered and stood out like a patch of clear blue sky between two dark storm clouds as Helyas had wedged her in between Quar and himself.

Helyas looked at me with more hope in his eyes than even she did.

I reached into my pocket and took the Key out of its hiding place. Everyone in the crowd gasped, especially Helyas.

I was just about to put the Key into the Priestess's hand when she said, "No. I dare not assume myself worthy enough to hold such a scared relic. Please hold it for me."

Helyas was practically drooling. "The Third Essential," he said, sounding as if it took every ounce of his willpower to keep from snatching it out of my hand. "It's the Key. At long last . . . it truly is . . . I can't believe my good fortune. The Knife and the Key. All in one day!" Helyas slowly reached out his trembling fingers but stopped and snatched his hand back just before he touched the Key. A sudden look of recall flashed over his face. His whole body began to shiver as he repeated over and over, "At long last you've come; at long last . . . "

Helyas suddenly blinked and bent his head closer to my hand. "Wait a minute," he said. "Turn it over, boy. It's . . . it's broken!" he exclaimed as I did what he'd asked me to do. "You come to us with a broken Key?" The crowd started murmuring.

"The Dragon," I said. "It's . . . it's got the other half."

"It can't be!" someone cried out.

"What are we to do?" someone else exclaimed.

"I'm here to get it from him," I said.

Everyone fell silent.

"You? How are you to get the Key from that beast?" demanded Helyas. "You are just a boy! Where is your armor? Where is your sword?"

Tessa stepped closer to me. "He . . . we will slay the Dragon, regardless," she said.

Seemed to me like Tessa had more faith in us than I did.

Helyas laughed. "We shall see," he said. And then he turned to the crowd. "The future of Emogen is in the hands of ill-prepared children!"

The crowd began murmuring again.

"What will become of us?"

"How could this be happening?"

"Mother Yegra have mercy!"

"You may put the Key away," the Priestess said to me. Then she turned to the crowd. The murmuring stopped. "Yes. It is so. They are to confront the Stone Dragon, just as the girl has said."

Quar stepped forward and placed his hand on my shoulder. "In their possession are the Three Essentials!" he announced. "Are we to question the method by which Mother Yegra has ordained the salvation of Emogen? They have the Stones, the Knife, and the Key. The spirit of Yegra is with them!"

A few villagers clapped. Then several more joined in. And then a few more, until all the villagers were clapping and cheering. Only Helyas stood, unmoving.

As crazy as it might sound, the feeling of Quar's strong hand on my shoulder and the sound of the cheering crowd made the fear inside of me slowly melt away. I suddenly felt a strong sense of justice rushing through my veins.

But there was no doubt I hoped the outcome this time would be very different than it was the last time I felt this way. It was the same burning feeling I had the day Mad Dog bullied Gil. The same overheated-thermometer feeling, the like-I-was-going-to-burst-at-any-second feeling.

But this time the bully I was to face was seriously tougher than a boy named Marion.

33 The Stone Dragon

It wasn't going to be long before the dark shadow of Emogen crossed in front of the moon again for the third night in a row.

Quar, Tessa, and I had spent most of the night before—after the Second Eclipse—sitting up and watching Rama brew an extra-potent batch of the Yegra Root tonic. Quar told us he wished he had a list of instructions for Tessa and me to follow, but he didn't.

"I just hope the spirit of Yegra inspires you quickly," said Quar that night, "since it's likely the Dragon will kill both of you the second it sees you."

That's when Rama stepped in and offered us all an extra-large slice of bloodberry pie. And a bowl—not a cup—of Yegra Root tonic. Besides filling our bellies with the tonic, all we would be armed with as protection against the Dragon were our Stones and Drofgum's Knife.

Quar said thank you, but he also asked her not to interrupt while he was speaking to us.

Rama said she didn't like the way he was frightening us, and she just wanted to offer us some "comfort food."

"That's all fine and well," Quar said, "but they need to know the reality of the danger they will be facing out there. They must defeat the Dragon. This is the one and only chance they have. Should they fail, they'll be killed, and Emogen will perish along with them."

That's when Rama set an entire pie in front of Tessa and me and said, "Eat!"

"Can I ask you a question?" I asked Quar.

"Certainly."

"Last night was the second time the Dragon came to life, right?"

"Yes."

"So why didn't everyone just go underground and hide? You saw what it's capable of doing the first night it awoke. Why did you choose to fight it?"

"It is within the heart of every Emogenite to fight for justice," said Quar, "to confront evil and do whatever we can to help preserve what little good there is left in this world; to assist in the restoration of Emogen to her pre-rebellion state, no matter the cost or how small or insignificant our contribution may seem. Fighting the Stone Dragon is our way of telling Demlock he has not won! He may send a dragon. He may send some other horrible beast. But we will not cower and hide. To do so would be our greatest failure, marking our betrayal to Mother Yegra. It is by her hand we have life, and it is our pleasure to live for her and be advocates for the restoration of her Elements."

"Besides, it wouldn't take much for the Dragon to burn us all alive in the cave," said Rama. "Just one blast of its breath down that tunnel . . . At least attempting to fight the Dragon off holds it at bay until the moon reappears."

• • •

The ground began to rumble as the massive Blue Moon slowly disappeared from sight. I expected to feel something as the good luck was supposed to kick in. But I didn't feel a thing. Except for my heart pounding against my rib cage and the goose bumps popping out all up and down my arms.

The rumbling seemed to start from the very core of the island and vibrated up through each layer until the rocks shook and the water in the lake rose and fell like a massive chest gasping for air. There was a trumpet blast, a horrible, deafening sound as the marksmen took their places at the water's edge. The villagers were all on guard throughout the village, just in case we needed some backup.

Tessa's grip tightened around my arm as we witnessed the first signs of the Dragon coming to life: The stone began to crack. What seemed to be a thin outer shell crumbled as the Dragon rose slowly out of its chair. It shook the dust and stone flakes from its body and stretched its neck.

It didn't take long for the Stone Dragon to realize that it wasn't alone on its island. And just as Quar had said, it only had eyes for us; our blood seemed to call out to it.

It took a heavy step off its throne and let out the most awful roar. Yellow sulfur and black ash spewed out of its mouth. It swooped down, and with one clawed hand, it picked both of us up. I let out a grunt as it squeezed the air out of my lungs with its firm grasp. It lifted us to its eye level—I guess so it could check out its meal before devouring it. The Dragon sniffed us long and hard, pulling our hair towards its nostrils on its inhale. It turned its head to the side and exhaled a long stream of fire. It turned back to look us in the eyes. Its hot breath was as wretched as rotting fish and eggs left for days in sweltering heat. It licked its drooling jaws with its purple tongue. It squeezed us tighter in its fist and licked the side of my face. I started thinking that if the inspiring Spirit of Mother Yegra didn't show up soon, my head would end up in the Dragon's mouth like a pea sucked from a pod.

Suddenly its red eyes blazed with fury. Its attention was fully drawn to the Stones around our necks. They blazed a deadly glow matching that of the Dragon's eyes. It let out another horrendous shriek, its whole body writhing this time, as if in agony.

But unfortunately for the time being, the Dragon didn't seem afraid enough of the Stones to give up a perfectly good meal.

I sure hoped there was something written on the Stones. I had to see. The only problem was that the Dragon had my arms pinned to my sides. And the Stones would be no good to us if they were still tied around our necks after it bit our heads off.

"Can you free one of your arms? Mine are pinned," I yelled to Tessa.

Tessa wiggled and squirmed and finally got an arm free.

"Good! Now hold my Stone so I can see what it says."

The Dragon let out another bolt of fire and screeched at exactly the same time I spoke.

"What?" Tessa asked.

"My Stone! Hold it so I can see what it says!"

She reached over and grabbed hold of my Stone.

"It . . . it doesn't say anything," she said.

"What? Are you sure you just can't read it? Hold it up! It's got to say something! It's glowing like a lightbulb!"

She held it up.

"It doesn't say anything!" I shouted when I saw Tessa was right.

The Dragon shrieked and sniffed us again. It looked like it was enjoying the presentation of its food.

"This can't be happening!" I shouted.

"Wait!" said Tessa. She grabbed her Stone. "Does mine say anything?"

"It says, 'Dragon's Throat'!"

"Am I supposed to throw it down its throat?" Tessa asked.

"I guess! Do it!"

Tessa grabbed hold of the string, and just as she did that, the Dragon stretched out its arm and put its head back, opening its jaws wide so it could pop the two of us into its mouth like a couple of jellybeans. Tessa got such a jolt that the string broke and the Stone slipped out of her hand.

"No!" she shouted, desperately clawing at the Stone in midair. But it fell to the ground below with a soft thud.

Tessa screeched at the top of her lungs. The Dragon roared and spewed fire from its open jaws. The heat singed my hair as we torpedoed through the air towards its mouth.

Suddenly the high-pitched screech of a bird all but drowned out the screech of the Dragon.

It was Melchior!

The eagle swooped down from above and grazed the Dragon's head. The Dragon shrieked and swatted at the eagle with its spiked tail. Melchior dodged the tail and circled around for another attack. This time he dug his talons into the Dragon's head and ripped scales from it.

The Dragon furiously thrashed its tail, trying to hit the eagle. The eagle managed to dodge it a few more times, but the Dragon eventually met its mark and sent the eagle tumbling to the ground. Melchior landed in a dusty, feathery heap on the other side of the lake.

"Smudge!" Tessa yelled. "Read your Stone! Quick!"

Luckily, during the skirmish, the Dragon had loosened its grip and I was able to free my arms. But I wasn't thinking about my Stone.

"Melchior," I whispered. "He's hurt."

"Smudge, you must focus!" shouted Tessa. "We can't do anything about him! It's too late for the eagle, but it's not too late for us—yet! Read your Stone!"

"But we were supposed to throw your Stone down his throat!" I screamed. "Mine didn't say anything!"

"Give it to me!" She grabbed my Stone. "Look! It says something now!" She turned the Stone to face me.

"'Knife!'" I said. "It says 'Knife'!"

(Dragon's Throat. Knife.)

The Dragon turned its full attention back to us, and resumed snacking mode. We were moving through the air at an incredible speed, right towards the Dragon's gaping jaws.

Tessa shouted, "Stab it!"

Dragon's Throat. Knife.

I tried pulling Drofgum's Knife from the sheath, but the snap was stuck.

"It's stuck!" I shouted.

Tessa screamed so loud it reminded me of the eagle's squawk.

Actually, it was the eagle's squawk! Melchior had regained some strength and he was flying above us. He swooped down at the Dragon's head and pecked at the Dragon's face as he flew by. The eagle circled around again and raced right back towards the Dragon's head.

"Duck!" I shouted and pulled Tessa's head down with mine.

The Dragon let out the loudest, most ear-piercing shriek. I felt something wet and hot land on the back of my neck.

I peeked up and saw the Dragon scratching at its face with its other claw. Its eye was missing! The eagle had pecked out its eye! And the wet stuff I'd felt on the back of my neck was dragon blood. It was gushing from the open wound.

Dragon's Throat. Knife.

I fumbled with the sheath, trying to focus on what I had started to do before the eagle had returned. I finally loosened the snap and pulled the Knife out.

Dragon's Throat. Knife.

The Dragon wasn't about to give up, though. It lifted us, with one clumsy claw, towards its mouth as it still scratched at its empty eye socket with the other. When we were close enough, I leaned in and sunk the blade deep into the Dragon's throat. It let out another screech that opened its mouth even wider than it had been before, like it was the Bermuda Triangle ready to swallow a passing ship.

Tessa reached over and grabbed my Stone again, this time breaking the string.

"Just in case!" she shouted as she hurled it towards the massive opening. The Dragon choked and screeched and finally released its grip on us, sending us careening to the ground.

No sooner had we landed on the ground that an awful moan escaped from the belly of the beast. It swayed back and forth, clawing at its own belly, scraping scales and flesh from its thick hide. After another deafening moan, it toppled over and landed with a heavy thud on the dirt. It quivered for a moment, and then a steady stream of steam escaped with a loud belch from its nostrils.

As the dust settled, a red glow came from the Dragon's chest. It grew and grew until it broke through what was left of its shredded hide, splitting the beast's body in half. The two sides of the carcass fell open and disintegrated, revealing the form of a lifeless boy lying in its place.

34 A Familiar Pasty Face

"Good job," I whispered to Tessa as we lay sprawled out on the ground, staring at the body lying in front of us.

"Thanks," she said with a weak smile.

Melchior glided down and landed with a louder thud than I was used to him making. He stepped towards us, limping on a leg that appeared to be broken. He picked two things up from the ground and nudged my foot. I held out my hand.

The eagle dropped our Stones onto my palm.

"Thank you," I whispered.

He squawked and lifted off. I watched him fly up and up against the backdrop of the reappearing moon.

I handed Tessa her Stone. She tied it back around her neck. My Stone was covered in green slime. I wiped it off on my pant leg before tying it back on.

Then I crawled over to the body.

I sat at the head of the still figure.

The pale glow of the reappearing moon cast my shadow, long and lean over the lifeless form. I blinked away the dust from my eyes as I couldn't pry them off the body that lay perfectly still in my shadow.

I looked hard at the pasty face.

The pasty face that I had seen before. Twice, actually. Once in the mirror and then again in my sketchbook. His hair was a lot longer than I had thought.

Holy crow! Maximillian Snute!

"Maximillian," I whispered.

Tessa gasped. "How do you know that's Maximillian? He was hardly at the school long enough to . . . and that was before you even came!"

"It's complicated," I said as I reached down.

"Ew! Don't touch him!" Tessa exclaimed. "He was eaten by a dragon!"

"He'd look like cat food if he was eaten," I said.

This is too weird.

I touched Maximillian's shoulder.

Nothing.

I touched his arm.

Nothing again.

I waved my hand in front of his closed eyes.

Not a thing.

The Knife was lying beside him. I picked it up.

Then without warning, there was a cough and a sputter. Maximillian rolled onto his side, spit something out of his mouth, and opened his eyes. He gave a crooked smile, propped himself up to a sitting position and said, "It's about time you got here."

Suddenly the sound of drums filled the air, and there were hoots and shouts of victory from the village across the lake.

I could hear children laughing for the very first time since we'd been there.

Maximillian reached down to where he'd spat and picked up the object that he had spit onto the ground. He held it out to me.

"Here. You'll be needing this," he said.

I looked at what was in his hand.

It was a mirror twin of my Key.

"Oh, I'm sorry," he said as he wiped it off on his sleeve a few times. "It's a bit slobbery, but I'm sure it will still do the trick."

He held it out to me again.

I just kept staring.

"Simon, it's okay. You can take it," said Maximillian. "I guess you still don't remember, huh? It's me, Maximillian. Your brother."

"My brother?" I exclaimed.

"You're his brother?" Tessa asked at the same time.

"I knew you must be someone familiar . . . but you're my brother?" I asked again.

"You're his brother?" Tessa asked again. "Did you know you had a brother?" she asked me.

I didn't respond.

"I don't think he knew he had a brother," she said to Maximillian. "I sure didn't know he had a brother. But then again, he has forgotten to tell me other things in the past, so for all I know he could have known. Did you know you had a brother?" she asked me again.

"No, no, I didn't," I said, putting my hand up to signal for her to stop talking. I needed a moment to think.

But I never got that moment. Just then, Quar and Rama, along with about a dozen other men and women, docked their boats on the rocky shore of the island and ran towards us.

"Who is this?" Quar asked when he saw Maximillian.

Maximillian stood up.

"I am Maximillian Snute," said Maximillian, bowing his head in respect before continuing. "Demlock used the powers of Sorgol when I refused to cooperate with him in obtaining the other half of the Key for his benefit. I had put my half of the Key in my mouth, threatening to swallow it, so he got the Dragon to swallow me instead."

Quar rubbed his chin. "And why, tell me, did he not kill you and take the Key for himself?" He sounded unsure, almost like he didn't believe what Maximillian told him.

"I wondered that myself, and the only thing I can conclude is that perhaps he is afraid that if he touches it, it'll disappear just like the Elements did. Perhaps he thought it best to not take a chance."

Quar nodded as if he believed him now, as if that answer satisfied him.

"Demlock then placed the Dragon here, to torment you," continued Maximillian. "I am truly sorry for the grief I have caused you." He bowed his head again and knelt in front of Quar. "Strike me, if you must."

Quar raised his sword high. "On this day . . . " he shouted.

He's going to kill him! I thought, horrified. He's going to kill him right here!

" . . . all of Emogen shall know the true meaning of freedom!" Quar brought the sword down. Tessa screamed and hid her face in my shoulder.

But Quar only rested the flat side of the blade on Maximillian's head. "Rise and be set free from any guilt. Tezema Raha bears no grudges, except against one." Quar held out his hand and helped Maximillian up.

A couple of men lifted Tessa and me high on their shoulders as the villagers on the mainland shore surrounding the lake cheered and hooted and called out our names. They carried us to the Stone throne of the defeated Dragon and stood us on its seat. The villagers on the shoreline cheered even louder as Tessa and I stood there, not quite knowing what to do next.

"You have saved us!" Quar shouted. "And you have recovered the other half of The Key!"

The villagers cheered.

"Soon all of Emogen will be set free! Let the first of many celebrations commence!" shouted Quar as the people cheered yet again.

The drums got louder and the Priestess stood at the edge of the water, her sapphire robes hanging gracefully to the ground. She nodded and then turned and disappeared through the crowd as the villagers on the island lifted us off the empty throne and carried us to the boats.

• • •

"Demlock made a couple of serious mistakes," said Maximillian as Tessa and I sat with him around a huge bonfire in front of the House of Sacred Writings. The victory celebration continued all around us, late into the night.

"What do you mean?" Tessa asked.

"Would I be standing here if the Dragon had chewed me up?"

"I guess not," she said and screwed her face up.

"Nor would I now be able to pass the Key on to you," he said to me.

"What was his second mistake?" I asked.

Maximillian pushed his hair back from his face. "Underestimating you. How much do you remember now, Simon?"

I told him about my sketches, the flashes, and the information Drofgum had told me.

"Shall I tell you the parts you're still missing?" he asked.

I nodded while Tessa blurted out, "Oh, absolutely. Everything right from the beginning, and make sure you don't leave anything out. I'm tired of only being told things in shorts bits, especially since I'm the kind of person who likes to know the whole story."

Maximillian and I just stared at her.

"Whaaaat?" she asked.

Was she really oblivious to the fact that this was actually *my* story and that maybe I was the one Maximillian would want to tell all the bits to?

"All-righty then," Maximillian began. "So, as you know, Demlock tried to steal the Elements, and they were automatically hidden in a Casket undergound. It was our mother's responsibility to keep the Key to the Casket safe. She was the Guardian of the Key."

"Do you know where she is? Do you know what happened to her?" I blurted. "Can I see her?"

Maximillian sadly shook his head. "No one knows where she is."

"Demlock has her! I just know it!" I shouted as the image of the creature in my dream flashed in my mind.

"I'm not sure if he does," said Maxmillian.

"Well, if Mom had the Key all along, why didn't she just use it to resummon the Elements herself? That way everything could have been taken care of a long time ago and none of this other horrible stuff would have happened!"

Maximillian looked deep into my eyes. He had dark chocolate-brown eyes, like me. Like our mom. "Because you are the Son of the Seventh, Simon. It is your destiny."

"But why? Why is it my destiny?" I asked. "How am I the Son of the Seventh? Why me? I still don't understand."

"Because you were born on Saturday, Epoch 7th, at 7 a.m."

"Epoch 7th?"

"Well," piped in Tessa, "Epoch could mean an historical period or an era or an interval of time or—"

"Or in this case," interrupted Maximillian, "a month. The seventh month."

"Oh. So?" I asked.

"The Elements operate by the Order of Sevens," explained Maxmillian. "They cannot be released from the Casket until seven years have passed. We are now in the seventh year. And since you are the son of the Guardian of the Key, and born within the Order of Sevens, it has to be you who frees them. No one else." He paused while I let the information sink in.

"Demlock didn't know anything about the Order of Sevens or the Key for a long time," continued Maximillian. "He just thought he had just sent the Elements to their doom, which was fine by him. But somehow, about nine months ago, he found out about the Key and the Order. Of course, now he wants to open the Casket himself. Who knows what will happen if he touches it and tries to take control of the Elements. That's why Mom had to send you away to Grimstown, to make sure you were protected from Demlock."

"Nine months ago? You mean to tell me I lived here up until nine months ago?"

"Yeah, that's right," said Maximillian. "Mom gave you a powerful Blessing of Protection to ensure your safety in that extremely mortal realm. But sending you through the portal with such a strong Blessing caused your memory to fail."

"So that's what happened!" I exclaimed. "Grampa told me I had been in some kind of accident."

"Well, I suppose you were," Tessa said. "It sounds like your memory loss wasn't supposed to happen."

"That's right," agreed Maximillian. Then he looked at Tessa out of the corner of his eye.

Tessa was fluttering her eyelashes at him!

"But . . . if that's the 'accident,'" I said, trying to refocus the conversation, "then . . . then what happened to our dad? I just always assumed he was killed in the same accident I was in."

"His death was no accident, that's for sure," said Maximillian through gritted teeth. "Demlock killed him in cold blood in the Woods of Kai, on the very same day he tried to take possession of the Chalice."

I didn't know what to say. My dad. Dead because of Demlock. I shuddered as I couldn't help but wonder what had happened to my mom.

"I hope that one day soon you'll regain memories of our father, Simon. He really was a wonderful man." A stray tear slid down Maximillian's cheek and his jaw relaxed a bit.

"I hope so, too," I whispered.

Maximillian cleared his throat. "So knowing Demlock's thirst for revenge knew no limits, Mom decided she had to be more proactive in guarding the Key. She split the Key in two and, since I'm your older brother, she gave half of the Key to me to keep safe and she kept the other half herself until it was time for you to have them both. And when we discovered Demlock had found out about the Key and the Order, she sent you away.

"She wanted so desperately for us all to stay together, Simon. But she had no choice. And the thought of you forgetting who she was tormented her. That's why she had Melchior bring you to her in your dream. She wanted to visit with you on your birthday and give you the Key in person, in hopes it would somehow jog your memory."

I nodded, remembering how I had gotten my first memories back in that dream.

"And since then," continued Maximillian, "it seems Melchior's taken it on himself to keep an extra eye on you, since it seems Demlock's got his extra one again."

"What do you mean?"

"Did you ever hear any rumors about me? At the academy?"

"Yes!" said Tessa. "That you were tortured in Detention Hall and that you shattered glass into The Rat—er, Mr. Ratsworth's—eyes! Is it true? Did all that really happen?"

"Well, part of it's true. I did shatter glass. And I did use it . . . to gouge out his eye."

"What?" shouted Tessa and I at the same time.

"Mr. Ratsworth had somehow obtained Sorgol."

"Sorgol . . ." I said, "You mentioned that name before, when you were talking about being swallowed by the Dragon."

"Yes. Sorgol is a black stone that's energized with the powers of evil. It is Demlock's strength. Somehow Mr. Ratsworth got a hold of it and had it hidden in his eye socket."

"He did?" I asked and then shivered at the sudden memory of the ghostly green flicker in his bare eye socket the day he lifted his eyeglass.

"He did. And when I discovered he had it, I immediately went to the school to take it from him—to destroy it."

"And did you?" Tessa asked with a sickened look on her face.

"Well, I did get it from him, but I couldn't destroy it. It didn't matter what I did to it; it remained whole. And I have a funny feeling it called to Demlock the entire time I had it because he easily tracked me. He caught up with me the day I called to you from the mirror."

"The day you called to him from the mirror?" Tessa asked.

"It's complicated," said Maximillian.

"Apparently a few things are with you guys," Tessa said, giving me a look. I knew I'd eventually have to explain everything to her.

"What happened when he caught you?" I asked, remembering how Maximillian had left so suddenly the day I saw him in the mirror.

"We fought over Sorgol, but Demlock's strength overcame me. Then once Demlock had the stone again, he demanded I reunite the Key halves for him. I refused. And that's when he had me swallowed by the Dragon. I thought I was dead for sure. I thought I would never get the chance to give you this."

Maximillian took my hand and placed his half of the Key onto my palm. I turned it over several times and then reached for the Key that was in my pocket. I held a half in each hand and stared at them.

"Well, they're not going to come together on their own," piped up a voice that came from somewhere behind me. I looked over my shoulder to see the Priestess standing on the bottom step of the House of Sacred Writings. "The time has come," she said.

I brought my hands together, slowly, and lined the keys up. As if drawn together by some kind of magnetic force, the two halves snapped perfectly into place.

35 The Key to the Gateway

As soon as the Key halves joined, the Priestess climbed the steps of the house and stood on the platform in front of the doorway. She raised her hands in the air. It was dawn by this time, and the villagers who had been partying all night long suddenly stopped what they were doing and all went quiet. They waited for her to speak.

The platform the Priestess was standing on began to rise. It rose until it was level with the roof of the house. The Priestess stepped onto the roof, her hands still in the air. She turned and faced the island and shouted, "Powers that be, open the way!"

The earth rumbled and the ground all around the village shook, loosening it from the inner edges of The Darkness. We all stared in disbelief as the village rose into the air, leaving The Darkness below, as if it were traveling up an elevator shaft. It rose until the rim of the gorge and the floor of the valley were even. Then The Darkness of the Unknown rose into the sky and disappeared like a storm cloud after it's cried all its tears.

The water in the lake churned even more furiously than it had before, as if it were looking for an escape. The fierce rocks dove into the water, drowning themselves in the madness.

The base of the Dragon's throne split open and continued cracking right through the ground, creating a deep crevice and allowing an escape for the water. It drained until there was nothing left but a big, shallow mud puddle.

Once all the water had drained through the crevice, the broken stones reassembled themselves on their own—shifting and scraping and rumbling—into the form of a crooked archway. Just inside the archway I could see the top of a set of steps leading straight down into the blackness of the crevice.

The Priestess stepped back onto the platform and was lowered down to the steps of the house. Everyone watched in admiration as she made her way down the steps and joined us where we were standing.

"Rejoice!" she shouted. "The time is at hand!"

The Tezeman people let out another loud victory cry. Tessa and I stood stunned once again as they began rushing towards us. The women of the village wrapped strings of brightly colored beads around our necks and gave us bunches of grapes.

"The time of the Restoration has come. You must open the Gateway and get to the Elements quickly, Son of the Seventh," the Priestess said to me above the excitement of the crowd.

"Open the Gateway?" Tessa and I asked at the same time as the villagers sat us on beautifully decorated chairs and lifted us onto their shoulders.

Maximillian reached up and grabbed my hand and turned it over. "Ever wonder why you got this?" he asked, pointing to the black scar Drofgum had burned into my palm with his Knife.

"How'd you know I had that?"

"I saw it. And remember, I know the prophecy. It's another Key."

I just blinked at him. "This is a Key?"

"The Gateway to the Crypt can be opened only with it," said Maximillian.

"The Key to the Gateway," the Priestess said. It almost sounded as if she was surprised to see it.

"What are you saying?" Tessa asked as a Tezeman woman wrapped a beaded anklet around one of her dangling legs. "Ooooh, pretty," she said, lifting her leg to get a better view of the jewelry.

"That Key is the only means to opening the Gateway. But it is only a temporary Key that will disappear once it has been used."

"So how do we get to this Gateway?" I asked, looking around.

The Priestess pointed to where the Dragon's throne once stood tall. "We shall go through the archway and follow the tunnel. It will bring you to the Gateway. Look for the ruby on the northern wall."

"We?" I asked.

"Yes. I must lead you to a certain point. From there I can go no farther."

"Use this to keep the metal Key safe," said Maximillian as he unhooked a silver chain from around his neck and passed it to me. I threaded the chain through the top of the Key and put it on. The Key clinked against my Stone. "Mother Yegra's blessings on you," Maximillian said to me. Then he started walking away.

"Where are you going?" I called after him.

"I've got to distract Demlock from finding you."

The villagers let out another cheer as they started dancing with us still on their shoulders. They all started singing and chanting; some played tambourines and wooden flutes, and some waved flags in the air.

"It won't be long before he discovers you've got the complete Key and are heading to the Gateway," Maximillian shouted over the music and singing. "Then there's no saying what he might try to do!"

"But what are you going to do?" asked Tessa.

"I'm not sure I'll have to do very much. Once he discovers his dragon is dead, he'll come looking for me. I'm sure of that. I'll just hide out a bit, to make his hunt a little more challenging, and let him come to me. At least it should provide a short diversion from him finding you."

"Yes," said the Priestess. "It should give you enough time to get to the Crypt. Once inside you must find the Casket, unlock it, and resummon the Elements."

"Resummon the Elements," I said. "How am I supposed to do that?"

"Call to the North Wind," said Maximillian. "She's the one who will take care of it for you. Just call to her."

"And before you go, my child," the Priestess said to Maximillian, "I must sanctify you with a Blessing of Protection. Come." She turned towards the House of Sacred Writings.

"Do it here," he said.

"A blessing of such magnitude must be performed in the Inner Sanctuary," the Priestess replied.

"But you've got to lead them to the tunnel, don't you? I'll be fine without the blessing." Maximillian turned to leave.

"No!" the Priestess shouted, grabbing his arm. "Helyas!" she called out to the crowd. Helyas came forward and bowed.

"Yes, oh wise one?"

"Take Maximillian to the Inner Sanctuary and prepare him for the Blessing with holy water."

"Yes, madam. It is my honor to do as you wish."

"I will lead them on, and then I will return to you to perform the Blessing," she said to Maximillian.

Maximillian sighed. "Very well," he said.

Helyas escorted Maximillian inside the House.

"You ready?" I leaned in and whispered to Tessa.

"Hmmmm?" she said. She looked like she'd just lost her best friend.

"You've got a thing for my brother?" I asked. "I mean, not that it would bother me or anything if you did."

"Of course not," she answered as she slapped my arm.

The way her face turned different shades of red told me otherwise.

"Now we must go," the Priestess said to us. "Onward!" she shouted to the crowd. They all sang and danced as they carried us on their shoulders.

When we reached the shoreline, the people paraded us across the dried-up lake to the spot where the Dragon's throne once was. The Priestess stood in the archway that led to a damp underground tunnel. We were lowered and helped off the chairs. The music and singing suddenly stopped. Everyone was quiet, waiting for the Priestess to speak.

"They will open the way," she said as she hovered her ringed fingers above my shoulder. "The Restoration of Emogen is at hand!"

The villagers cheered again.

Rama and Quar made their way through the crowd and stood beside us. Cayenne wedged herself in between them. Rama put her arms around us.

"I am so very proud of you, my darlings," she said. "Now, I know I didn't tell you too much. In fact, if we had more time I could brew us up some nice tea and we could sit a while as I recount all the events of the—"

"Rama, we do not have more time," Quar interrupted. "Time is now of the essence. We must let them finish their journey. Perhaps another day."

"Oh, yes, yes," said Rama as she blushed. "Yes, of course. Oh dear there I've gone on again. Now, I know I really should stop that. I really must learn to listen to the voice inside my head when it says—"

Quar cleared his throat, a little too loudly.

"Oh, yes," said Rama again. "Yes, I understand. Keep well, my dear ones," she said as she gave us each a strong hug and stepped back.

Quar stepped forward and put his hands on our shoulders. "Thank you again," he said with tears in his eyes.

"You're welcome," Tessa and I both said.

"I will travel with you, but as I have said, it will only be for a short distance," said the Priestess. "Discoveries beyond your wildest imagination await you. Now we must go."

Tessa grabbed my arm. "Well, what are we waiting for?" she said. "You heard her."

I hate to admit it, but I blushed at Tessa's forwardness. But it wasn't because of what she said or even how she said it. I was way used to that by now.

It was because she was holding my arm.

And didn't let go.

I wasn't quite sure what to do about that.

Let's just say she stepped up her friendliness a few thousand notches.

The Priestess offered me an unlit torch. Not sure what good an unlit torch would do inside a dark tunnel (but not wanting to offend her by asking), I took it from her. The moment my fingers gripped the handle, the top of the torch burst into flames.

Tessa and I, still arm in arm, stepped towards the archway, with the Priestess leading us and the crowd cheering us on.

36 The Silver Door

The steps that led us down into the blackness of the tunnel were wet and slippery. And once we were inside the tunnel, the walls of the cavern gave off a strong smell of algae and fish. I could hear the steady dripping of water.

I sure hope this leads us to Gil, I thought as I looked around at the damp walls that reflected the flickering torchlight like orange fireflies.

I reached up and undid the chain that held the Key around my neck. I held it in a tight fist. For some reason I thought it would be safer in my hand than swinging loosely under my shirt.

"This place is giving me the creeps," I said.

"Shhhhh," whispered the Priestess. "You mustn't speak."

We followed in silence. Tessa still clung to my arm like a remora on a shark. I decided to just ignore her and see if she would let go.

She didn't.

The Priestess grabbed hold of the torch handle just above my hand and stopped me. She leaned the flame towards the wall.

The firelight bounced and danced on the surface of a huge door. It looked like it was made out of pure silver and it had a picture engraved on it: a huge apple tree with blossoms and grass growing under it. There was a waterfall flowing over the branches of the tree, making a river that ran around the bottom of it. The picture was imprinted in the middle of a circle of gold fire that looked like the flames were trying to reach out and lick me, like they would burn me with their hot tongues if I got too close.

The door suddenly swung open towards us. The opening behind the door was just a hole in the stone wall that was about waist height. It was just big enough to crawl through. A bad smell wafted through the damp air.

"This is as far as I'm permitted to go," said the Priestess. "Now you must enter. The tunnel is easy to follow. It leads straight to the Gateway, which guards the Crypt. In the Crypt you will find the Casket of the Elements. I will close this door behind you and stand guard so no harm comes to you."

Tessa looked at me.

I looked at her.

"Well, I guess we should go," Tessa said.

"I guess," I said. But for some reason, something didn't quite feel right to me.

"Doesn't look like there are any other more pleasant options available," Tessa said in a more nasally sounding voice than was usual for her. She was holding her nose. "You first."

I lifted my knee and crouched down to squeeze myself through the hole. Surprisingly (and luckily, considering I had a lit torch to carry) I only had to crawl about six paces before I came out the other side into a tunnel that I could stand up in. It looked like this tunnel had been hacked through the ground with a pick axe. It was barely high and wide enough for one person.

Tessa slid out of the hole and stood behind me. The silver door clanged shut from the other side of the hole.

"Now where are we?" Tessa asked.

"I have no idea, but I guess we should follow the tunnel."

We walked on and on the best we could without cracking our skulls open on the jagged stones above our heads. The tunnel was extremely straight and narrow. I did actually end up with quite a few scrapes on my knuckles and elbows. Actually, it was a good thing Gil wasn't with me. He'd have a panic-induced asthma attack for sure.

"Wait a minute!" I said as I suddenly remembered something and stopped in my tracks. Tessa crashed into me.

"Please don't do that again," she said, steadying herself on the wall. "What is it?"

"Drofgum mentioned that the tunnels to the Gateway and the Crypt were really confusing, like a labyrinth."

"Well, maybe they'll get more confusing the farther we go," Tessa said.

We kept walking. Finally we arrived at another opening that dropped down a step or two onto the floor of a small, circular room. We hopped down. There was another opening that looked exactly like the one we'd just hopped out of, on the opposite side of the room.

"Oh, it feels as though I haven't stretched out my arms in ages!" said Tessa as she reached up and behind her, twisting her body this way and that. I treated myself to a few arm and leg stretches, too, but I didn't notice the colorful, half-moon-shaped mosaic under my feet until it was too late.

Exactly like the time I was in the root cellar at the school, the colors exploded into a bright kaleidoscope, spinning and blinking around us.

It was another portal!

"Not again!" Tessa shouted. She covered her eyes and screamed.

The walls started spinning, and then my torch went out and everything went black. This time it didn't feel like I was falling through the darkness. It was more like I was being swept along a strong river current.

And when I stopped, it felt like I'd hit a wall. And maybe that was because I had.

"Ouch!" screeched Tessa. It sounded like she'd crumpled to the ground beside me. "I didn't think that was supposed to happen."

"It wasn't!" I replied. "We were tricked, Tessa. Terrible and beautiful colors equal The Powers of Darkness!"

She gasped. I stood up and helped Tessa to her feet. My torch mysteriously relit.

The area we were in looked like a cave. And it only had one exit off to the right of where we were standing. The light from the torch only reached a few feet beyond that exit. It was pitch-black. As I strained my eyes to see past where the light drew its line on the floor, I thought I saw something waver in the shadows. Maybe a bat. I decided not to tell Tessa. Things were bad enough already.

"What. Is. That?" said Tessa, grabbing my arm.

Too late. She saw the thing in the shadows, I thought.

"Yeah, I know," I said.

"How can you know? You're looking the wrong way," she said.

"What?"

"Look at that! Diamonds!"

I turned to see what she was pointing at and was stunned: The torchlight glittered off thousands of tiny diamond-like stones that were pressed into the wall behind me.

Tessa let go of my arm and ran to the wall. "Smudge, look. It says something."

The diamonds were positioned around a circular-shaped word maze. There was a ruby about the size of a walnut in the exact center of the maze. The message started at a large diamond, and the words formed a spiral that moved in towards the center point.

"What does it say?" asked Tessa.

I had to position myself really awkwardly in order to read the message, but I managed. I read it out loud.

"The Dragon is dead, the Key is complete.
The lake water's dry, the threat obsolete.
The way must be opened; the pure onyx scar.
The Chalice is waiting. Be swift; it's not far."

"It's the Gateway," Tessa said. "Put your hand on it. Isn't that what Maximillian said to do?"

"Tessa, we got here through Dark Magic!" I exclaimed. "That can't be the Gateway."

"Well, it sure looks like it could be! And we'll never know if it is or not unless you put your hand on it. It can't hurt to try."

Out of the corner of my eye, I saw something move in the shadows again.

Of course it's just a bat. Bats always live in caves, I thought as I turned back to face the supposed Gateway.

"I guess you're right," I said and raised my hand. As I held my palm over the message, the ring of words that read, "The way must be opened; the pure onyx scar" shone bright silver. At the same time, I felt an insane heat coming from the scar. The ruby in the center of the word maze suddenly turned to the left and then to the right and then to the left again before it disappeared into the wall. There was a loud click and a rumble as the huge chunk of stone that held the diamonds slid backward and then to the side, disappearing behind the cave wall. A shower of dust and stone bits sprinkled the entryway.

The heat in my hand slowly cooled down, and when I looked at it again, the black scar faded, bit by bit, until it was completely gone. Just like Maximillian had said it would.

"It is the Gateway!" Tessa exclaimed.

So Demlock knows about it, too, I thought. And before I even had another thought, the air inside the cave changed.

I can't explain exactly what it was that changed, because it seemed like everything and nothing had changed at the same time. It all looked the same, but it didn't feel the same. It felt like a cold, clammy blanket had settled on my shoulders and wrapped itself around my whole body.

And at the very same time the familiar yet mysterious music I'd gotten used to hearing at the most bizarre times seeped through the darkness.

"Do you hear that?" I asked.

"Yes," Tessa replied. "I do this time."

And then suddenly the torch was snuffed out again. It was pitch-black again. Tessa screamed.

"It's okay," I said. "Just stand here by me. I'll protect you."

I heard a slight grunt as something whooshed past me through the shadows.

Must have been that bat, I thought as I ducked.

"Tessa?" I asked as I felt around the dark emptiness for her.

I heard a pair of feet shuffle up next to me. Then a hand gripped my arm and slid down to hold my hand.

It felt warm and soft, a nice contrast to the cold, clammy feeling that was wrapped around my shoulders. Of course, I assumed it was Tessa.

The Key was wedged in between our hands. Her grip suddenly tightened.

"What's wrong?" I whispered.

There was no response, but her breathing got heavier. She began wheezing and panting and a strange sound came from her throat.

"Tessa, what's wrong?" I asked. "Are you okay?"

"Smudge!"

The blood froze in my veins. Tessa's voice called to me from much farther away than I'd expected. She wasn't standing beside me at all.

If she's not, then who the heck is this?

I screamed as I pulled my arm away from the now sweaty palm. I swung the torch around my body with both hands in hopes of hitting whoever it was that wasn't Tessa. I closed my eyes tightly expecting to hear the sound of a thud as I landed a blow. But my ears were only met by the hollow whooshing sounds of the unlit torch sailing through the damp air.

Suddenly the cold, clammy, wet-blanket feeling lifted off my shoulders and the torch relit with a puff of fire.

And the music stopped, too.

I was standing there, alone.

I panted heavily as I stood with my knees bent, in midswing. I looked around, keeping my battle stance.

I remained ready to land my torch on anyone who might jump out at me from behind the rocks.

The hollow drip-dripping sound of water rolling off the cold stone in icy drops ricocheted around the empty cave.

"Tessa? Tessa?" I called out.

The only response I got was the rocks mimicking my words.

All at once, but not soon enough, I noticed that it wasn't just the cave that was empty; my hand was empty, too.

The Key was gone!

I immediately fell to my knees and searched the cavern floor. The flickering torchlight made it hard to see, but I did find something: an empty silver chain.

Suddenly I heard a muffled cry over the sound of the dripping water.

"Fmmm! Fmmm!"

I looked around, but the jagged overbite of stalactite and stalagmite teeth got in the way. I stretched out the torch in the direction of the cries and saw movement. I walked over and nearly tripped on Tessa, who was wriggling like a worm on the ground, her hands and feet tied, a gag stuffed into her mouth.

"Fmm! Fmmm!" she mumbled. Her eyes were as wide as Frisbees.

I untied her feet and then her hands, noticing the rope had scratched her wrists.

She yanked the gag out of her mouth. " . . . and just when the light blew out, I was grabbed from behind by horribly cold and rough hands!" she blurted. "Something awful and smelly was shoved in my face, and that's all I remember. I woke up like this!"

"Whoever it was must have been waiting for us," I said.

As if on cue, we both looked towards the open Gateway.

"Waiting for you to open the Gateway," Tessa said. "But how . . . ?"

I pointed towards the part of the tunnel where I thought I had seen the bat moving around in the shadows. It seemed maybe it hadn't been a bat after all.

"Who knows where that leads," I said.

"Please don't say you want to find out," Tessa all but begged.

"On any other given day . . . " I said. "But there's a bigger problem to deal with right now."

Tessa sighed a great big sigh of relief. "What's that?"

"The Key is gone."

"What?" she shouted, her voice bouncing off the walls.

Just then, the echo of a murderous shriek bellowed from inside the Gateway.

37 A Formal Introduction

"It's coming from in there," I said, pointing through the Gateway.

Tessa grabbed my arm. "That's why we're going this way," she said, pulling me in the opposite direction, back towards the cramped tunnel.

"Let go of me!" I said, shaking her off my arm.

She turned to face me, about to protest, when she shouted, "Smudge, look! Your Stone! And look! Mine, too!"

It was almost as if I'd suddenly remembered something that I'd shoved to the back of a dark closet and forgotten about for years.

The Stones.

How could I have forgotten about the Stones? The last time I'd seen them glow was . . . I couldn't exactly remember. Was it when we fought the Dragon? And not since?

"When was the last time the Stones glowed?" I asked. "Besides right now."

Tessa thought about that for a few seconds. "I . . . I think it was when we defeated the Dragon," she said.

"Oh, man! Did I ever mess up!" I shouted as I covered my face with my hands. I suddenly remembered what Drofgum had told me. I dropped my hands and groaned.

"What do you mean?" Tessa asked.

"We were supposed to go back to the waterfall with the Key!"

"The waterfall? Is that what Drofgum told you?" Tessa asked. "Why didn't you tell me that before? I would have remembered! How could you forget that?"

"I know! I know! Save the lecture for another time," I said as I grabbed her by the arm and headed through the Gateway. "Whoever or whatever was waiting for us in the shadows down here—probably Demlock!—now has my Key and is headed for the Crypt ahead of us!"

We ran along a short dark corridor that snaked downward. When we reached the end of the corridor, we found ourselves in another open cavelike area that had many dark crevices and gaps along the walls. Any number of cave creatures could have been hiding in the shadows and we would never have seen them.

The walls were decorated with symbols that looked like they'd been sketched with charcoal and roughly colored in with chalk. They looked like symbols of the Elements: one was obviously shaped like fire, one like choppy waves of water, one was a circle with a diagonal line through it, and one looked like a funnel cloud with three horizontal lines through it. The symbols were about as big as I was tall, and they were spaced out evenly around the perimeter of the cave.

On the wall directly opposite the corridor we had come from was an archway. Strings of flat, smooth stones and wooden beads hung from the top, blocking our view of what was on the other side.

"Do we or don't we?" Tessa asked, motioning towards the archway.

Our Stones were still glowing, so I was about to say, "I think we should," but someone else beat me to it. And it wasn't Tessa.

"Who said that?" I shouted. "Who's there?"

Tessa and I spun around a few times and then stopped, standing back to back.

"Tessa, hide your Stone," I whispered over my shoulder as I tucked my Stone under my shirt. I didn't want whoever was in there with us to know this was where we were supposed to be.

Then, as if created by smoke and mirrors, an image appeared before my eyes. It was the woman who was in my dreams.

It was my mom.

She was standing between the archway and me.

"Mom?"

"Yes, darling," she said as she came closer and held out her hand. "Let me take that from you. You won't be needing it anymore." I passed her my torch. She threw it aside and an invisible, magneticlike force pulled the torch to the stone wall where it stuck, giving light to the whole room.

"Smudge?" Tessa said as she stepped around and stood beside me.

"Shhh . . ." said my mom as she reached out and put a finger on Tessa's lips. Tessa closed her eyes and was silent. "Come closer, darling," my mom said to me. "Dreams are funny things. Sometimes they seem so real, don't they?" She walked towards me. "Don't you wish you could live in your dreams?"

"Yes," I said as a feeling of stillness passed over me. I closed my eyes as she reached for me.

"Simon, don't give in! It's not her!" shouted a familiar voice.

"Oh, shut up!" shouted my mom, snapping me back to reality.

My eyes shot open just in time to see Maximillian, hands tied at the wrists, running out of the shadows. He lunged at me and pushed me to the ground.

"Stay away from him!" Maximillian shouted. He stood between my mom and me.

"Yes, yes, dear Maxi," said my mom. "Aldusa should have let you run and hide. Then I wouldn't have to deal with your insolence."

I was confused.

"Mom?" I asked, standing up beside Maximillian.

"Of course," said my mom. "Look me in the eyes. You do remember my eyes, don't you, son?"

Maximillian stepped between us again. "Don't look at her, Simon. She's not who you think she is."

"Now, Maxi," said my mom. "Step aside. I want to look at my son."

"Not if I can help it!" Maximillian grunted as he lunged at her.

"Maximillian!" I shouted, but before I knew what was happening, my mom transformed into the hideously pale, crusty-faced creature that had torn into my dreams. It shot a flash of green light from one of its eyes, throwing Maximillian to the ground.

"Why do you continue in your feeble attempts to stall me? Can you not see I am on the threshold of my victory?" the creature shrieked.

"Your victory?" shouted Maximillian, laughing in a forced and angry way as he wiped blood from his mouth on his shoulder. "You'll never be victorious, Demlock!"

"Demlock," I repeated, staring at the dark creature that stood in front of me. The dark creature who, I suddenly realized, had a dark eye with a three-point star in the middle of it.

"How rude of me indeed," said Demlock as he rubbed his hands together like he was warming them before offering me a handshake. "We haven't been formally introduced. However, it does seem a rather waste of time to do it now, considering how my title shall soon be promoted. Oh, what the heck." He extended his hand towards me. "I am the new Sustainer of Emogen!"

"You will never overthrow the Sustainer!" cried Maximillian.

"Pity he's not around to have a say in the matter," said Demlock, dropping his hand. "Pity he isn't here to witness his own dethroning. Perhaps I shall have Aldusa send him word by way of a personal prophecy." He laughed.

"Aldusa?" I said. "The Priestess?"

"Yes, precious, isn't she? She has been a great asset to advancing my cause this last little while, what with helping you find your way to my portal. Both of you, actually."

I looked at Maximillian.

"Remember how Helyas took me to the House of Sacred Writings to prepare me for that 'Sacred Blessing of Protection'?"

I nodded.

"Well, the blessing was a load of bunk. He just took me there because there's a tunnel that runs under the House of Sacred Writings to the portal."

"Helyas is in on this, too?" That didn't surprise me.

"Of course!" said Demlock. "We're all in on this." He motioned behind me, towards one of the many dark crevices in the rocks. "Don't be shy. Come out where they can see you."

I turned to see a wolf step out of the shadows. It was unmistakably the same wolf that had just about killed me in Tezema Raha. He was holding the end of a metal chain in his jaws. The chain clinked and scraped along the ground as the wolf padded towards us, pulling the chain tight. He growled as he gave a hefty tug, and a boy came tumbling out of the shadows. It was Gil, all bloody and sweaty, wearing an ankle cuff that was attached to the other end of the chain.

"Gil!" Tessa and I exclaimed at the same time. But he didn't respond.

"How rude," sneered Demlock. "Have you children learned no manners? Stand up, will you? What with the way Fangrot had to practically drag you to the portal the whole way, if you ask me it's the least you could do for all the trouble he's gone through just to get you here."

Gil stood up. The chains clanged against his ankle cuff.

"What have you done to him?" I shouted. "Gil!"

He still didn't respond.

"Don't waste your breath," Demlock said. "He's only got ears for me."

I looked at Gil. He was standing there, totally clued out to everything that was going on. He appeared to be so deeply entranced by Demlock, that I didn't think I had much hope of ever seeing him come out of it.

"Nothing more than was necessary," Demlock said. And then he suddenly looked towards the corridor we had come through. I heard the hollow echo of heels bouncing off the stone walls.

"Ah, Aldusa," he said. "Impeccable timing. The children had just been asking about you."

38 Aldusa

"You know, you really shouldn't be so trusting, Maxi," Aldusa said as she stepped out of the darkness of the corridor and took her place at Demlock's side.

"Ah, my exquisite creation," said Demlock as he traced Aldusa's jawline with a long, yellow fingernail. Aldusa giggled.

"Your creation?" asked Tessa.

"Of course," replied Demlock. "An invention of my sheer brilliance. Why else do you think Maxi's alter ego didn't kill her along with the other vile villagers on its debut rampage? It was her blood spatterings on the door frames. Evil knows the scent of its own kind."

"Absolutely, darling," Aldusa said in an all too familiar voice as she fixed her eyes on me. "Why, I believe even urchins know the scent of other urchins." She looked from me to Tessa and back again. It was then that I noticed she was smoking a cigarette. And she was wearing high-heeled shoes.

"Griselda," I said, stunned.

"I see you're not as stupid as you used to be. The academy must have done you some good after all," she said.

"How . . . ? When . . . ?" I stammered.

"Oh, it really wasn't difficult to sway her," said Demlock, stepping in to take full credit. "All I had to do was promise her beauty, fame, and the performance of a lifetime. And ta-da! Look at her now. Quite a treat for the eyes, if I may say so myself."

"Darling," said Griselda, "you flatter me."

"But how . . . ?" I asked again.

"Perhaps you'll recognize this shape a little better." Demlock transformed his image right before my eyes and stood, looking me square in the face with Sorgol in one socket and a wandering eye in the other. The eyeglass was gone, but there were two obvious puncture-wound scars where the staple had been.

"Mr. Ratsworth!" cried Tessa and Maximillian.

"The Rat," I said at the same time.

"Ah, yes," he said. "Though I do take offense to your pet name for me."

"Edgaaaaar," sighed Griselda.

"You were Mr. Ratsworth?" exclaimed Maximillian. "He was you?"

"You . . . you . . . " stuttered Tessa.

"Yes. Me. Me! You like?" he said, spinning as if he were on a fashion show runway. "Mr. Ratsworth, my grandest creation, if I may say so myself. So unique, so articulate, so diabolical, so—"

"So blind!" retorted Tessa, either in a spontaneous act of rebellion towards her former favorite teacher or in an act of impulse, not having time to consider her choice of words. But for whatever reason she said it, I was proud of her. Way to say it like it is, I thought.

The Rat—er, Demlock—took major offense. "How substandard! And to think I was about to put you on the honor roll! I thought we were tight," he said with a smirk as he lifted his hand and crossed his fingers. "Isn't that what you told everyone at the academy?" Tessa's face went red and she looked down at her feet.

"I'll have you know, young lady," continued Demlock in a firm voice, "that it's not as easy as it may seem for a superior being such as myself to arrive unscathed at such a substandard—ugh!—wretchedly human destination as Grimstown. Easy for you, of course, being bred of an inferior species—to land in a superior destination such as Emogen intact. I'm just relieved it was only my vision that was jumbled and not something horrendous, like . . . like my lexis!"

"His 'lexis'?" I whispered to Tessa.

"His vocabulary," she explained.

"Oh, geez, yeah," I said. "How lucky for all of us."

"I'm sure you're just dying to find out why I chose this form at this particular time in history?" Demlock said.

"Not really," I said.

"It's simple," Demlock continued, ignoring my response. "I want to rule the universe!"

"By being Mr. Ratsworth?" asked Tessa.

"Yes, by being Mr. Ratsworth," Demlock said, sounding offended. "How dare you question my ingenious method! It was a magnificent plan! How else do you propose I was to retrieve the other half of the Key from Grimstown?"

Tessa just shrugged her shoulders.

"Well, if you don't have any intelligent suggestions, then I recommend keeping your comments inside that pathetically human brain of yours. Now, no more interruptions.

"When I discovered that Simon and half the Key had been sent to that despicably—ugh!—mortal realm, I immediately traveled there. And I will say again that it was an ingenious decision on my part to become the self-appointed headmaster at the school. Why, after the former headmaster's 'mysterious accident'—in which he fell headlong off the roof—rendered him, well, lifeless, it only made sense that I should step in to become his successor."

"That wasn't an accident!" Maximillian shouted. "You killed him!"

"And I couldn't have killed him at a more convenient time, I must say," said Demlock.

"And was it convenient for you to get Mom out of the way, too?" spat Maximillian.

Demlock growled. "Absolutely. And she was so easy to deal with," he said. "And in the end, so were you. You turned out to be much more agreeable encased in stone."

"And your music was much more agreeable in Grimstown," said Maximillian.

My mind suddenly flashed back to the night Gil and I were spying on Psycho-conductor through the door: There was a potted plant . . . it was limp . . .

"Do something!" he had shouted at the plant. "How can I work my magic if you won't cooperate in this wretched place?"

"That was you?" I blurted. "You were Psycho-conductor?"

Demlock shot me a withering glare. "Curse that inferior realm! Curse that inferior, mortal realm infinite times!"

"There, there, darling," Griselda said as she stepped closer to him and attempted to massage his shoulders. Demlock slapped her hands away. She looked crushed.

"DO NOT mock my greatness!" he shouted at Maximillian and me. "You should bow to me! Honor and revere me—a true artiste! For I am not so limited now."

A wicked smile curved and cracked Demlock's lips as the three-point star began to blaze.

39 Thank You for Coming

As Demlock's eye shone, a haunting melody seemed to creep out of the crevices and crawl along the ground and up the walls until the entire cave was filled with music.

"The music—" I said.

"Not *the* music! *My* music!" shouted Demlock, flashing the blazing Star in my direction.

"Simon! Look away!" shouted Maximillian.

I did. Which only made Demlock fume even more.

"I can clearly see you are all in desperate need of a demonstration to fully comprehend the supremacy of my music." He directed our attention to where Gil was standing.

The music swelled and suddenly massive vines sprouted from the ground all around Gil. The wolf yelped and dropped the chain. He got up on his hind legs, trying to avoid contact with the vines, and stepped back until he was almost lost in the shadows. The vines grew at an incredible speed, wrapping themselves around Gil's shoulders and head in rhythm with the tune. But just like the last time I saw it happen to him, he didn't respond. He just stood there and let the vines swallow him alive. Tessa screamed.

This can't be happening again! I thought. I've got to stop him this time, but how? The Knife! It was such a sudden, awesome idea, I almost shouted it out loud. I got that snake between the eyes. Demlock's head is a way bigger target!

I quickly reached down to unsnap the sheath, but it wasn't snapped. It was already open!

"Looking for this?" asked Demlock with a sneer as he pulled something out of his cloak and swung it like a pendulum by the handle.

"My Knife!" I shouted, stunned. "How'd—?"

"I have my ways," he said, throwing a sly glance towards Gil. "I'm sure you've noticed by now that your little knife isn't the only thing you're missing." He put my Knife back inside his cloak.

Griselda threw her cigarette holder over her shoulder and clapped her hands. "Lovely, darling. Absolutely astonishing!"

The music stopped. Demlock took a bow. "Do tell me," he said, swinging his cape around as he turned to face us. The fire in his eye had died down. "Have you ever seen an artiste extraordinaire such as I? I must say, the years I've devoted to the craft of composing incomparable works of art certainly have paid off. Wouldn't you agree? Soon the realms will be at my beckoning as the Elements will have no choice but to succumb to my greatness as well!" Demlock stepped away from Griselda.

"Of course, you weren't aware of the prophecy that condemned the Elements to the Crypt the first time you tried to gain that kind of power, were you?" Maximillian asked with a massive amount of annoyance in his voice.

Demlock cleared his throat and slowly smoothed back his stringy hair. "That's where this Gilbert comes in," he said with forced calmness, referring to Gil who was still wrapped from head to toe in vines. Luckily, the vines had stopped growing and I could see Gil was still breathing. "This Son of the Seventh," Demlock added.

"I don't understand," I said.

Demlock snorted. So did Griselda.

"I wouldn't have expected him to," she said.

"Nor I," said Demlock.

But then suddenly I did understand.

Gil's birthday was the same as mine. Same month and year, anyways. And the Elements' resummoning could only be done by the Key and by a boy born in the Order of Sevens—the Son of the Seventh. And technically speaking I guess Gil was a Son of the Seventh.

But would it really work? I wasn't sure.

"When I learned about the Order of Sevens, I knew I needed to have a Son of the Seventh open the Casket. At first I thought I needed Simon. But then I discovered this Gilbert. And now my Son of the Seventh has finally obtained the Key," said Demlock. "Ahhh . . . there's nothing like the smell of refined, Emogenian metal. Don't you agree?" Demlock said as he leaned in and sniffed Gil.

That's why The Rat kept sniffing me at the school, I thought. He could smell the Key!

"As we can now see, it has all worked out in my favor, despite my . . . challenges," said Demlock. "Despite the fact that this Gilbert couldn't properly be swayed to clue in to the plan in his own realm. Despite the fact that you escaped death by viper and having your throat torn out by a bumbling idiotic wolf." He glared at the wolf. The wolf whimpered and hung his head. "Despite the second Key, the Key for the Gateway, that I was unaware of until very recently. Tricky, tricky," he said as he wagged a long finger at me. "You'd almost think there's someone up there watching out for me," he said as he mockingly looked upward and put a hand over his heart. "Luckily for me, my story does have a happy ending."

"Your story?" shouted Tessa. "*Your* story?"

"Aw, are you jealous?" teased Demlock. "Why, I do believe your face is turning green with envy. Awww . . . the little orphan girl wants a happy ending, too!"

"She's not an orphan," I said, stepping up to Tessa's defense. "She has parents. And they'll come to get her one day."

"Is that what she told you?" asked Demlock, raising an eyebrow at Tessa. "Is that what you told him?" he repeated.

"Yes," she whispered.

"Liar!" Demlock shouted as if he'd won a game of BINGO. "She's a liar! Murdered in cold blood while they were on an exotic vacation, weren't they? One of many vacations they neglected to take you on, wasn't it? Although I do suppose it was lucky for you they left you behind that time."

"Stop it!" shouted Tessa.

"I really must insist you find yourself some new friends, Simon. The two you have are absolutely unacceptable: one is a traitor and one is a liar!"

"Just stop it!" Tessa hung her head. And cried.

"Oh, shame. Have I hurt your feelings?" Demlock mocked. "I suppose this hasn't helped you get any closer to your own happy ending, has it?"

I reached over and took hold of Tessa's sweaty, shaking hand.

"But you can both rest assured that your friend's story will have a happy ending." He stroked the vines on Gil's head like a loving mother. Gil rested his head on Demlock's chest. Demlock reached into the front of his cloak and pulled out a gold chain with a small, blood-filled, tear-shaped glass vial hanging from it. He moved towards Tessa and dangled it in front of her face. She looked at it, confused.

"He has made a blood contract with me. He now belongs to me. The Son of the Seventh belongs to me!"

"It can't be!" exclaimed Tessa.

"Oh, but it can and it is," said Demlock. He stepped around behind her and placed his white hands on her shoulders as he whispered in her ear. "It never ceases to amaze me just how trusting you humans can be."

"And stupid," said Griselda, snickering.

She's forgotten that she's human, too, I thought.

"Yes," said Demlock, eyeing her. "Very stupid. Although," he continued, tossing the vial in the air and then snatching it back, "come to think of it, if my lexis were hindered, I'd be tempted to sell my soul, too." He laughed as if he had just told the funniest joke ever.

"You're a monster!" shouted Tessa with tears still in her eyes. "How could you prey on such an innocent person?"

"I believe I have already answered that question," said Demlock, suddenly serious again, as he put the vial back under his cloak.

"So you're telling us that you're going to cure Gil's stutter?" I asked.

Demlock broke out into hysterical laughter again. "Of course not!" he said.

"Then how is his ending going to be happy? You said his story was going to have a happy ending."

"Well, now that you put it that way, I can see it is all a matter of perspective. I said it was going to be a happy ending, but I suppose not necessarily for him."

"You are a monster!" Tessa shouted again.

"Oh, I'm sorry," Demlock said. "Have I ruined it for you? Oh, shame," he said as he looked at me, obviously mocking the expression on my face. "You pathetic humans and your need for acceptance and meaningful relationships!" He growled through gritted teeth and smoothed back his greasy hair as he shot his withering glare from Gil to Tessa and to Griselda.

"Darling?" she asked.

"Shut up, Griselda!" Demlock shouted.

"You . . . you mean 'Aldusa,'" she said. "I'm your Aldusa."

"It's time to break it to you," said Demlock, taking Griselda by the hand. She sighed. His wandering Rat eye started twitching violently, and his face got so red it looked like his head might explode right off his shoulders.

"Darling?" asked Griselda.

"I am not your darling!" he growled. "And you are nothing to me! Nothing but a pawn in my glorious hand! You have served your purpose. You have ensured the safe arrival of the Key into my possession. That is all. One simple task."

"Have I not pleased you?" she asked.

"Of course you have! By the way," he said as he turned to me, "if I were your grandfather, I'd be more than a tad peeved that you stood me up." A wide, wicked grin curled his cracked lips up at the corners.

What's that supposed to mean? I wondered.

"If you are pleased with me," Griselda said, interrupting my thoughts, "then—"

"Then nothing!" shouted Demlock. "The deluded honor and respect you received from those wretched Tezeman villagers is your prize. I have no further use for you. Thank you for coming."

All at once, the star flashed and the music swelled. Demlock shrieked as he morphed back into the hideously ugly, crusty-faced creature. The vines that were wrapped around Gil unwound their grip on him and shrank back into the ground. Then a single vine popped out of the ground right by Griselda's feet. She screeched and hopped from one foot to the other. Then another vine popped out beside the first one. And then another and another, until there were thousands of little vines snaking and climbing their way up Griselda's legs. She screamed and pulled and scratched at the vines, but they grew and climbed and grew some more.

"Edgaaaaaaaar!" she screamed. The vines entered her ears, her nose, and her open mouth, choking her. They grew at such a fast speed that she was completely covered in a matter of seconds. Then, the vines started pulling her still-thrashing body into the ground. They pulled and heaved until she was gone.

Tessa and I just stood and watched in horror. There was nothing else we could do.

40 The Crypt

The music stopped. Demlock inhaled and exhaled deeply a couple of times. He smoothed back his stringy hair and turned to me.

"Back to happy thoughts," he said as he smoothed the front of his cloak. "Now, let's get to the real reason we're all here." He eyed the archway. "Fangrot!"

The wolf growled.

"The prisoners," he sneered, not taking his eyes off the archway.

The wolf slinked out of the shadow and picked up Gil's chain in his jaws. He dragged him to where Maximillian was and then bit and held Maximillian's arm, pulling both of them forward. He then stood behind them with his neck bent down, the hair on the back of his neck bristling. He growled again, letting them know that they had better obey.

"Just so you are aware," Demlock said to me, "there is only one reason I haven't killed you yet. You or your brother. There seems to be a little problem that I'm guessing one of you can fix for me." He motioned towards the archway. "After you."

Tessa, Maximillian, and I walked slowly towards the beaded stone and wood curtain. Fangrot growled, and I heard Gil's chains clanging behind us.

Just as I reached out to part the curtain, the stones that hung there started glowing. I quickly dropped my hand. The stones pulsed, becoming brighter and hotter with each beat. And I could feel my Stone doing the same thing under my shirt.

Tessa shot me a look and took in a quick breath. Her hand flew up to where she had hidden her Stone.

"Interesting," said Demlock, glaring at Tessa's hand through vertical eye slits that had become even narrower. Tessa slowly lowered her hand. Demlock smiled and looked at the curtain. "This didn't happen when I peeked inside earlier on, before you arrived. Now, like I said, after you."

I inhaled deeply as Tessa and I parted the curtain. We took a few steps through the entryway. The rest of them entered and stood behind us.

As we stepped into the large, round, dark space, the walls lit with a sudden hot, pulsing, glowing light. It was the same kind of light that was in our Stones. The room was a completely empty space, like it had never seen the existence of anything—a total void. It was like we'd stepped into nothingness and were standing on air, suspended inside a glowing bubble. Only we weren't floating around every which way, the way you'd expect astronauts do in space. We were firmly grounded, but on nothing.

"This must be the Crypt," I whispered, my voice getting sucked into the emptiness. When I spoke, the

Crypt didn't even have an echo. The space seemed to absorb the sound of my words as soon as they left my mouth.

"Yes, I've gathered that," said Demlock swishing past me, his cloak twirling around him as he stopped suddenly to face me. "But what I don't understand is, where are the Elements?"

"Yegra's smarter than that," said Maximillian. "Seems she's always a step or two ahead of you."

"Yes, I'm sure she is," said Demlock. "It's the very reason you're both still alive, it seems. I'll try to remember to thank her for you when it's all over. Now, where are they?" I think he meant to shout at me, but his voice got lost in the void.

"I . . . I have no idea," I said. My Stone was so hot it felt like it was going to explode. I was afraid it might be shining through my shirt, so I slowly put my hand over it, trying really hard not to make it noticeable.

But Demlock noticed anyways. "Sons of the Guardian of the Key! Did your mother leave you with no instructions? I'm sure someone did!"

He glided towards Tessa and wrapped his thin, white hand around her neck. Then he pulled her Stone out from under her shirt by the twine. He cried out in pain as the light from it burned his eyes, but he didn't let go of Tessa or take his eyes off the Stone.

"Take yours out!" he shouted at me. His grip on Tessa's neck tightened.

"Smudge, don't do it," Tessa wheezed.

Demlock squeezed tighter still. "It wouldn't take much to snap this little neck," he said.

I pulled my Stone out. The light was so bright it outshone Tessa's and even the glowing walls. Demlock cried out in pain again.

"Now give him yours!" ordered Demlock. He let go of Tessa and stepped back. She was gasping for air as she removed her Stone and gave it to me. There was a horrible red handprint on her throat.

"Now read them!" Demlock demanded.

Tessa shook her head. "Don't do it," she whispered.

Just then, the music started up again. Only this time it was very faint because, of course, it was getting sucked into the nothingness.

"I said, read them!" Demlock said again, the star blazing.

Suddenly a tiny vine popped up right by Tessa's foot. It just appeared from out of nowhere and from nothing. There was no ground beneath our feet but the vine popped up anyways, as if from underneath an invisible line. Beneath the vine, I saw no roots.

Tessa screamed. Then another vine popped up from nothingness right by her other foot.

"I do have ways of making you speak," Demlock said as he raised his hands. The music got louder.

The two vines slowly wrapped themselves around Tessa's ankles. She screamed again. She tried pulling at them, but they just grew faster. I pulled at them, too, but it was no use. Maximillian rushed to help us and dropped to his knees. He tried to pull the vines out of the ground with his bound hands, but he couldn't. They wouldn't budge. They grew so fast; they were already around Tessa's waist, pinning her arms to her sides, and then they wound around her shoulders. The vision of Griselda's gruesome death was fresh in my mind.

The vines were crawling up Tessa's neck when I read her Stone and shouted, "Fire!" The letters pulsed on her Stone, and the word disappeared into the air as I spoke it.

"Smudge! No!" Tessa screamed as the vines tried to enter her mouth. She bit a piece off one and spit it out. "No!" she shouted again. Maximillian had stood back up and was trying to keep the vines from suffocating her.

"Water!" I shouted as the vines kept growing. Demlock laughed and shrieked with pleasure.

"Smudge! Stop!" Tessa shouted as Maximillian pulled another vine out of her mouth.

"Stop now and she'll be dead," warned Demlock.

I held my Stone up. "Air! Earth!"

When I said the word "Earth," the light in the Stones suddenly went out, and they turned to dust in my hand. The same happened to the stones in the archway. There was a loud sprinkling sound as the dust fell to the ground. Only the walls remained lit.

Demlock's music stopped, too. The vines went limp and fell off Tessa.

Demlock stood tall, slowly looking all around the room in anticipation.

Everything was quiet.

Then there was a low rumbling that filled the room, vibrating the air around us as the nothingness of the Crypt suddenly changed. The air itself seemed to shift and move, magically bringing into view the features of the room.

A solid floor formed beneath our feet. It was made of dirt, and more than a few huge cockroaches skittered across the ground and attempted to climb up the walls. About fifty popping sounds shot through the Crypt as each giant bug exploded from the heat.

Then at four points around the perimeter of the circular room, four stone statues slowly emerged. Each statue resembled one of the four Elements—Air, Water, Fire, and Earth. They were all female, except for Fire. Their arms stretched out towards the center of the Crypt. Each held an empty bowl in one hand and pointed with the other.

"The hosts," said Demlock.

The object the hosts were pointing to slowly materialized in the center of the Crypt. It was a simple wooden stool with a hand-carved wooden box on it.

"The Chalice," Demlock said, his voice trembling.

That wooden box must be the Casket, I thought.

The stool with the Casket on it stood in the exact center of a huge compass rose that was embedded into the floor. It looked like it was made of pure silver; the needle of pure gold; the letters of the four points of pure bronze. And it was covered in clear, thick glass. The compass pointed west.

The rumbling in the room suddenly stopped. Everything was quiet again.

Demlock spun around. "Your hours are numbered!" he shouted at me. "When my Son of the Seventh inserts the Key and unlocks that box, the Elements will have no choice but to obey my commands!"

"The Elements will never obey you!" Maximillian shouted. "The Key is not rightfully yours!"

"Rightfully?" Demlock shrieked. "Rightfully? I've heard about enough from you! Curse you!" The Star in his eye socket suddenly shone brighter as he flung his arms in Maximillian's direction and shot a flash of colorful light from his fingertips, throwing Maximillian against the glowing, hot wall of the Crypt. He fell to the ground. He rolled away and tried to get up, but Demlock shot another flash of colors. The dirt floor around Maximillian softened, swallowing him to the waist.

Maximillian gasped as he sank farther into the ground.

"I have every right to that Key!" Demlock shrieked at me, the three-point Star still blazing. "Look at me when I'm speaking to you!"

"Don't do it, Simon!" screamed Maximillian. "You must resist the powers of Sorgol! He's trying to overpower you!"

I tried looking away, but it was too late. The pull was too strong. I was drawn deep into the Star, almost to the point of being in the scene I saw.

There, in the widening Star, was an image of my mother surrounded by flames. She was frantically looking for a way out.

And screaming.

"No," I said, trying to find my voice as my knees buckled underneath me.

"You ran! You could have tried to help her, but you ran away, didn't you, you cowardly little imp?"

I did.

"And, if I'm not mistaken, you couldn't even stand up to a little tenth grade bully on your own best friend's behalf, could you?" he said with disgust.

"Don't listen to him!" screamed Maximillian. "Close your eyes!"

But I couldn't help it. I had to look; I had to face the facts. And the facts said I was a failure. The feelings I had the day Mad Dog tormented Gil came back like a flood to drown me, and that flood was pouring right out of Demlock's eyes.

"He's right," I said.

"Yes, of course I'm right," said Demlock. "Son of the Seventh indeed!" he mocked. "A failure!"

"It's not true, Smudge," pleaded Tessa. "Please don't listen to him!"

"You can't deny it!" shouted Demlock, speaking over Tessa. Only this time when he spoke, his lips weren't moving. I could hear his voice without him speaking. He had tilted his head and was speaking to me through the Star.

I shook my head.

"Forget your friends," Demlock said without speaking a word. "What I want to make clear is that when you heard your mother's tortured screams for help, you ran, afraid of what you might have had to face. Isn't that right?"

"What's he saying to you? Don't listen! Close your eyes!" begged Maximillian.

"Coward!" Demlock shouted at me through his telepathy.

I am a coward. I am a coward.

"What a shame you failed her—your own dear mother. She was right there with you, and you ran."

I failed my mother. I am a failure.

I hung my head and slumped to the ground. I was so ashamed of myself.

"Simon!" Maximillian cried as he sank farther into the quicksand.

"Hold your tongue!" screamed Demlock. "I shan't prolong this any further."

Demlock locked eyes with Tessa as he made his way to Gil and put his arm around him. He guided him towards the Casket.

"This Gilbert here is such a compliant boy. Now," he said as he turned Gil to face him, "don't fail me! Do as I say! Open the box!"

Gil took the Key out of his pocket and knelt in front of the Casket. He robotically inserted the Key into the iron lock and turned it to the right.

41 A Bad Mistake

Nothing happened.

"The other way, fool!" Demlock shouted.

Gil twisted the Key to the left.

Nothing happened.

"Again!" shouted Demlock.

But before Gil could turn the Key again, the sides of the box collapsed outward, revealing a sparkling silver Chalice.

Demlock stood in awe, trembling, as he looked at the Chalice.

I was stunned, too. How did Gil open the Casket? Was Demlock right? Is there really more than just one Son of the Seventh?

"Such ultimate power is here for the taking," Demlock whispered. "Power over the entire universe." He suddenly shrieked a laugh. "Did you really think you could stop me from harnessing the powers of the Elements? The power to alter the destiny of every living creature is in that Chalice. Mine now, forever to do with as I please! Foolish boy."

"Leave him alone!" shouted Tessa as she tried to stand tall and sound brave.

"Hush, hush, my dear," he said as he put a long, thin, white finger to his lips. "Let's have a pretty face to remember you by, not a sour one." He took a few steps towards the Chalice.

"NO!" screamed Tessa. She ran to where I was still slumped in a heap and shook me. "Smudge! Snap out of it, Smudge!"

"I'm afraid he can't hear you, my dear," Demlock said with a satisfied sneer. "Seems he's nothing without his Key. He has succumbed to my power at long last. And so will the weakened Elements. Now, watch closely."

Demlock spun around and took steps towards Gil with his greedy hands reaching out for the Chalice. His whole body trembled in his excitement. "Watch now as I alter my destiny and the destiny of Emogen forever. I will have the power to create what I wish and destroy what I wish." His fingertips all but touched the Chalice when he stopped.

"Wait," he said. "I must go no farther without some assistance." He turned to Gil. "You must pick up the Chalice for me, fourteen-year-old boy. Certainly they will not feel threatened by a Son of the Seventh."

Demlock started his music and cringed in nervous anticipation as Gil dutifully picked up the Chalice.

Nothing happened.

"Yes," Demlock said. "Now pass it to me, slowly." Gil held the Chalice out to Demlock's shaky hands. Demlock slowly reached out and, finger over finger, took hold of the Chalice with Gil's hands underneath his.

His body shuddered with satisfaction as he knelt down and lifted the Chalice high above his head. His music got louder as he poured the Elements onto himself as if showering in them. They ran down the full length of his body, soaking into his clothing, right through to his skin. When the excess reached the ground, it formed a puddle around him.

When Demlock finished, he stood and threw the Chalice—and Gil—to the ground. The Chalice spun until it slowly lost its energy and came to a stop.

He raised his arms in the air and spoke. "All power is mine! The four Elements I have poured out, and the four Elements belong to me. Be loosed and do the will of the one who released you!"

Demlock's music got louder still as the host of the Earth moved and spread out her arms.

Immediately a rumble began beneath Demlock's feet. The floor cracked where he stood. The rupture widened and spread, circling the compass on the floor and creating a deep, empty ditch around it. The crack splintered around the edges of the ditch and continued to grow, the lines spinning their way across the floor like spiderwebs. The main crack split into four veins, and each stopped at the feet of one of the four stone hosts.

Another rumbling was heard, only this time it shook the walls and came from up above. Rocks loosened and fell. Then the ceiling of the cave split and separated, like the roof of a convertible car. Layer after layer of rock did the same, until the starless Emogenian sky could be seen far up above.

"Yes! Yes!" shouted Demlock.

One by one the statues raised their bowls, offering them up to the damp, cold air. The Water statue opened her cloak. From inside the sleeves a waterfall flowed over the palms of her outstretched hands and ran through her fingers. The water gushed out and filled the cracks on the ground. The host of the Earth blew into her hands and scattered seeds around the cave that instantly sprouted into every plant you could imagine.

A great snapping sound shot out from the one named Fire. Demlock turned and faced him as he raised his left hand and shot a blast of flames into the air that billowed and hung above Demlock like a glowing blanket. Demlock looked so small and insignificant compared to the majesty and terror of the statue that glared into the night sky.

"Fire, I bid you—go!" Demlock commanded as he circled his left arm around and around.

Fire, under the spell of Demlock's music, formed a ball. As Demlock flung his arm in Gil's direction, the fireball hurled itself at Gil and encircled him with flames.

"Gil!" Tessa screamed.

Fire's dense walls slowly closed in on him.

Demlock raised both arms in the air and called out, "Water! I bid you, come!"

All at once, the water from the ditches on the ground gathered together into a massive whirlpool. At Demlock's command, the swirling water arched high into the air and surged downwards, directly towards Tessa. She crouched down and shielded her head with her arms, but it swallowed her up anyways, completely surrounding her in a dark inky-blue water bubble. Her eyes opened wide in horror as she kicked and punched at the walls of her watery prison.

"Stop kicking!" shouted Maximillian. "Conserve your energy! Stop kicking and hold your breath!"

"Enough out of you!" Demlock shouted at Maximillian. Once again he raised his arms in the air, swirling his hands above his head, and shouted, "Earth! I summon you!"

Suddenly the ground surrounding Maximillian rumbled and he started slipping downwards—fast.

"The Chalice! Pick it up, Simon! You must call them back! Call to the North Wind!" he shouted just before his head disappeared under the quicksand.

Demlock laughed a deep, satisfied laugh. The volume of his music lowered. "Look around you, boy," he said to me. "This is the power I now have: the power to control the very Elements of Emogen." He walked to where Tessa was quietly floating in the bubble. He swirled a finger in the water. "And I am going to make you a proposition, one I'm sure you cannot possibly refuse. I am willing to make you my protégé. You will be like my own son. Your days of being a lonely orphan can finally come to an end."

A lonely orphan.

"O.W.N.O.," I whispered.

Suddenly something clicked in my mind's eye as it replayed specific scenes: Gil nicknaming me "Smudge" in the hallway at the academy; Drofgum entrusting the Knife of Creation to me; Tessa at my side as I searched for the missing half of the Key and my friend; Quar and Rama taking care of me and believing in me; Maximillian telling me he was my brother.

Although I still had no clue where or how my journey would end, at that moment I did know one thing: I definitely wasn't an O.W.N.O. I had ditched that label the day I was sneezed on in the hallway at the academy.

"Did you hear me, boy?" Demlock shrieked.

I looked at Tessa, suspended in the water bubble. She looked deep into my eyes from within her watery grave. A few bubbles escaped from her mouth.

"Look at me when I'm speaking to you!" Demlock shouted. "Do you not comprehend the magnitude of what I'm saying? I am offering you the chance to become somebody others will fear and respect throughout the rest of history!"

I looked at each of the hosts, and as I looked at Water, I could have sworn I saw a big, heavy tear slide down her face. And that's when I heard her whisper to me, "You're *our* boy."

I nodded and slowly stood up.

"Ah, yes. There we are. You are coming to your senses at last," Demlock said as he took steps towards me, stretching his arms out as if to hug me.

But I ducked under one of his arms and ran to where the Chalice lay. I picked it up.

"No!" screamed Demlock. "Stop! What are you doing? Don't touch that! Get your hands off it!" He stood tall and raised his hands, heightening the sound of his music. And then he pulled my Knife out of his cloak by the handle.

At the exact same time, I lifted the Chalice high above my head.

And just as he bent his arm back to fling the Knife in my direction, I closed my eyes and screamed at the top of my lungs, "North Wind, I summon you!"

The statue called Air immediately opened her cloak, and a deafening wind blew and raged from inside of it. The North Wind encircled me and spun her fierce cyclone around my body, intercepting the path of the Knife. I held the Chalice tightly against my chest.

The North Wind continued spinning around me, faster and faster. The whir of it in my ears got louder and louder, drowning out Demlock's music. Suddenly, when I thought I couldn't stand the sound anymore, everything went still and quiet inside the cyclone, even though the North Wind was still raging around the outside.

Then she whispered in my ear, "What is your bidding, Master?"

Maximillian had never told me what to say if the North Wind talked to me!

Think! Think!

"What is your bidding, Master?" she asked again.

"Do as you see fit," I blurted out, "so that Emogen can be free and you can take your rightful place."

It was all I could think of to say, but I had the feeling that it was okay. Maximillian had told me that the North Wind would take care of everything.

Suddenly the North Wind spun off and away from me.

Demlock shrieked as the North Wind gathered all the Elements together into her cyclone. Tessa fell to the ground, sputtering and gasping for air. Gil thudded to the floor of the cave in a limp heap, his hair and clothes steaming.

Demlock fell to the ground as well and crawled backwards away from the cyclone. "What's happening? No!" he screamed as his body suddenly warped into a horrific shape.

He writhed on the ground; his whole body twisted and turned as the Elements—one by one—entered his body. Earth, Air, Fire, and Water covered him and consumed him. The Fire Element first burned him, turning him into a live flaming torch. His screams were almost unbearable as he rolled on the ground, trying to put the fire out. Then the Water Element must have taken pity on him and soaked him, causing his scorched skin to sizzle and steam. Then the North Wind blew over him, long and hard, freezing his nearly lifeless body solid. Finally the Earth Element disappeared down his throat as the North Wind lifted him high in the air. They twisted and wrenched his charred and frozen body, eventually causing it to explode into a shower of dry, brittle pieces. The ground where he fell singed and turned black.

The powers of the Elements then rose together to where the ceiling once was and angrily circled the room.

"Smudge!" Tessa screamed above the deafening roar as a bolt of fire zigzagged from the middle of the Elements and headed straight towards me. I held the Chalice even higher above my head as the Elements funneled furiously downwards—one by one—with deadly energy, draining into the Chalice.

The noise stopped unexpectedly as the last Element was sucked back into the Chalice like lint into a vacuum.

Everything was silent.

Clutching the Chalice to my chest, I ran to where Maximillian had disappeared. I dropped to my knees and put the Chalice down beside me. I furiously started digging.

Tessa was beside me in a flash. We were up to our elbows in dirt when Tessa cried, "Gil!" She reached over and hugged him.

"Tessa? What are y-you doing here? What are you doing? Ow! W-watch the b-blisters!" he said as he pried her off his waist.

"Sorry," she said as she let go of him and smiled.

"D-did you just s-smile at me?" he asked in disbelief.

"Yeeesssss," Tessa said as she turned back and continued digging.

"W-what are you doing?" asked Gil.

"Looking for Smudge's brother," said Tessa.

Gil looked really confused.

"We're not going to find him!" I shouted and sat back on my heels. We'd already dug a few feet down and there was no trace of him. "It's no use!" I wiped my forehead and slumped to the ground, exhausted.

"I . . . I don't know what to say," Tessa stammered as she pushed her wet hair back from her forehead with a mud-caked hand and looked at the hole we'd dug. A few of her tears fell and disappeared into the black earth.

"There's nothing to say," I whispered.

We stood up. Tessa picked up the Chalice and handed it to me.

I saw Gil standing by the barren circle of scorched ground where Demlock had fallen. Tessa and I joined him. In the middle of the singed area was a black stone with a dimming three-point star. That was all that was left of Demlock.

Tessa reached over and held my hand. For real. But I didn't even mind. My hands were blistered from the friction of the Elements as they siphoned into the Chalice. The pressure of her grasp burned, but I didn't care. I squeezed her hand.

As we stood looking at the scorched ground, a black crow suddenly swooped in through the open ceiling and scooped up Demlock's eye in its beak. It circled the cave once, as if it was checking the place out, and then flew back the way it came in.

As soon as the crow was gone, a lone ivy sprouted from the center of the burnt area and crept its way along the earth, creating a complete circle around Demlock's remains before the shoots gathered all the particles and wrapped them in a vine cocoon.

Then the vine heaved and tugged at Demlock's cocoon, squeezing and pulling it under the ground until it had completely disappeared.

We stood and stared at the empty space for quite a while.

"Now what?" Tessa finally asked.

As if on cue, a loud, familiar squawk rang through the Crypt.

42 Living Stones

Melchior swooped in and landed on the cold Crypt floor with his distinctively silent thud. He stepped towards the center of the Crypt. It looked like his leg had healed.

"Now we must undo Demlock's mischief," came a familiar but tired-sounding voice from on top of the bird.

We stepped around Melchior and saw Drofgum, barely hanging on to the oily feathers. Melchior lowered his body to the ground.

"Grizzly Goat's guts," said Drofgum slowly as he looked at us out of the corner of his eye. "You're all a bloody mess, you are. Jes look at you." He winked at me.

He was a mess, too. His face was deathly white and his beard was matted. Even his hands seemed to be withered.

"Help me down, will you?" he said in a weak voice.

Tessa and I took him by the arms and helped him slide off Melchior's back. He could barely stand on his own. I put his arm around my shoulders to support him.

Melchior did not move.

"Drofgum, you look really sick. You shouldn't be here."

"No, no, I shouldn't. I should be at da waterfall. Which was where I was. Waitin' fer you. But no worries about dat now. Dere's work to be done. And quickly, too. I can sees we're missin' a comrade."

I looked at the hole Tessa and I had dug. "Yes. Demlock had him swallowed in—"

Drofgum cut me off. "Da Chalice, please," he said in a barely audible whisper. "I needs da Chalice."

I handed it to him.

"What did I tells you? Demlock's a real dim dolt, he is. Didn't even know wheres to pour da Elements out. T'ought he'd pour dem on himself. Knuckle'ead. Dey've gots to be poured out in dem dere bowls. What'd he t'inks dem bowls was fer? Decoration?"

Drofgum closed his eyes, lifted the Chalice—the best he could—and recited a short chant.

"Bless da re-pourin'
Now done wit' clean hands
By da One you'd foretold
When Emogen began."

"Now," he said to me as he opened his eyes and lowered the Chalice. "Take dis and fill each of dem bowls 'til dey're full, right to da top."

I took the Chalice from him and took a couple of steps towards the host of Earth. I stopped and turned back to look at Drofgum, to make sure this was really what he wanted me to do.

"Go on," he said. "We've all been waitin' a long time fer dis."

I stood in front of the first host, Earth, looking way up to the bowl, wondering how the heck I was supposed to reach it.

"You've gots to climb," said Drofgum. "Nut'in' wort' havin' comes easy."

I stepped up onto the foot, climbed up the folds and creases of the cloak, heaved myself up onto the shoulder, and inched my way across the outstreached arm like it was the branch of a tree. Not an easy feat while holding on to a Chalice, I'll tell you.

When I finally reached the bowl, I poured until it was full. Suddenly the host breathed deeply and came to life. She was still stone, but she was moving. I almost fell off her arm, but she caught me and gently lowered me to the ground.

I repeated the procedure for the other three hosts, making sure to wrap my legs tightly around their arms as I poured.

"Dey t'anks you kindly," Drofgum said feebly when I finally finished. "Dey don't takes too nicely to bein' all messed up and poured out all over da ground."

Then he asked me for the Knife. The Knife! The Knife! I thought, a bit panicked, searching the floor around my feet.

Oh, right. I looked back to where Demlock had thrown it at me. It was on the ground, right around where I'd been standing. I darted over to it and picked it up. I gave it to Drofgum. He held it to his heart.

"Takes dis," he said to me as he struggled to take off the sack he had strapped across his back. I helped him with it and put the sack on the ground.

Then Drofgum took off his hooded cloak.

Two awfully familiar-looking pointed ears popped out from under one of the biggest comb-overs I'd ever seen.

"Grampa?" I spluttered.

Then it hit me.

"Drofgum!" I exclaimed.

"Drofgum Ecaroh, to be exact," he said.

Drofgum Ecaroh—Horace Mugford!

"Of course! Your name was backwards!"

"Backwards on Eart', maybe." He let out a low whistle. "I'm sure glad you've finally discovered me secret identity," he said with a weak grin and a wink. "I was bustin' to tells you." He squeezed my shoulder.

"So why . . . why didn't you tell me?"

"You was too overhwelmed as it was. Besides, it wasn't da most critical t'ing you needed to know, and I knew you'd find out sooner or later anyhow. Now, we'll chitchat some more later. Da Sustainer of Emogen's been waitin' too long fer dis moment to waste anudder second. He's got work to do if we ever wants to see dat boy again." He nodded to where Maximillian had disappeared.

"The Sustainer?" I asked, looking around the Crypt.

Tessa elbowed me in the ribs. "I think he's talking about himself," she said as Grampa rolled up his sleeves.

"You . . . you're the Sustainer?"

"Can't get much crazier den dat, huh?" said Grampa, winking at Tessa. He gave me a weak smile, exposing his two glittery silver teeth. "Here, spread dis on da ground, over dere." He held his cloak out.

I did what he asked me to.

"Dat's a good boy. Now helps me sit on it," he said, gasping.

Tessa and I helped him sit cross-legged on the cloak. He was sitting exactly in the middle of the Crypt.

He took in a long, deep breath and carved an *F* on the palm of his left hand with the blade of the Knife. Immediately the host of the Fire Element came and knelt his heavy stone body in front of him. Grampa took the left hand of the Fire host and carved the word "FIRE" into it. Then he placed his own cut hand over it and squeezed. Their blood mingled and dripped to the ground, sending sparks flying around them. When Grampa let go, I saw that the word "FIRE" had turned into a raised symbol of actual fire on the host's palm. The host raised his hand in the air, and the fire shot out of it like a blowtorch. The heat and light from it was almost unbearable in the Crypt.

Grampa then placed his cut hand on the host's head and gave him a blessing. After the blessing, the host stood up and said in a hissing, crackly voice, "Our dear, dear Simon. How we've missed you."

I don't know why, but I flung myself at him and hugged his knees (that's where I came to). As I held on, I had a memory. A real, live memory. One without flashes or pencils or dreams.

In my mind I was transported to a grassy lawn in front of an enormous castle. I was running around the perimeter of the castle walls. I stopped at one corner, panting, and looked up, up, up. The host of Fire was standing at the southeastern corner of the castle, his red robes flowing in the breeze like outdoor curtains. I flung myself at him and hugged his stone ankles—that's as far as I could reach then. He whispered, "You're our boy. Never forget." I laughed as I let go of him and ran off around the corner of the building towards the blue-robed statue, Water, eager to hear what she'd say to me. All at once I knew that was my favorite game. And I knew I'd always loved the hosts and that they'd always loved me.

When I let go of Fire, he lumbered to the wall and raised his arms up, sending the Fire Element out the open roof of the cave and back out into the environment.

Once the Fire Element had been sent out, Grampa seemed to sit a little taller.

He did the same for each of the other Elements, first carving the Element's initial onto his own palm and then the Element's word onto its host's palm. One by one, they knelt at his feet, and each time their blood mixed, the Element regained its power, spilling it onto the ground: Water, Air, and Earth.

And before they sent their Element out into the environment, I hugged each one of them.

With each Element's release, Grampa seemed to get stronger, to the point of standing up on his own as the Earth Element was sent on her way.

When the Earth Element had been sent out, she immediately went to the place Maximillian had sunk into the ground. The ground shifted and then started heaving and lifting as if a buried platform was being raised. The dirt fell away, leaving Maximillian's lifeless, dirty body lying there.

That was the second time I'd seen him that way.

Tessa and I ran and knelt beside him.

"I'm so sorry," she said, and she put her hand on my shoulder.

There was a sudden and ferocious howling sound as the North Wind spun back into the Crypt and entered Maximillian's nose and mouth. His chest heaved several times before he suddenly started coughing and spewing sand and leaves out of his mouth and nose. He rolled over to his side, letting the sand pour out of his mouth, and continued coughing.

Tessa and I helped him sit up.

"Whoa, what a close one," Maximillian said, thumping his chest.

"Close one?" I sputtered. "Any closer and you would have been sprouting daisies from your nose!"

Maximillian locked eyes with me and whispered, "Demlock?"

"The Elements blew him up," I whispered back.

"Any sign of Sorgol?"

"A crow came and—"

"The crows," said Maximillian, shaking his head. He turned to watch Grampa.

By the time Grampa was done, the cave looked like a completely different place. It wasn't cold and barren and dark and smelly anymore. It was warm and bright and smelled like a fresh rainfall in spring. There were trees of all shapes and sizes, with colored leaves and blossoms, growing right out of the Crypt floor. There were musical birds and perfumed flowers and a warm breeze and a crystal-clear river flowing from the base of an amazing underground waterfall.

And the big compass rose embedded in the floor in the center of the Crypt was pointing north.

Once all the Elements had been blessed and sent out, Grampa raised the Chalice high in the air and said, "Create in dis land a spotless heart. Renew in her people a loyal spirit. And restore to Emogen da pleasure of your liberation. Now, out of harm's way."

The Chalice shone as bright as the sun, causing us all to shield our eyes. And by the time I lowered my hands, the Chalice was gone and Grampa was looking up to the sky.

"Well, dat's dat," he said as he wiped his forehead.

That was when I saw the palm of his left hand.

After he had sent each Element back to the environment, the Element's letter healed into a shimmering golden scar.

"Where'd it go?" I asked, following Grampa's gaze upward.

"A place where it can't be touched," said Grampa. "A place known only to Mudder Yegra."

Grampa gave a satisfied nod to the sky and walked to Melchior, who was still crouched on the ground. He laid his hand on the eagle's head.

"T'anks, me friend," he said and kissed the bird lightly on the beak. "A job well done."

Melchior stood and squawked loudly, ruffling his feathers. The sound echoed off the walls. He squawked again and lifted off, disappearing into the night.

Grampa turned and looked at me. His eyes were bright, and he looked healthier than ever.

"So dis is da girl who went on your journey wit' you," he said.

"That's right," I replied.

"Does da girl have a name?" he asked, looking at Tessa.

"Oh, yeah. Tessa. Tessa, this is Drofgum—I mean, Grampa," I said. "Grampa, this is Tessa."

"Pleased to meet your acquaintance," said Tessa.

"Right proper, ain't she?" asked Grampa. "Looks good on you." He winked at me. "Nice to meet you, too, m'dear. Trust he took good care of you on da journey?"

Tessa smiled. "Oh, yes. He did."

Speaking of journeys, before he left with Melchior, Grampa had said he was going to look for someone.

"Did you find Mom?" I blurted out.

43 No Sense Worryin'

Grampa looked at me, surprised by my words.

"You said you were going to look for someone," I said. "That's who, isn't it?"

Grampa nodded at first, and then he shook his head and said, "But I didn't find her."

"I . . . I saw her in Demlock's eye!" I exclaimed. "Surrounded by flames—"

"Da bugger better have just made you imagine dat! So help me," said Grampa, pounding a fist into his palm, "if she's sufferin'!"

Maximillian suddenly put his head back. "The North Wind, Grampa!" he said. "She's blowing again!"

"Right you are!" said Grampa, giving him a knowing look. He raised his hands in the air and shouted, "North Wind! I summon you!"

Grampa put his head back, and his lopsided hair unravelled and whipped and whirled around his head as the North Wind entered the Crypt again. She rustled the leaves on the trees and stirred up the dust on the ground. She filled my lungs, and I felt her cool breath reach right through me.

Grampa said,

"Find da one we seek!
Seek da one we wish to find!
Da one of whom we speak,
Cherished of all Emogen-kind!"

The North Wind howled as she exited the Crypt and passed across the open space up above the ceiling. After a few moments there was just a soft breeze left in the Crypt.

Grampa lowered his arms and fixed his hair with impressive speed and accuracy.

"Now dat we have da speed and agility of da North Wind, we should hopefully get some answers soon. Good t'inkin', boy!" he said to Maximillian.

Then he turned to Gil, who had been standing off on his own, quietly, the whole time.

"Come here, boy. I believes you've gots somet'in' dat belongs to me."

Gil nodded and reached into his pocket. He took something out and handed it to Grampa. It was Grampa's compass. He flipped it open.

"Well! Dis has certainly been a long time in comin'!" Grampa passed the compass to me.

It was pointing north.

"Jes like in da good old days." He kissed it and put it in his cloak.

Then he wrapped one of his arms around me and one around Tessa and led us towards the archway. "Come on, da two of you!" he called to Maximillian and Gil. Tessa and I parted what was left of the curtain. There were only scattered wooden beads on it now.

We walked back up the corridor and through the Gateway.

And this time we didn't go through a portal. We went the right way—the way we should have taken the first time. Wandering through confusing passageways was something I was getting used to, but it was a good thing the tip of Grampa's cane acted like a flashlight, because this confusing passageway was definitely the most confusing.

"And so the rule about no one being allowed in the Inner Sanctuary was just a cover-up so Demlock, Helyas, and Aldusa could dig the tunnel and set up the portal to the Gateway without anyone finding out. The Inner Sanctuary is just an empty room," Maximillian concluded just after we'd turned a corner into yet another long, dark corridor,

"So you mean the Sacred Writings that Helyas was supposed to be engraving onto a silver tablet don't even exist?" asked Tessa.

"Nope. All part of the scam," said Maximillian.

"How disappointing," said Tessa.

"Does Quar know?" I asked. "Does he know about Helyas?" I really hoped he didn't.

"No," said Grampa. "And I knows it would break his heart to find out. He really t'inks a lot of him, he does."

"We need to go back!" I said. "We need to go back and warn the Tezeman villagers about him!"

"Dere's no rush fer dat," Grampa said. "He's already gone."

"Where did he go?" Tessa asked.

"Not sure about dat. But wit'out Demlock and da Priestess, he won't be tryin' anyt'ing any time soon."

"Unless he gets his hands on Sorgol," said Maximillian.

Gil made a strange squeaking noise.

"How would he get Sorgol?" I asked.

"The crow," replied Maximillian.

"All's you needs to be t'inkin' about now is dat you're safe," Grampa said, putting his hand on Gil's shoulder. "And start enjoyin' da benefits of da Elements. No sense sittin' and worryin' fer da sake of worryin'."

"B-but, you just never know w-with p-people like them," whispered Gil.

I wondered if Gil knew something we didn't know.

As we hiked on, Tessa yapped on and on to Gil about all he'd missed. And Gil just walked quietly along and listened, until she got to the part about Maximillian. When Gil realized Maximillian was who he was, he stopped in his tracks and stared at him. Maximillian laughed and put his hand on Gil's shoulder. "It's all right, mate," he said. "It's all right. Who'd you think I was?"

Gil just shrugged his shoulders and shook his head, wide-eyed.

As it turned out, Gil didn't have much to say, even after he got over the shock of being in the presence of the infamous Maximillian Snute, because it seems that he couldn't remember anything that had happened to him after he had met Demlock in the woods. But even if he could have remembered something, I'm sure the way Tessa was talking, he wouldn't have had a chance to get a word in edgewise anyways.

But the funny thing about that whole scene was that I didn't even mind hearing Tessa yap on. Somehow the feeling I had inside from finding out about Grampa kind of made me feel really settled, as if nothing could ever happen again that would disturb me.

But from time to time I'd look over at Gil and he'd look away from me.

We finally came to the place where the tunnel opened up behind the waterfall. As soon as we stepped out onto the ledge, the opening behind us closed up. Stones had magically materialized out of thin air, filling in the entryway, until there was no trace of an opening to be seen. Because of the sound of the rushing water, the closing of the tunnel seemed to happen without a sound. If it weren't for Tessa saying, "Look at that!" I would have missed the whole thing.

We took our time climbing down.

"Ah, yes. Dis is what it's all about!" Grampa said as he planted his feet on the ground. He took a deep breath and spread his arms out.

Emogen looked totally different. The trees were green and strong, and the ground was covered with green grass and every kind of wildflower you can imagine. Squirrels and chipmunks were running up and down tree trunks, and birds were singing as they flew from branch to branch. The air smelled fresh and felt warm. And the sky was a brilliant shade of blue.

"Let's head back to me clearin'," Grampa shouted over the roar of the water. "From dere I can sends you back to Eart' t'roo a proper portal: me reflectin' pool."

"What do you mean by that?" I asked.

"Guess you never did figure out da reason I sent you da mirror, huh?"

"The mirror? Ohhhhh . . ." I said as it suddenly dawned on me. Right. The note—it said the mirror would help me not get too lost. And Grampa had been talking to Maximillian through the mirror. And Maximillian must have been looking through the reflecting pool, even when he'd contacted me.

"I was supposed to have come here through the mirror!" I said. "Now I get it. A bit late, huh?"

"Better late den never. And regardless of how or when you got here, you got here. And you got your job done, too. You've sure grown up, me boy," he said, messing my hair. "You've changed a lot."

I guess I had.

"And you've done a good job, too," said Grampa. "You've certainly left your mark on Emogen. And fer dat, she'll be eternally grateful."

44 A Little Squeeze

I was barely awake the next morning before Tessa came and sat on my blanket.

"What's up?" I sat up and rubbed the sleep out of my eyes.

I hadn't slept very well that night because I kept thinking about stuff. And for some reason, I was all of a sudden overcome with a strange feeling of guilt. Guilt for treating Tessa the way I'd treated her all that time at school. The reality of her family situation and the way Demlock had tormented her about it came back to me in the middle of the night, and I suddenly felt really awful about it, especially since my story was turning out to have a good ending and hers maybe never would.

"Although I do think he's a bit of a dimwit, you need to talk to him," Tessa said motioning to Gil. "He feels rotten about what he's done." She looked across the little clearing to where Gil was scooping water out of the river with a bowl. He took a drink.

"Oh. Yeah," I said.

"It really wasn't his fault."

"Of course. I know. It's just . . ." I don't know why I was having a problem. It was just awkward.

"So are you going to talk to him?"

"I guess."

"You should do it now," she said. "And pleeease give him back his glasses while you're at it. Even if they are ruined."

"Uh, okay," I said, wondering what that was all about. I had actually forgotten that I even had Gil's glasses. I had been carrying them around with me ever since I found them. The last time I'd thought about them was when I thought I saw Gil at the bottom of the gorge with the wild dogs.

"But before I talk to him . . . uh . . . I need to talk to you," I said.

Tessa couldn't hide her surprise. "About what?" she asked.

"Uh . . . about something I did . . . have done. To you. Something I'm . . . sorry about."

Tessa blushed. "I had a feeling it was you," she said. "The locker?"

I nodded. "And the mirror."

She blushed an even deeper shade. "Oh," she whispered as she looked down at her hands.

"I . . . I didn't know. About your family. Or else I wouldn't have—"

"I didn't want you to," she said.

"I know. But . . . it was really rotten of me anyways."

She nodded. "Me, too," she whispered.

"What do you mean?"

"I . . . I've been rotten to you, too." She suddenly turned away. "You need to talk to him," she said as she stood and started waving madly at Gil. And before I knew it, he was crouched down beside me.

"Hey," Gil said. He offered me the bowl of water.

"Hey," I said. "Thanks." I took a drink and put the bowl down.

I looked at Tessa.

"Just trying to help some friends out," she said. And then she smiled at me.

I smiled back.

Gil looked like he wasn't sure if he should smile or not. He did anyways. Sort of.

Tessa left to sit with Max and Grampa by the fire.

Gil and I sat in complete silence for a while. He kicked a hole in the ground with the heel of his shoe. We were so awkward with each other. It felt just like the first day we'd met in the deserted hallway at the academy.

Only he didn't sneeze a whack of snot on the back of my neck this time.

"Tessa reminded me that I had these," I said. "She really wanted me to give them back to you." I reached into my pocket and pulled out Gil's twisted glasses frames.

"M-my glasses!" he said as he took them from me. "W-well, m-my *frames* at least. Thanks."

"How've you been doing without these? Not that they'll be much good to you now, anyways."

"I don't really r-remember," he said. "B-but s-since I've come out of that t-trance, I've just b-been w-walking really s-slow. It hasn't really b-been that m-much of a p-problem. Although—"

"What?"

"I did m-mistake T-Tessa for M-Max this m-morning. That w-was really awkw-ward."

"Oh no. What'd you do?" It didn't sound good.

"I s-snuck up b-behind her and gave her a w-wedgie. An at-tomic."

"What?" I screeched. I burst out laughing.

"W-well, I thought she w-was M-Max," he said.

"What?" I screeched again. "How could you confuse those two? He's like six feet tall, Gil!" I could hardly breathe, I was laughing so hard.

"Yeah, w-well, she w-was s-sitting on a rock. And they b-both do have l-long hair. You could at l-least give m-me that."

By this point, I was practically rolling around on the ground, laughing. That's why she'd insisted I give him his glasses back right away.

"What . . . would possess . . . you . . . to even give . . . Max a . . . wedgie?" I managed between gasps.

"He gave m-me one first," Gil said, sounding defensive. He didn't seem to find it as funny as I did.

"How . . . how did she . . . take it?"

"Once I exp-plained it all t-to her, she just s-slugged m-me in the arm and s-said, 'Don't ever do that again!'" he said, putting his hands on his hips and doing his best Tessa imitation.

"Wow, you got off easy," I said, stunned. And "wow" was right. If he had done that to her while we were at the academy, I would have been planning his funeral.

She must have been feeling really bad for what had happened to him.

"Yeah," said Gil, nodding. "I w-wonder if I c-can fix these," he said, suddenly changing the subject. He held his twisted frames up.

"For your sake," I said, "I hope you can." I tried to hide the fact that I was about to burst out laughing again. I snorted as I held it in.

"M-maybe Drofgum can help m-me," Gil said, ignoring me. He stood up and brushed his pants off. But just as he turned to walk away, he sneezed right into his hands. All over his glasses frames.

He turned back. "Hey, Smudge?"

"Yeah?"

"Y-you got a tissue?"

That did it. I burst out laughing again.

Gil stuffed his hands—along with the frames—into his pockets and went back to sit with the others around the fire. As soon as he sat down, I heard Tessa scream.

"You're disgusting!"

"What? It'll j-just dry, l-like glue. Then I c-can j-just peel it off!"

"Ugh! Get away from me!" she screamed and sat somewhere else.

Max and Grampa just laughed.

I joined them a few minutes later. I sat down beside Gil just as Grampa said, "Are you kiddin'? Dose tings have given up da ghost! Best to jes bury dem and put dem out of deir misery! I'm sure you can gets yourself anudder pair when you gets back. Good mornin'," he said to me.

"Good morning, Grampa."

I looked down at the river. The water shimmered in the morning sunlight.

Sunlight. It was twinkling like pieces of shattered glass through the branches of the trees above our heads. I couldn't remember the last time I'd seen real live sunlight.

Grampa followed my gaze. "So have you decided wedder you're goin' to stay here or not?" he asked me.

Gil stared at me, along with Tessa. "You . . . you're going t-to s-stay?" he asked.

"I don't know yet," I said. I looked from Max to Tessa to Gil to Grampa. "Grampa said we could all stay if we wanted to. Right?"

Grampa nodded. "Dat's right."

Tessa suddenly reached over and put her hand on my arm. "I'll stay if you do," she said as she gave my arm a squeeze.

A little squeeze.

Why were my legs becoming weak?

Why was my stomach feeling all fuzzy?

Holy crow! Get a grip, man!

She put her hand back in her lap. The fuzzy feeling disappeared.

Grampa snorted. "Why don't you go spend some time down by da river and t'inks about it. Take your time. You're in no hurry." He patted my knee and winked at me. "Da sunshine and water'll help clear your head. It'll do you some good."

Tessa and Gil came with me. We sat in the sunshine on the riverbank.

"W-what do you think you're going t-to do?" asked Gil.

"I'm thinking maybe I'll stay," I said. "I mean, just look at this place now. Why would anyone ever want to leave? Besides, I've got nothing to go back to. None of us have anything to go back to, really."

Gil's face clouded over and he started pulling at the grass.

"What's the matter, Gil?" I asked.

"Uh . . . w-well . . . I've never t-told anyone this b-before, b-but I've b-been doing s-some res-search. T-to find my p-parents. And I'm t-telling you right now, I don't think any of m-my l-leads are p-pointing t-to Emogen."

Gil was left on the steps of the school as a baby. His parents are probably out there, on Earth, somewhere. I totally knew how he felt, wanting to find them and all. But at least I had Grampa and Max looking for my mom, too. Gil was on his own.

"Well, Gil. If you want to go back, I'll go with you." I said. "I'll help you find your parents."

He snapped his head up. "You w-will? You really w-will? You m-mean you'll give all this up for m-me?"

"I'm sure I can come back anytime I want," I said. "And who knows? Maybe while I'm helping you, I'll discover some leads to finding my own mom.

Besides, I think it's time I went somewhere with you. We all know you've followed me around enough."

"Well, I'm certainly not going to stay here by myself!" exclaimed Tessa.

"So what do you say, then?" I asked, looking at each of them. "We going back?"

Tessa put on a pouty face. "But I kind of like your idea," she said. "This place really is beautiful." Her face suddenly lit up. "Can we at least stay here for the rest of the summer? That way we could have a real vacation for once."

I shrugged and looked at Gil.

"Uh, I'm not sure," he said and then started pulling at the grass.

I guess I couldn't blame him for wanting to leave.

"Well, how about at least just a few more days, then," Tessa countered, rubbing the back of her neck, "I was really hoping Smudge could ask his grampa to conjure up a day spa. I seriously need to destress."

Gil looked at me out of the corner of his eye. "W-well, I guess that s-sounds okay." And then he whispered, "Especially the p-part ab-bout her d-de-stressing."

I nodded and scrambled to my feet. "I hear ya, Gil. Uh, Grampa?" I called as I climbed back up the river-bank and headed towards the clearing.

45 The Beginning of the End

Summer's over. The room's chilly. It's almost dawn. And I'm sitting in front of a mirror in my dorm room, talking. I'd seen Grampa do this a few months ago and thought he was totally nuts. But a lot has changed since then, and now I'm doing it myself.

Gil's still wrapped up in his blankets, sleeping. And he's snoring away.

"Morning, Grampa," I say as his image becomes clear in the glass.

"Mornin' Simon. How's da wedder dere today?" He asks me the same question every morning.

"It's raining a bit now, but I can tell it's gonna clear up and be sunny a little later on," I say.

Grampa smiles. Gone are the days of Grimstown being a dry, dead town. And gone are the days of "invisible, havoc-wreaking gremlins," too. It didn't take me long to figure out that the "pranks" Grampa used to pull weren't pranks at all. He had been trying to keep Grimstown from drying up and dying completely. Since his powers were seriously limited while in the realm of Earth, he had made messes everywhere every night so that the neighbors had to use their hoses to wash up every morning. And that watered the earth, just like the rain's doing now.

"Did you have a good sleep?" he asks.

"Not really."

"Why not?"

"Oh, I just kept thinking about stuff."

"Like what?"

"Lots of stuff. Like . . . Mom."

"Ah, yes," says Grampa, nodding. "Me too."

"And what would happen if Demlock ever shows up again."

Grampa says nothing for a while.

Then he says, "Don't t'ink you needs to be worryin' about seein' Demlock's hideous face ever again. But I do t'ink dere's good reason fer your sleepless nights. I t'ink it's well wort' your time to be t'inkin' about dose t'ings."

"Why," I ask, "if you don't think Demlock will come back?"

"Da resummonin' of da Elements was a wonderful t'ing," Grampa says, "A grand t'ing. And all of Emogen is well on her way to bein' made right. But she hasn't been freed from evil."

"Because Helyas is still out there?"

"Because dere always has been and always will be evil, Simon. Dere ain't no wipin' it out. In fact, da power of evil will soon gain momentum again."

"What do you mean, Grampa?" I whisper, suddenly hoping our conversation hasn't woken Gil up.

"I just received news dis mornin' dat Helyas has obtained Sorgol. And a vial of human blood."

Gil snorts and I look over my shoulder to where he is sleeping. He pulls the blanket off his face and rolls over to face the wall.

"Yep," says Grampa quietly. "His blood. I'm afraid his part in da story ain't over. It's just beginnin'."

IT TAKES A VILLAGE TO RAISE A BOOK

Acknowledgments must be made to...

Jon, for not trying to haul me out of the trenches, but for hunkering down beside me. That's the best kind of friend.

Matthew, for being my very first reader and for lending me the name "Demlock." Yes, I know, I owe you.

Jesse, for being my #1 promoter and asking the most questions.

Abby, for being the girl I always wanted to be. You make me happy.

My dad, Joe, who said the difference between him and me is that I actually did it.

My mom, Linda, for dreaming bigger dreams than I do.

Special thanks and gratitude also to...

Veda, for being the most "persistent advocate" I know. If it wasn't for you, I may never have finished the first draft.

5 – You were there with me in the early days, before anyone else knew. Thanks for your support, for the sharing of your lives, and for laughing with me.

Dimiter Savoff. Thanks for being a risk-taker and considering the potential of a new author. I am forever grateful.

Kallie George. Thanks for making me work harder than I ever have before. You have certainly been instrumental in the evolution of this book. Stephen King nailed it and I can't think of any better way to say it: "To write is human. To edit is divine."

Colin Thomas, for your heartfelt encouragement and professional guidance. You've helped me become a more confident writer. Thank you.

Tonya Martin. Although our virtual paths crossed ever so briefly, thank you for lending some of your expertise.

Elisa Gutiérrez, who's used her magic to transform paper and ink into a beautiful treasure.

Jade Chan, for having the eagle eyes necessary to spot the mistakes we overlooked.

Kim Aippersbach. Your help was very valuable. Thank you for sharing your skills.

Veda and Joanna, my reader friends. Your insights and remarks were much appreciated.

And last, but not least, Gillian Hunt for the heart-stopping email that got this crazy ball rolling.